# THE BIG OVERNIGHT

## BOOK 3 IN THE STELLA REYNOLDS MYSTERY SERIES

Libby Kirsch

Sunnyside Press

Sunnyside Press
www.LibbyKirschBooks.com

Publisher's Note: This is a work of fiction. Names, characters, places, and incidents are a product of the author's imagination. Locales and public names are sometimes used for atmospheric purposes. Any resemblance to actual people, living or dead, or to businesses, companies, events, institutions, or locales is completely coincidental.

Book Layout © 2015 BookDesignTemplates.com

The Big Overnight/ Libby Kirsch -- 1st ed.
ISBN 978-0-9969350-3-6

To my friends, especially Sherry and Matt. Thanks for always being my first readers.

# CONTENTS

# 1

The news van screeched into an open spot in the parking lot behind the police department, and Stella was out on the pavement before her photographer had even cut off the engine.

"They're walking!" she called back, craning her neck to see over cars in the packed lot. "They're already walking!"

"Take the mic, Reynolds. I'll be right behind you," came Bob's gruff response as he climbed stiffly out of the driver's side of the live truck.

Bob was older and he moved slower, but nothing seemed to faze him and he hadn't missed a shot in the nearly two years she'd worked with him. Stella grabbed the stick microphone and took off across the parking lot, flipping the switch at the bottom of the mic to the "on" position as she walked.

The blondish-gray, day-old stubble on the homicide detective's face glinted in the late afternoon sunlight as he strode across the blacktop, as did the handcuffs clamped around the wrists of the man walking in front of him. The prisoner, pushing six feet tall, was long and lanky, and his baggy jeans and T-shirt left skin exposed to the harsh winter air. Detective Brian Murphy slowed when he saw Stella hurrying over and she shot him a grateful look.

"Cas Rockman," she said, extending the microphone toward the pair. "Did you shoot Oliver Bennet?"

Rockman's eyes raked over Stella from head to toe and he smiled a slow, deliberate smirk before answering.

"Yeah, Red," he finally said, bobbing his head twice, "I shot him."

"You did?" She was so surprised by the admission that she stopped walking, and Bob swore under his breath as he crashed into her from behind. She winced and started moving again, first catching Murphy's victorious look and then noticing that Rockman's smile was gone.

She had to scramble to come up with another question. She'd never had anyone confess on camera before—usually they didn't say anything at all.

She stole another look at Bob and was surprised to see him staring back at her, eyebrows raised. The interest on his face was almost enough to shake her brain loose.

"You know you're admitting to shooting someone right now," she said, only realizing when she heard Bob groan that she hadn't actually asked a question.

As they neared the side door to the county jail, Rockman slowed to a stop. Seconds later, the lock clunked over and the door swung toward them. Stella peered inside. Even with the door wide open, the winter sunshine couldn't penetrate the gloom within.

"Why?" Stella finally asked, as Detective Murphy's pen scratched out his signature on a form.

Rockman stared straight ahead, all emotion wiped from his face. Murphy pushed him inside the secure facility, and they disappeared into the darkness without another word. Moments later, the heavy, metal door swung closed with a clank. The lock flipped over soon after, and Stella found herself staring at Bob.

"Why did he shoot him, or why did he just confess?" Bob asked, taking the camera off his shoulder.

"Both," she answered, somehow dissatisfied, even though they got their exclusive. Her hair blew wildly around her face with a sudden gust of wind, and she hastily smoothed it with her free hand. "Call it in. We'll need to wait here for sound with Murph, but we can be live at five with the story." She flipped open her notebook and started outlining her live shot. She'd been working here for almost two years and still couldn't believe her luck at landing the job. Stella had done her time in tiny TV markets and felt like a seasoned pro with nearly four years as a reporter under her belt.

While they waited for the detective, she looked around downtown Knoxville, realizing she felt more at home in the concrete and asphalt surroundings than she did in her own apartment.

Her roommate, Janet, was an old friend who was full of surprises. They shared an apartment in an up-and-coming neighborhood in town, and her two former flames lived just miles away in what was an oddly cordial friendship triangle that she had to spend a lot of time telling herself not to overthink.

It was times like this, however, when she had nothing to do but wait in a live truck with a crotchety old photographer, that she found it difficult to keep her mind off the men in her life. Despite the fact that one had a girlfriend and the other was too busy to date, she spent a lot of time thinking about them both.

***

"Thanks for the call, Murph," she said, after the detective walked out of jail twenty minutes later.

"No problem. Glad you made it," he added with a sly smile.

"You said you were going to walk him at three thirty! We pulled up at 3:28 and you were already halfway across the parking lot!"

"Oh, stop your bitching. You got your perp walk—and a confession. I'd say you owe me."

She nodded grudgingly. "Yeah, yeah. How's Annie?" she asked, changing the subject. Murphy's wife had been Stella's soccer teammate in Ohio when both women were in high school. Annie had seen her on the news right after Stella had taken the job in Knoxville, they'd reconnected, and now, thanks to Annie's husband, Stella had one of the best sources at the station.

"She's good," he answered. "She says you girls need to get together for coffee soon."

"I'll call her this week."

A throat cleared behind Stella and she ducked her head.

"Sorry, Bob. You ready?"

"Been ready for half an hour, Stella. Let's go."

She winked at the detective and started the interview. Murphy didn't give out much information about the arrest, refusing to divulge a motive, what led them to Rockman as the suspect, or anything about the victim beyond his name and age of forty-six, so the interview didn't last long. Before they wrapped up, though, Stella felt another set of eyes boring into her from behind. She looked back and saw a stranger staring at her, his eyebrows drawn together. His expression wasn't angry, exactly, but it wasn't far off.

While Stella waited for Bob to get the live truck up and running, she walked over to the stranger, who was now sitting on a bench and staring at the cement under his feet.

"Check your sources," he said, looking up. The glare was back, and she stopped short, not wanting to get too close.

"Excuse me?"

He blew warm air into his cupped hands and then dug a pair of winter gloves out of his coat pocket. A black skull cap followed, and after he'd adjusted it over his shaved head, he glared up at Stella.

"I said, check your sources. My son did not shoot that man any more than you did." He had a funny way of speaking; it was very proper, which was unexpected, given his distinctly rough appearance.

"Well, uh, my source is the suspect, himself. He just told me he shot him." She shifted on her feet and added, "I'm sorry that, umm," but clamped her mouth shut, unsure of how to phrase why she felt bad. She shook her head and fell silent, instead.

He brushed her words off and stood. She was five-foot-nine and wearing heels, but he still towered over her. The sound of popping joints and cartilage made Stella wince, but she sensed an opportunity.

"Did you want to—"

An annoyed wave of his hand cut her off mid-sentence and revealed a sleeve of tattoos up his arm. "No, I do not want to talk, but I do want you to do your job and find out who the shooter was. That guy is not *the* guy."

He walked away, weaving through cars in the packed municipal parking lot, and disappeared into a throng of people crossing a busy street. She stared after him thoughtfully. Why would Rockman lie about shooting someone, and why should she believe Cas's father over his own admission? She blew out a breath, preparing to forget the entire exchange when Bob whistled for her attention.

"Hey, Red!" he shouted. "What did Harrison Keys want?"

"Who?" she asked, looking behind her and catching a glimpse of her hair, which wasn't red, for heaven's sake, but definitely auburn.

Bob took a pack of cigarettes out of his back pocket and tapped the bottom until one slipped forward. He carefully plucked it out and took his time lighting it. He blew a giant puff of smoke toward Stella before answering, "I guess it was before your time, but I figured you'd have heard of him by now. That man you were just talking to served twenty years in prison on murder charges."

She spun back around to look at the intersection Harrison had melted into. Like father, like son, or was Harrison onto something and his son actually *was* innocent? She felt her heartbeat surge and fingertips tingle. This could be the beginning of something big—only time would tell.

Her cell phone rang, interrupting her mounting feelings of intrigue. It was Lucky, but before she could answer, a second call beeped in from John.

*Oh, boy*, she thought, tossing the phone back into her shoulder bag without answering either call. Suspense and intrigue seemed to be building on so many levels these days.

Usually an on-camera confession was the end of the story, so why did Stella have a sneaking suspicion that today's confession was only the beginning?

# 2

Hours later, Stella was headed home for the night. It was after midnight, and the streets of Knoxville were deserted. Her hair was pulled up into a messy bun, and she'd kicked her heels off as soon as she'd gotten into her car and was now driving barefoot through the quiet downtown as the heater blasted warm air throughout the vehicle. She picked a route that took her past the most blinking yellow lights, so she wouldn't have to stop the car, and as she cruised down the road, she couldn't help but think about all the people with normal jobs who were already in bed for the night.

Before she could sort out her feelings about it, her cell phone rang. After taking one hand off the wheel and digging around in her bag, she felt out her cell phone and answered.

"I need you to do me a favor." Janet's words barely cut through the din of the crowd around her.

"What's up?" Stella asked suspiciously.

"Well, I'm closing the bar tonight, and I forgot to move the RV." Janet spit the words out rapid-fire.

Stella groaned. "Janet, it's probably already too late! Besides, you know I hate driving that thing." She cradled the phone between her ear and shoulder, so she could use both hands to spin the wheel at a corner.

Stella and Janet had met back when she'd gotten her first TV reporting job in Montana. Their relationship had begun contentiously enough, but they soon became friends. When Stella left the state for a new job on the other side of the country, she assumed she'd never see the Montana native again. The two had reconnected the following year, however, in Alabama, of all places.

At the time, Stella had been working for a station in Tennessee to solve the mystery of an explosion on the NASCAR track. Janet had rolled up in a giant RV—and had never really left. When Stella took this job in Knoxville, Janet had decided to come with her, saying she wanted to finally set down some roots. So, the two unlikely friends had gotten an apartment together. At the last minute, though, Janet had decided she couldn't part with her RV.

City zoning didn't allow her to simply park the RV on the side of the road and leave it there, and their apartment complex wouldn't allow her to use the lot, so Janet had to move the RV to a new spot on the street every forty-eight hours, or she would risk getting a ticket. She forgot more often than she remembered, and now she had a sizable stack of unpaid Knoxville parking tickets on her bedside table. One more ticket and the RV would be towed.

"Ugh, I'll do it," Stella said with a sigh.

"Thanks, hon, you're a doll." Janet hung up without waiting for Stella's reply.

She frowned and set the phone down on the bench seat of her old Plymouth Reliant. After a few more turns and stoplights, she pulled up to her apartment complex, eased into spot, and scanned the street for Janet's RV.

It wasn't difficult to find. The giant monstrosity stood gleaming under a street lamp just a block from her front door. Stella looked longingly at the entrance to the apartment, but slung her bag over her shoulder and walked in the opposite direction. This wasn't the first time she'd had to move Janet's ride—in fact, it happened so often that she kept a key for it on her ring.

The street was both deserted *and* packed. Not a single car or person was on the road, except for the crowd of parked vehicles along the street.

Stella climbed up into the RV, turned the key absent-mindedly, and flinched as the engine roared to life. She rolled it slowly down the road. Five blocks later, she found an opening large enough and spent a considerable amount of time wedging it into place. She finally threw the vehicle into park and got out.

Before she could take even one step toward her apartment, though, her cell phone rang again. "Sorry I had to rush off the phone there, Stella," Janet said, still breathless. "The bar is slammed tonight and I had a line of customers wrapped down to the door."

"Tell me honestly, Janet, did you forget to move the RV, or did you see that there weren't any spots free nearby?" Stella asked her roommate skeptically.

She ignored the question. "Hey, your dad called. Also, your old man didn't look too hot when I left for work."

"Oh, *my* old man, huh?" Stella asked.

"I just mean that he looked sad. I think you need to give him some extra attention tonight," Janet said matter-of-factly.

"Hmm. Thanks for the heads up. Are you closing tonight?"

"Yep; I should be home around three."

"I guess I'll see you tomorrow, then."

Stella disconnected the call and walked the last few steps into her apartment building. She always felt slightly guilty when the topic of her dad came up, because Janet's father had died years ago. For some reason, Stella felt guilty for having one.

She opened the door, wondering what fresh drama was awaiting her. To her surprise, the place was dark and quiet. The light was blinking on the phone console by the kitchen, and she picked it up and listened to a message from Lucky Haskins. Her ex-boyfriend would be back in town the following week and wanted to get together. She placed the phone back into the console and crept down the hall.

A sleeping figure was lying in the middle of the bed in Janet's room. He didn't move, so she quietly backed out. Finally, at close to one in the morning, she climbed under the covers in her own bed and fell, exhausted, to sleep.

\*\*\*

Stella woke up slowly on Saturday. The sunlight streamed in through her metal, mini blinds, letting her know it was well into mid-morning.

Heat radiated from the other side of the bed, and when she rolled onto her side, she saw that she wasn't alone.

"Hey," she said, poking the sleeping figure between his shoulder blades. He snorted and rolled over toward her, pawing her arm. "Hey," she said again, batting him away. "Wake up, lazy bones."

He gave another snort, but this time she heard his tail thump against the mattress, and she reached out and stroked his head, stopping to scratch between his ears. He let out a low, grumbling moan, and his tail thumped harder.

"Did Janet kick you out?" Ole Boy yawned, his jaw opening wide enough to gulp down a groundhog. His tongue curled up and his back arched. "She said you were feeling blue, but you look fine to me."

Ole Boy was a mutt Janet had adopted about a year ago after Stella's station had featured him on their weekly pet segment. He was a massive dog at over one hundred pounds, and his coat was a mottled mix of black, gray, and white. The shelter guessed he was Newfoundland mixed with some kind of shepherd and was likely seven or eight years old.

He pressed his cold, black nose under her arm and then stood up and stretched out with a noisy yawn. He gave her a nudge, which nearly rolled off the bed.

"Argh!" she yelped, barely catching herself on the bedside table. She sat up, swung her legs off the side of the mattress, and Ole Boy gave her a final push. "All right!" she laughed, standing up and slipping into her robe. They padded out of the bedroom together, and the smell of waffles, syrup, and coffee filled the air.

Ole Boy galloped past her and skidded around the corner, crashing into a small side table. A vase and the phone console landed on the floor with a thud, but somehow, nothing broke.

"Slow down!" she admonished, picking up the mess and turning to face Janet. "You're up early," she observed as Janet slid a waffle onto a plate.

"You want one?" she asked, pouring more batter onto the sizzling iron.

Janet was medium everything. She stood about five-foot-six and had medium-length hair that wasn't dark brown or light brown, but that fell somewhere in between. She was a little rough around the edges and tended to wear her clothes a bit too low at the neck and too high at the hemline. The first impression she gave was that she was a hard woman, but Stella knew Janet had a big heart, was a loyal friend, and worked hard.

"No, just coffee for me, thanks," Stella answered. She poured a cup, and both women walked to the couch with Ole Boy bumping between them, his nose raised high in the air and drool dripping to the carpet.

Janet set her breakfast on the coffee table and picked up the remote. She bopped Ole Boy on the nose when he moved in for her waffle, and then she pressed the button to turn on the TV. Ole Boy huffed out an irritated sigh and cantered past them to the front door, whining.

Stella set her coffee down, tightened the ties on her robe, and slipped her feet into her slippers by the door. "All right, let's go."

She opened the door and was unexpectedly shunted to the side as the dog raced over the threshold. She had just recovered her balance when she heard a crash. Her head whipped around, and she saw her dog crumpled into a heap on the floor of the hallway with a pair of arms and legs flailing under his weight. She started running toward the pile up with an apology on the tip of her tongue when a man rounded the corner, swearing.

"Jesus Christ almighty! What the hell?"

Stella cringed and ran forward. "Oh my gosh—Cheryl, I'm so—"

The woman pushed Ole Boy off of her and heaved herself up to a sitting position. She shot Stella a grin, gingerly stood, and brushed off the seat of her pants. Cheryl had recently moved in across the hall from them. She was an actual crime scene investigator for the city police department and always had an air of professionalism about her, even on the weekend. Her no-nonsense brown bob was now messy from the collision and she used both hands to smooth it. Her smile froze, however, when her companion's voice rose another notch. Cheryl's cheeks colored slightly and her brown eyes squeezed shut, a grimace taking over her features.

"Keep that horse under control, or I'll call the police. What kind of maniac allows such an out-of-control animal off leash?" The man was glaring at Stella, and his words had come out with such force that tiny bits of spittle at the corners of his mouth had flown toward her.

She looked apologetically at her neighbor just as Ole Boy nudged his head under Cheryl's hand so she would pet him behind the ears. The sound of the dog's delighted moaning interrupted the man's lecture, and he looked down just as Ole Boy leaned into Cheryl, his tail tapping out a happy beat against the wall. Cheryl took a bracing step and continued scratching Ole Boy; the dog was so big that she didn't even have to bend over.

"Tim, it's all right. This is my neighbor, Stella, and her dog, Ole Boy. I just wasn't expecting you two to be out and about so early."

Tim tried to soften his glare upon learning that Stella and the dog weren't strangers, but she could tell that Cheryl's comment about her late-morning routine had him judging her all over again.

His disapproving expression lingered, and he tried to smile at Cheryl, but it came out looking more like a sneer.

Tim was tall with narrow shoulders, and his lanky arms and legs were tense from the recent confrontation. His salt-and-pepper hair was cut short, and gray had taken over the sides of his head more than the top, giving him a reverse skunk look that he somehow managed to pull off with panache.

"Well, honey, I guess we should let Stella and her... uh, *dog* start their day."

Cheryl smiled up at Tim and they walked toward her apartment. Stella grabbed Ole Boy's collar before he could lunge after them and snapped his leash into place. As she pulled the dog toward the door, she heard Tim mention something about Section 8 vouchers being unfair to full rent-paying lessors. She felt a grin crease her face as she pushed the door open and breathed in the sunshine and fresh air.

Five minutes later, she and Ole Boy were walking back into the apartment.

The hallway was bare of decoration, but the carpet was new and lush underfoot. The realtor had told them that the building was in an up and coming neighborhood; only time would tell, but it felt like it had a long way to go before it would arrive. The apartment, itself, was spacious with two master suites, plus a guest bath off the main hall. The neighborhood, however, wasn't the best, and crime seemed to creep closer to their building every month. Just a week earlier, management had hung reminders to lock doors and windows at all times after a rash of car break-ins in the parking lot.

Janet dropped her plate noisily into the sink when Stella reached around her for the coffee pot. "Jeez, you're jumpy! I just needed a refill."

The news program Janet had been watching blared in the background as she laughed and piled the mixing bowl and spoon on top of her plate. "I've, uh, I've got to head into work."

"Now?" Stella looked at the clock over the oven. "It's not even ten in the morning!"

"Cookie quit last week, so we're short-staffed," Janet said, frowning.

"Why do you work at that hole-in-the-wall bar, anyway?" Stella asked, searching her friend's face. "You could get a job at any upscale bar or restaurant. It's almost as if you went out of your way to find the worst place in town."

Janet stared stubbornly at the sink and remained quiet. Stella continued, "I worry about you being at that place at night. Do they even have a bouncer working with you, or are you all on your own?"

"It's not like it's just me," Janet said. "My regulars are there—they wouldn't let anything happen to me."

Stella wasn't convinced, but she decided to drop the subject. In the silence that followed, a music pop for the local news station across town sounded throughout the apartment. She turned toward the screen with anticipation on her face, and her reaction wasn't lost on Janet.

John's face filled the screen as he read off news teases for the day ahead. He was the weekend anchor at ABC6, which was a really great step for him, career-wise. She sighed as she watched him on screen. He looked good—he always looked good.

"You've got to move past your past," Janet said, watching her friend watch John. Stella continued staring at the screen, but nodded. "Well, then, what's the problem?" Janet asked.

Stella shrugged, and it was her turn to avoid eye contact. "It's just," she took a deep breath and cleared her throat before starting again. "I know that I don't want to date anyone seriously—nothing exclusive, you know? For some reason, though, I don't like that he's serious with someone else. Does that make sense?" She pulled her hair back into a ponytail and groaned at her own indecision.

Janet smiled, "Yup." She raised one eyebrow, "Speaking of serious, did you hear that voicemail Lucky left last night?" When Stella nodded, she continued. "Lord, even that man's voice is sexy. I swear I got so hot and bothered that I listened to it three times in a row just to finish—" Just then, the sound of the bedroom door opening and closing interrupted Janet's memory.

"Is somebody here?" Stella snapped out the question as

she tightened the ties on her robe.

"Umm..."

"Hey, sugah, you got some coffee or somethin'?" The slow, southern drawl of a stranger rumbled down the hallway. Stella narrowed her eyes at Janet, who smiled wickedly as a man rounded the corner into the kitchen. He was short and stocky and wore more earrings than the two women had combined.

He looked from Stella to Janet and back again, finally crossing his arms in front of him. "Babe? You gonna introduce me to your friend?"

Stella had to stifle a snort at his peeved tone. He had no idea that he was just a random hook-up for Janet. If history told her anything, she'd never see him or his earrings again.

"Excuse me," she said, sliding past him and heading to her bedroom. As she sauntered down the hallway, she heard him say, "So, I'm going to need a ride home and all, since my car is in the impound lot. Can I get your number..."

Stella quietly closed the door to her bedroom, thinking back to Janet's advice just minutes before. Her roommate talked a good talk when it came to men, but Janet spent all her time going from one loser to the next without a break. Stella wondered why that was.

# 3

Just over a week later, Stella was wrapping up a live shot on a Tuesday night. It was cold and dark outside, and Stella reeked of smoke. A fire at a vacant house blazed behind her, orange-red flames licking up the wooden siding. Smoke billowed into the sky. She was cold, her feet were killing her, and she couldn't help but wonder how much it was going to cost to dry clean her entire outfit.

If there was one thing Stella had learned over the last few years, it was that the smell of a house fire didn't come out with a regular wash.

"Standby, Stella. Coming to you for the live tag in ten seconds."

Stella straightened and looked at the camera expectantly.

**STELLA**
**After firefighters get this blaze under control, they'll begin to sort out how the fire started in the first place. Reporting live, I'm Stella Reynolds. Chet, back to you.**

**CHET**
**Stella, a quick question. Any word from authorities on what started the blaze?**

Stella's eyes widened and she glanced behind her at the dozen firefighters hustling around the scene, spraying water on the still-furious flames. It took some effort, but she was able to keep her expression neutral when she turned back to the camera.

**STELLA**
**Not yet, Chet. As I said, the fire chief tells me that once the blaze is out completely, they'll be able to begin their investigation into what sparked the fire. We'll certainly have the latest for you tomorrow morning on**

### Daybreak.

"Clear." The woman opposite Stella poked her head out from behind the camera. Melissa Doyle was short, squat, and looked even bulkier because of the fishing vest she always wore over her clothes. Her dark brown hair had flecks of ash sprinkled in tonight, and she grinned slyly at Stella as she took the camera off the tripod.

"Stupid cow. Why does he insist on asking questions during every reporter's live shot, but refuse to listen to what they say during their report?" She patted one of her many pockets and pulled out an extra battery for the camera.

Stella clicked off her microphone and shook her head. Melissa was one of her favorite photographers to work with, but she wasn't about to get into a what's-wrong-with-the-anchor discussion at 11:04 at night. She was ready to tear down the live shot and get home, but with an active scene behind them, they'd have to wait until the overnight crew arrived to relieve them.

Her cell phone rang, and she and Melissa locked eyes.

"Uh-oh," the older woman said, as she rolled up a coil of cable. "What'd we do wrong?"

Stella took her cell phone out of the bag at her feet, a sinking feeling in her stomach. It was never good to get a call from the station immediately after a live shot. She raised the phone to her face and answered. "Stella,    it's Del."

DeLaura Esposito was the nightside assignment editor at the station. Her job was to listen to dozens of police scanners and send news crews to different parts of the city to cover breaking news and other events to fill the newscast every night. Del had pulled Stella and Melissa from a city commission meeting earlier that evening so they could cover the fire on Knoxville's east side. The fact that she was calling Stella now at 11:05 p.m. likely meant there would be a change in Stella's schedule.

"I've got some bad news."

Stella's nose wrinkled. "What?"

"Piper called off sick."

Stella let the sentence hang there, not wanting to make Del's job any easier. After another moment of silence, the other woman continued. "There's no one on call tonight, so that means you'll need to stay on and get us through the morning shows."

Stella blew out a sigh. Piper, the morning reporter, had a habit of calling off at the last minute; this wasn't the first time Stella had to work a "big overnight," as her boss liked to call it.

"Melissa, too?" Stella asked.

"Nope, Melissa can head home after Jim gets there."

A fresh wave of annoyance rolled over her as she disconnected the call. Jim Blunt was Stella's least favorite photographer at the station. He loved to say that he was "blunt, like his name" and "told it like it was." She found it difficult to maintain her own politeness when she was around him for too long.

Stella and Melissa finished packing up the equipment from their live shot and soon, both were sitting in the front seat of the van waiting for Jim. Melissa had enough video of the flames and all they needed was a soundbite from firefighters, which for some reason was taking longer than usual.

Ice covered the shrubbery, grass, windows, and siding of neighboring homes as water from the fire hoses froze solid. The scene was lit only by headlights from the cars and firetrucks on scene. Every surface in the rundown neighborhood looked shiny and sparkly—even the trash and broken porches. It was an oddly festive backdrop for a burning house.

Two hours later, Stella stifled yet another yawn.

"What is *taking* so long?" Melissa complained.

She didn't know if Melissa was talking about the fire chief giving them a sound bite or Jim Blunt showing up to relieve her. She looked at the dash clock. It was half past one. Melissa grumbled about not wanting this particular bit of overtime, but her words trailed off when an un-marked car pulled up to the scene.

Detective Murphy and his partner, Dave Gibson, stepped out of the maroon Crown Victoria. Murphy glanced up at the news van and waved, but Gibson glared directly at Stella before turning toward the blackened house.

"What's his problem?" Melissa asked, and Stella knew she was asking about Gibson. She side-stepped the question with one of her own.

"Why did homicide just roll up to this vacant house fire?"

They watched the detectives walk past the last remaining firefighters putting away their equipment and head into the still-smoldering house. Before Stella could comment on how funny it was that Gibson used the front door to enter the home, even though there was a truck-sized hole burned out of the wall just a few steps away, she heard tires crunching on gravel and turned in time to see Jim pull up to the scene.

"Finally," Melissa breathed. She shot a sideways look at Stella and said, "No offense—I'm just ready to turn in for the night."

"I know. Me, too," Stella agreed.

"I guess someone wanted to go out in a blaze of glory," Jim said as he strolled up to Stella's open window. He waited for the women to laugh at his joke, and unaffected by the silence that followed, he tried again. "I bet it's a hot mess in there."

A sudden flurry of activity at the house in front of them made everyone stop and stare; the two homicide detectives were coming back out of the house with grim faces and their eyes swept the street.

The crowd that had gathered when the flames were dancing high had long since dispersed, and now it was only Stella and her coworkers, along with a photographer from one of the competing stations.

Stella waved Detective Murphy over, and as he picked his way through the smoldering trash on the ground, Gibson made a beeline for the other photographer's unmarked car. By the time she got out of the truck, Gibson was gone.

"That's weird," Stella said, watching his taillights disappear.

"I'm out of here," Melissa said, swapping keys with Jim and taking her equipment to the news car he'd driven to the scene.

Stella headed toward Murphy. "Not just a fire in there, huh?" she asked.

Murphy held out a hand. "Got a body in there. Off the record, ID says it's Luanne Rockman. The coroner's on her way."

Stella started at the name. "Rockman? Related to your shooter from last week?"

He shrugged. "Might be. We won't put anything on camera now, but we'll make sure you get an update before five."

Stella nodded, thankful that he was aware of her deadline. She flagged Melissa down before she could drive away. "Let Del know that we've got a homicide investigation underway. With a twist."

# 4

On a normal day, Stella slept from around one in the morning until nine or ten, depending on how long Ole Boy let her hit snooze. Now, at four in the morning in the dark, cold van, she was really dragging. With nothing to eat since dinner at five-thirty the night before, and after breathing in smoke all night, she was parched. A half-full bottle of water beckoned her from the drink holder, but if she took even a sip, she'd have to pee. There wasn't a bathroom nearby, and she was waiting on Detective Murphy's soundbite, so she was stuck. Add to that the constant drone of Jim's voice, and Stella was seriously on edge.

A new set of headlights swept across the ruined house in front of them. Stella turned to see who had arrived on scene and felt her cheeks flush when she caught the driver's eye. John raised a hand in greeting and walked over to Stella's live truck. She rolled down her window and smiled.

"Hey, stranger." A smile played at the corners of his lips.

"Hey," she said and bit her lip. Why did her voice sound so funny? "What are you doing here?"

"I was just wrapping up some work at the station when Russ called off sick. I offered to cover for him."

"Hmm," Stella narrowed her eyes, "Piper called off, too. Are they..." She made a twirling motion with her finger. At John's blank look, she elaborated, "Are they together?"

"Yes," he laughed, wiggling all his fingers toward Stella, "they're together."

She smacked his arm. "Shut up." The silence between them felt awkward, and Stella searched for something to say. Aware that Jim was listening, she climbed out of the van.

"How's Katie?" she asked, doing her best to keep her voice neutral.

"Good," he said, bumping her shoulder with his. "She's fine. She really likes her program at UT."

She nodded like she cared. Katie had been an intern at John's old station in Montana, and the two had begun dating after Stella moved away. Whether that happened before or after she and John officially broke up was still up for debate. At any rate, he'd traded his pickup truck for a station wagon and followed Katie to Knoxville—although Stella often thought that, technically, they'd both followed *her* to Tennessee.

"What's she studying again?"

"Kinesiology."

"What's that again? The science of gym class?"

He snorted. "No. She's studying the way the human body moves. She wants to be a physical therapist someday, but first wants to—"

"Oh, that's right," she interrupted, "kinesiology." She bit her lip again; talking about Katie made her unhappy, and she didn't like to think about why that was.

He gave her a curious look. "You should come out to the apartment sometime. She'd love to meet you."

Now it was Stella's turn to snort. "Sure. Maybe someday we can, uh, we can make that work." She turned away from John and tried to collect her thoughts. She didn't want to date John, so why did the mention of his girlfriend make her feel so annoyed?

John put a hand on her shoulder and spun her around. He searched her eyes, and after a moment, opened his mouth. Jim's voice, however, broke in before he could say anything.

"Either of you try the new Golden Corral off of Clinton Highway, yet? I hear they have the best breakfast buffet."

John barked out a laugh and then looked past Stella into the van through the open window. "That's a thought.

Thanks, Jim."

Before the man could reply, Detective Murphy came out of the house toward them.

"Okay, crew, let's get this over with." Murphy looked as tired as Stella felt. He rubbed a hand over his short, blonde hair and moved it down his face, almost as if he were trying to wipe the exhaustion away.

Jim got his tripod into place while Stella clipped a microphone onto Murphy's lapel. John was doing the same when their fingers brushed; she quickly pulled her hands away, not acknowledging the touch. When she looked up, Murphy was watching her with a grin.

John's photographer asked, "Everyone ready?"

The interview was short. Detective Murphy wasn't willing to share many details of the investigation with the media just yet, and he ended by saying, "We'll have to wait on the coroner's report before we know the cause of death."

"Detective, do you have a name on the victim?"

Murphy shook his head, "Not yet." Stella made a face and he sighed. "We can't release anything until we can find and notify next of kin."

She grimaced, thinking it wouldn't take long. They knew right where to find Cas Rockman—the Knox County Jail.

Both cameras clicked off, and Stella and John retrieved their microphones. The fire chief was standing by, ready to give Murphy a ride, since Gibson had already left. Before the detective had gone five steps, though, another car pulled up to the scene.

Stella and John looked at each other in surprise when the mayor of Knoxville climbed out of the car fully-dressed in a business suit, polished wingtip shoes, and meticulously spiked hair. One glance at Detective Murphy told Stella that he wasn't too happy about the visitor.

Mayor Kevin Lewis looked younger than his actual age of forty-eight. A few sprinkles of gray just at the sideburns of his dark brown hair were the only clue about his true age. Otherwise, his round cheeks and twinkling eyes put him closer to thirty than fifty.

"I got a call about this homicide overnight," the mayor began as he walked toward the cameras. "I thought I should come out here to let everyone know the City of Knoxville is still safe."

Stella gave Jim a tiny shrug, turned the microphone back on, pinched the tiny clip between her finger and thumb, and held it out toward the mayor. He took that as a sign to keep going, and John scrambled to get his microphone back out of his bag.

"Last week's shooting and this homicide overnight represents a spike in violence we just won't stand for." The mayor had an easy, slow southern drawl and was as comfortable as Stella in front of the camera. Just then, his eyebrows were drawn down gravely. "I want the citizens of Knoxville to know that I have the police chief, fire chief, and arson investigators working overtime to solve both crimes. We've got one man in custody in the Bennet shooting—already a confession—and we won't rest until the same is true for Luanne Rockman's killer, as well. Gang-style retribution executions are not something we will stand for in our city. We will put an end to this kind of violence today."

Stella saw Murphy grit his teeth. He'd circled back to stand next to John when the mayor started talking and was clearly frustrated that the mayor released the victim's name.

Mayor Lewis continued grandstanding for a few more minutes before he finally ran out of things to say. Stella and John hadn't asked a single question—yet.

"'Gang-style retribution shooting?'" Stella said, "Can you elaborate?"

Lewis nodded gravely. "Cas Rockman's mother was gunned down in a cowardly—"

"No—no more comments," Murphy jumped into the camera frame, effectively ending the interview. "This is an ongoing investigation. That's all."

The mayor looked surprised and then contrite. The men walked away with Murphy talking low and fast into the mayor's ear, and Stella resisted the urge to follow them. It was 4:36 a.m.—there wasn't time for another follow-up question, anyway, and the five o'clock news would be starting soon.

Jim took the tape out of his camera and handed it to Stella as they walked back to the van. She shoved it inside one of the playback decks in the back of the live truck, ready to find soundbites for the morning news. After rewinding the tape to the beginning, she hit "play." Detective Murphy's face came up in crisp color and his mouth started moving, but there was no sound.

"Hey, Jim," she said, leaning back in her seat to find him smoking his cigarette outside. "What am I doing wrong here? I can't hear anything."

He blew out an irritated sigh and balanced his cigarette on the edge of the hood before leaning past Stella. He pushed a few buttons on the playback deck, messed with the toggle wheel to rewind and fast-forward, and then cursed under his breath.

"Well?" Stella asked, looking at the clock on the dash. Twenty minutes to pick a soundbite, write a story, and send the video back to the station was plenty of time, but not if she couldn't hear the interview. Jim continued fussing with dials and buttons for another thirty seconds before Stella broke in again. "What happened?"

"We've got no audio."

"Why?"

Jim stared at the control panel, his mouth working as silently as Murphy's onscreen. "Looks like I forgot to flip the switch on the camera for your microphone."

Stella looked at her photographer in disbelief. "Didn't you check levels as the interview started?" It was a basic procedure for any photographer. Just as she turned the microphone on before she started an interview, Jim needed to make sure the auxiliary mic input was selected on his camera.

Jim lashed out. "I thought I did, but obviously I didn't. I'm not used to working with you, Stella. You do things differently than Piper, so it's really your fault just as much as mine."

There it was, the other reason Stella disliked working with Jim. At least half of the dozen times the pair had worked together, some technical problem plagued them. It happened to everybody over time, but the number of times it seemed to happen to Jim made her think it was more than simple bad luck.

Disgusted, Stella pushed the chair away from the edit deck and climbed out of the truck. She picked up her cell phone and called the station. "I need the morning producer."

Stella quickly explained the situation. "I'm going to try to get a live interview with the mayor, but it might just be a straight live shot for the first hit."

Early in Stella's career, the live interview had always seemed to tangle her up. There were often difficult-to-understand eyewitnesses or unexpected information coming out live on-air. Over the last two years in Knoxville, however, she had gotten over that particular career hurdle and now a live interview was just as easy as any other. She looked at her watch and saw she had ten minutes until the morning newscast would start.

The burned-out, icy shell of a house was roped off by police caution tape with the phrase "Police Line Do Not Cross" repeated endlessly around the corner. After two minutes of staring between exposed studs, she finally saw movement as the mayor, fire chief, and Murphy walked out of the house. All three were headed toward their cars, and she called out to the mayor.

"Kevin, I'm so sorry to ask this of you, but could you stick around for a live interview? We had some technical problems..."

Kevin's face brightened almost imperceptibly. Murphy

muttered something to him, and the mayor nodded and headed her way. Kevin made a show of looking at his watch and wrapping his coat around himself a little tighter before he said, "Sure, Stella, I guess I can do that for you. Detective Murphy says I can't speak to any specifics of the case, though."

Stella smiled warmly at the mayor, gathered some equipment, and got ready for her first round of morning live shots. She'd been at work for fifteen hours—what was another few?

***

The monster block of morning news—two hours in all—was finally over, and Stella zombie-walked from the tripod back to the live truck, microphone tucked under her arm. She was on auto-pilot, just hoping to drive home safely from the station and fall into bed without any more glitches. She stumbled a bit on loose gravel and felt herself heading toward the ground. Just before her knee slammed into the asphalt, though, a hand reached out to keep her upright.

"Steady there, Stella," John said. She felt her face flush. He smiled through his own exhaustion, but his eyes showed the same intensity she'd gotten to know so well in Montana.

"Thanks. I've never felt so tired." She smiled up at him. He nodded slowly, his eyes never leaving her face.

"I just wanted to make sure you're okay. I want you to be happy, you know?"

They stared at each other for a beat before Stella started to feel too vulnerable. Maybe it was the exhaustion, or maybe it was the intensity of John's gaze. Whatever it was, she didn't feel equipped to deal with it.

Grasping around her mind for something to break the mounting heat between them, she said, "How about the mayor, huh?"

"Do you know his history?" At her blank stare, he continued. "He was first elected mayor maybe twenty years ago. Crime had been at an all-time high in the city—

especially here in East Knoxville." She looked around the neighborhood, her eyes taking in the rundown buildings, boarded-up windows, and random bits of trash smashed into the street gutters. John continued. "During his tenure, crime rates went down—nothing Earth-shattering, but the stats were good. He did his two terms and didn't run for reelection. Term limits," he explained, and Stella nodded to show she was listening. "Crime started to creep up when he was out of office, and the city council changed the rules so he could run again. They did away with term limits; that was maybe ten years ago, and he's been the mayor ever since. During the last two elections, no one even ran against him. People just love him."

Stella nodded again tiredly and looked longingly at the live truck. Her photographer was just slamming the rear doors, all his equipment finally loaded in. John, who'd been holding her arm throughout his history lesson, gave her a gentle squeeze that she felt in the pit of her stomach.

"I'll see you soon, Stella." He leaned in and brushed his lips against her cheek.

She felt a sigh escape as she looked up at him. "Bye."

She climbed into the live truck and tried to feel happy that her ex-boyfriend was happy. It was a good thing, right?

# 5

Back at the station, all Stella wanted to do was grab her car keys from her drawer and leave. Instead, she sat at her desk and started writing up her story. She was so tired that it seemed every fifth letter she typed had to be deleted and retyped. She quickly made notes for whichever dayside reporter would take over the story and got to work writing the article for the station's website.

The ding of an incoming email distracted her; determined to get home as quickly as possible, though, she ignored the flashing envelope icon while she worked. Finally, curiosity got the best of her and she clicked on the new message. It was from an anonymous emailer with the subject line, *Big Tip for You.*

"Oh, great," she muttered.

Stella got lots of feedback from viewers. Sometimes, a viewer actually wrote to comment on her story. Usually, however, it had to do with her outfit, makeup, jewelry, or winter hats. An anonymous email from someone with such a subject line could go a lot of different ways.

She quickly looked down to make sure she had the same shoe on each foot and then checked that she was wearing matching earrings. Certain she'd avoided any major outfit snafus, she allowed her eyes to move down the screen. The message read, *You missed something. Two victims, one shooter. More to the story than meets the eye.*

This kind of email would have normally captured her attention, but it was 7:33 in the morning and she had been up for almost twenty-four hours. Instead of grabbing the phone and making some calls, she closed her email account and finished writing her story. Once she uploaded the script to the news website, she logged off her computer and went home.

***

"Nice work last night," Patricia Eddy called across the newsroom. Stella had just arrived back at the office after a very unsatisfactory five-hour nap. She was grumpy, looked like crap, and still couldn't believe that she'd seen Piper and Russ at Panera when she'd made a quick stop on her way home that morning for breakfast. They'd been canoodling in a booth like long-lost lovers, and neither looked sick. It had made Stella ill.

She tamped down her bad temper and smiled up at her boss when she walked over. "Way to roll with the punches on that live interview this morning, Stella." Patricia had worked on air for years in a small market in Florida. Family obligations had forced her to come home to Knoxville fifteen years ago, and she'd worked her way up from associate producer to news director. Her long, dark hair had a thick streak of gray that floated down one side of her face like a silvery streak of light. She was heavyset—a byproduct of years of stress and sitting behind a desk—but she carried herself with the confidence of someone who was good at her job and well-respected by her employees.

Stella resisted the urge to complain about *why* she'd had to roll with the punches that morning and instead said, "Who's working on the arson today?"

"You are. We're short-staffed, and I didn't have anyone free. I need you to do the updates at five." She started walking back to her office, but called over her shoulder, "Oh, I guess that means you'll need to find the updates. Tick-tock, Stella—you're on the clock."

She set her bags down by her desk and logged onto her computer. The newsroom here had an open floor plan, just like her last station. Eight rows of desks ran the length of the space with half-height, fabric-covered dividers between them. Stella sat in one corner, near the photographers' area, where a camera was raised on a dais and aimed diagonally across the newsroom for reporters and anchors to use during different newscasts throughout the day. The assignment desk was in the corner of the newsroom directly across from Stella, where fifteen different scanner speakers were aimed at one unlucky employee charged with catching any kind of breaking news, crime, or violence that might erupt.

Currently, the dayside assignment editor was sitting on a swivel chair, typing furiously on the computer with the phone pressed into her ear and held into place by her shoulder. Stella's computer was taking forever and a day to boot up, so she walked over.

"Danielle, is there a photographer free? I need to get updated sound on the murder from overnight." She peered over her shoulder to read the newscast rundown currently displayed on her computer. "Looks like I'm live at five in front of the coroner's office downtown; you might as well send me with a live truck, too."

Danielle opened her mouth to answer, but then she paused as a tone rang out from one of the scanners. The call was for a drug deal in progress, and the dispatcher warned that there were possible weapons involved. Danielle tucked her short, blond hair behind her ears before grabbing the two-way radio microphone. "Who's near the intersection of Linden and Hatchett?"

A chorus of "Not me," came back, until finally a deep, gravelly voice said, "On my way, D."

"Thank God for Bob," Danielle said, typing a quick note to the producers about a possible new story for the evening news. She finally turned to Stella with a blank look on her face. "What did you need?"

"A photographer and a live truck."

"Right, right. Okay, let's see." The petite, younger woman looked down at a clipboard in her lap, and then her eyes moved up to scan the back corner where the photographers kept their gear. "Looks like Ernie's back there. Why don't you take him? He's got Live One today, anyway."

Stella nodded, walked away from the assignment desk,

and surveyed the newsroom as she headed toward the photographers' area.

Her station in Knoxville had the largest staff she'd worked with to date with ten reporters, nearly as many anchors, and a dozen photographers. Despite the record number of coworkers, Stella had really only gotten to know the handful of photographers she worked with on a regular basis.

Each reporter was expected to cover several stories each day, so no one was ever in the newsroom. Plus, with reporters working every possible shift, she was hardly ever working at the same time as any of the other on-air staff.

Stella loved her nightside shift and reveled in sleeping in and going to bed in the middle of the night. She loved hitting up the grocery store at midnight and never having trouble scheduling appointments in the middle of the morning. It would, however, have been nice to know more of her coworkers.

As she got close, Ernie looked up and smiled. He was young, fun, and really good at his job. After working all night with Jim, she was thrilled to be paired with one of the best cameramen at the station. His strawberry-blond hair was pulled back into a neat ponytail at the base of his neck, and he was surrounded by camera parts when she walked up.

"Can you be ready to roll in five?" she asked, looking uncertainly at the pieces of his camera carefully sprinkled around his bag.

"I'm ready now. This is a spare camera I'm trying to rebuild. Laffy says I can't do it—oh, ye of little faith."

Stella smiled. Ernie and Pat Lafragueta—Laffy to everyone in the newsroom—had been best friends since elementary school and were both excellent photographers at the station. They were constantly playing pranks on each other and other unsuspecting coworkers.

"I know you can do it, and so does he," she said.

"Yeah, but he said I couldn't get it done before the six o'clock news!" Ernie said with a grin.

"Oh," Stella said, looking again at the mess of pieces on the counter.

"He called off sick—I think just to make sure I'd be running around all afternoon. Oh well, I can still do it!"

"You guys are nuts," she said with a laugh.

When she walked back to her desk and quickly checked the newscast rundown and deleted several spam emails from her inbox, one new message caught her eye. It looked like it was from the same anonymous person who'd emailed her earlier. The note read, *Two victims, one shooter. Ask questions.*

She sighed; this anonymous emailer was starting to annoy her. There's no way the same shooter tagged both victims. Cas Rockman couldn't have killed his own mother, even if he'd wanted to—he was behind bars when her body was found. She looked at the wall clock and shook her head. *Some people just want to feel involved in crimes, and they make things up. That's probably what this emailer is all about.* She fired back a note, anyway. *Where do I start?*

She logged off her computer and grabbed her bags, caught Ernie's eye across the newsroom, and said, "Let's roll.

# 6

By Friday morning, Stella was starting to feel like herself again. She was sitting in a lovely, three-season room off the back of the house at Annie's, drinking ice water scented with lemon. She set the tall, sweating glass on the ceramic tabletop in front of her, and leaned back in the comfy, cushioned chair.

"I just love it here," she said, closing her eyes and turning her face toward the sun. The early days of February were still cold, but the mid-morning sunshine warmed the glass-walled room, and Stella could practically taste spring.

Curving flower beds rounded away from the patio just beyond the sliding glass doors, ready for flowers to pop up when the weather turned warmer. The grass was somehow lush, even in its dormant, yellow hue, and tinkling chimes sounded whenever a slight breeze blew. Both women were wearing stretchy workout gear, having just finished a robust walk around the stately neighborhood.

"So, the big day's coming up. Are you ready?" Stella asked, shooting her friend a sly smile.

"Ugh! Don't remind me. Just one year closer to thirty and I can't stand it!"

Stella laughed. Annie didn't know it, but Brian had asked her to help him plan a surprise twenty-eighth birthday party for her. It was still months away, but with her attitude about aging, she wasn't too sure Annie would be pleased.

"I just keep reminding myself that Brian turns fifty this year, so at least I'm not *that* old." She laughed lightly, and Stella nodded automatically, even though, in truth, she was slightly horrified that her high school friend's husband was practically twice her age.

"Tell me how you two met again. I lost track of you for a bit after we graduated. You came here right after high school?"

Annie drained her drink and walked into the kitchen; her words drifted back to Stella while she filled her glass from the pitcher in the refrigerator. "Yup, I came to UT Knoxville for a nursing program. I was working my first job as an ER nurse when Brian walked in with a stab wound to his arm." She sat back down on the couch adjacent Stella and tucked her legs under her while she talked. "He needed fifteen stitches to close the wound—he still has the scar." She smiled at the memory.

"Not many people can reminisce about a stab wound with such affection!"

A laugh burbled up. "Well, that's probably true. I like to giggle because I was so nervous to be working on such a handsome guy. He never did take his eyes off of me. He *says* he was mesmerized by my beauty," she laughed again, "but I think he was terrified I was going to hurt him with my shaking hands!"

Stella smiled, picturing the scene. "Do you miss working?" Annie had been married for nearly six years. She'd quit working a year after saying "I do."

"Not really. The hours were terrible—well, you know what that's like, Stella. It was fine when I was single, but it was impossible to see Brian, especially because he's on call with Gibson all the time. It just got to be too much."

"Don't they take turns being on call?" Stella was fishing for information, but Annie didn't seem to mind.

"No, they like to be on call together, so they can both get to the scene at the same time and bounce ideas off each other. You know, they've been friends forever."

"Really?"

"Both grew up dirt poor with no family to speak of. After a few years working in manual labor, they decided to enter the academy together. They wanted to give back and they've been on the job together ever since. Obviously, I think Brian is great, but I don't know where he'd be without David's support."

"Yeah, Gibson seems..." Stella trailed off, not sure of what to say. Every time she saw Murphy's partner, he glared at her, ignored her, and otherwise was a jerk. Annie obviously saw him in a different light, though. "He seems to really have Brian's back."

Annie smiled. "It's such a blessin'."

Stella looked up sharply when Annie's last word came out with a twang. "Annie, did you just hear yourself? Are you developing a southern accent?"

Her words were met with a sheepish smile. "Oh, God, did I drop the 'g' again? I swear, it creeps up on you, and before you know it, you're speaking slower and slower, and saying things like 'bless his heart,' and 'I declare.'"

"Maybe it's the sweet tea. I'd stick with water from now on!"

Both women dissolved into a fit of giggles. Once they had calmed, Stella stood. "I have to get going—last day of work this week."

"Won't you join us for dinner? David might come. We'd love to see you!"

"Oh, thanks," Stella said, grateful for once that she worked nightside, "but I don't really get a dinner break." Hanging out with Glaring Gibson on her off hours didn't sound like anything she wanted to do.

Annie picked up on her reluctance. "I probably shouldn't tell you this, but David is a bit... anti-media."

"You don't say?" Stella said, wrinkling her nose.

"Oh, you've noticed?" At her friend's look, Annie continued, "Well, I guess I'm not surprised. He wears his heart on his sleeve."

"What do you mean?"

"He used to date a reporter—from your station, actually. Clara. She broke his heart and totally screwed him over, pardon my language," she said, blushing.

"I've heard worse," Stella said dryly. "What did she do?"

"He told her something about a murder case he was working on. It was off the record, of course, but she reported it on the news and ruined the whole case. He got put on leave and didn't trust anyone in the media after that. I can't say I blame him," she added, looking apologetically at her.

Stella blew out a sigh. The background on Gibson certainly explained the glares and angry countenance. "How terrible," she said with feeling. "Where is Clara now?"

"I think I heard she got a job in New York City."

Stella was reluctantly impressed. New York City was the biggest TV market in the country; if you got a job there, you shared space with the network people, which often led to more opportunities. She noticed Annie watching her and said, "That kind of behavior gives us all a bad rap. I'd never sell out your husband—I promise."

Annie smiled warmly and nodded. "I know, Stella. I know."

***

Before she started up her car to drive home, Stella took out her phone to check for messages. She touched the mail icon on the screen, but looked up as a truck rumbled past, and when she glanced back down, she dropped the phone with a yelp. After a deep breath, she picked it up with shaky hands to see a picture of a dead woman filling the tiny screen. Her finger scrolled past the vivid image and her mind took a moment to process the words written below. *Start with this. Look at the evidence. Do your job.*

It looked like Anonymous was getting irritated—and graphic. She wasn't expecting to see a dead woman that morning, and frankly, she wasn't sure how it proved that the two recent shootings were connected. She closed her eyes and screwed up her face, preparing herself to look at the image again—the tipster had said she needed to look at the evidence. She opened her eyes and inspected the dead woman.

On her phone's tiny screen, it was difficult to make out

much. What first appeared to be a blanket covering the body was actually an unfolded newspaper, and a dark patch beneath the body must be blood. The woman's eyes were wide open, her mouth hung loose, and her head lolled off to the side closest to the camera. There were no obvious signs of what had killed her, and for that, Stella was thankful—she'd never seen a real dead body before.

She squinted, moving her eyes slowly over the picture and trying to find anything unusual. She could see where fire had burned part of the room, but the firefighters must have gotten to the house before it burned the body—*thank God*—and bits of trash littered the floor around the victim's head. Stella's eyes finally stopped on a shiny spot in the lower right corner. Was it a coin—a clue? Stella tossed the phone onto the seat next to her; it was impossible to tell on the small screen. She'd have to look at work later that day.

She barely remembered the drive home, because her mind kept wandering back to the victim's expression. It wasn't shock, or terror—it just *was*. Stella couldn't help but think that the woman had died with her eyes wide open, completely aware of what was happening. She shivered, not liking her train of thought. She'd rather think of the victims as faceless—nameless—and not as actual people. It made her often-gruesome job easier to handle.

She tucked her phone deep into her purse, determined to not think about the disturbing picture within until later, and walked slowly into the apartment building. Maybe she'd discuss the picture with Janet; her roommate always had good instincts when it came to crime. She snorted and tried not to dwell on why that was. Even though they'd lived together for nearly two years, Stella didn't know much more about Janet than she had when they'd first met. She had poor taste in men, clothes, and jobs, but Stella didn't know anything about her family or her past.

She tried to turn the doorknob to their apartment, but it was locked, so she dug into the depths of her bag. She jumped when her hand, searching for her keys, grazed her phone.

"Get a grip! It's not a dead body, just a phone," she muttered, finally unlocking the door to the apartment and pushing it open.

"I don't care what the hell you think I owe you," Janet's voice came snarling across the room. Her back was to Stella, and she paced in front of the sliding glass doors to the outside patio. "I'm not talking to you or anyone you want me to—you can't make me. I don't care who they are, I won't..." She caught sight of Stella and stopped mid-sentence. Janet's lips pursed shut and she pivoted away, muttering, "Don't call me again," before she clapped her clamshell phone shut and threw it down onto the couch with force. It bounced off the cushion and clanged against the edge of the end table before it landed with a quiet thwack against the carpeted floor.

"Dang it!" she shouted. She glared at Stella before stalking down the hallway into her bedroom, and the door slammed with a crack that echoed throughout the apartment.

A quiet whimper caught Stella's attention. Ole Boy was curled up under the end table. She scooped up Janet's phone, placed it safely on the coffee table, and then coaxed Ole Boy out with a few pats and whispers. He finally stood up cautiously and stretched out with a groan. His tail started wagging slowly, and he took three steps toward Stella before collapsing into a heap next to her.

"Don't like all that yelling, huh?" she murmured, rubbing the spot between his ears that always made his hind leg thump.

He groaned again, and Stella went to the hall closet for a treat. She tossed it his way and watched him leap and snatch the biscuit out of mid-air, all concerns vanished. She left him busily chewing the treat and went in search of Janet.

Stella knocked softly on her door, and after a moment of silence, Janet's sullen voice responded. "What?"

Stella pushed the door open. "You okay?"

"Sure," she said, looking at Stella through the mirror as she rimmed her eyes with thick strokes of black liner to match the smoky eyeshadow already filling her lids. In the five minutes she'd been alone in her room, she'd been busy. Her hair was already pouffed up high, teased to a gravity-defying height, and her bar "uniform" was hugging her every curve.

"Who was on the phone?" Stella asked more directly. If someone was threatening Janet at home, she wanted to know who, why, and what they were going to do about it.

"It was no one."

The women stared at each other silently for a moment before Janet broke eye contact and dug into her makeup bag. She picked up a tube of mascara and coated her eyelashes three times. The sticky liquid framed her hazel eyes with a dark, ominous fringe.

Janet spun around to face Stella. "I don't want to talk about it. Just leave it."

Stella held a neutral expression. "No problem. Let me know if things change."

Her friend blew out a breath and turned her back on her. "Sure."

She put her headphones on and resolutely turned up the volume, so even Stella could hear the music, as if from speakers—so much for her plan to talk to her about the anonymous emailer. She left Janet's room for her own and got ready for work.

Minutes later, she heard the apartment door slam shut and muttered to herself, "Bye, Janet. Have a great night at work."

When she was finally ready to leave the apartment, she looked at their chipped Formica countertops with distaste. Annie's house was full of upgraded finishes, including granite countertops, ceramic tile, linen drapes, and mahogany woodwork. Even though she was only three years older than Stella, she seemed like a "real" adult. Stella felt like she was play-acting—living in a slightly run-down apartment in a not-so-nice part of town, working second shift at a thankless job.

With a sigh, she locked the door behind her and then stopped short. As she scrutinized Cheryl's door across the hall, an idea formed in her mind. She would ask Cheryl to look at the picture of the crime scene. She was a forensic scientist—she'd be able to identify the so-called "evidence" right off the bat, and she might even be able to dig around for Stella on the Rockman homicide. No one answered her knock, though, so she hastily scrawled a message and her phone number on an old Post-it note from her purse and stuck it to Cheryl's door. She nodded to herself, happy to have a plan.

# 7

"I'll have a number three with extra guac and a cookie." Stella was standing on the sidewalk at the edge of downtown Knoxville where food carts lined the street, waiting for tipsy customers to pour out of the row of bars nearby. The area was called Old City, which was funny, since it hosted a number of new clubs and music venues. It was just past midnight, but still early for drunkards, so Stella was enjoying light crowds and no lines. She wanted a quick bite to eat before she went home after her shift, and the Hot Tamale truck seemed like the perfect answer.

The sizzle of onions and peppers on the grill soon gave way to warm, delicious smells that made Stella's stomach rumble. She'd been straight with Annie that morning—she rarely got a dinner break. That evening, she'd barely had time to gobble a snack out of the vending machines when she'd gone from breaking news about a shooting to a different call about a stabbing—which was alarmingly close to her apartment, by the way. Stella hadn't even sat down, except in the news car between crime scenes. Police had said both violent crimes were drug-related.

She was still tense from the day, and she tried to relax, now that the stress of her looming deadline was over. After taking one deep breath and then another, she looked around downtown and felt the chaos in her head start to quiet. Just as the food truck operator handed over her burrito, however, a tingle ran down her spine and her back stiffened seconds before a hand gently grazed her arm.

"Stella Reynolds."

Though the slight twang was normal around Knoxville, Stella recognized this particular voice. She steeled herself before turning around, but was still dazzled by Lucky

Haskins's handsome smile. His blond hair was perfectly tousled, as if he'd just come from a photo shoot. She happened to know, however, that he spent zero time on his appearance, and frankly, it made her even more irritated than when Jim had announced he'd forgotten to bring the light kit for her eleven o'clock live shot that night and had to use the van's headlights, instead.

Lucky was a top NASCAR driver; they had met when she worked at her last station in Bristol, Virginia, near both the Tennessee border and the huge Bristol Motor Speedway. They'd had a short-lived but emotional fling as they worked together to solve a mystery explosion on the track.

When they'd gotten back to reality, they hadn't worked out as a couple. He was still caught up with his ex-wife and was out of town more than in, and shots of him in different tabloid magazines and on gossip shows on TV with an annoying number of beautiful women had sealed the deal for Stella. When she left Bristol and moved to Knoxville, she'd figured their chance run-ins would come to an end.

She'd been wrong.

He'd sold his condo in Bristol and moved back to his home in Knoxville full-time just a few months after she did.

"When did you get back?" she asked, shrugging off his hand and taking a bite of her dinner.

He grinned, delighted. "No hug? No smile? I love that you don't pull any punches." His smile faded. "I've missed you," he added, staring at her intently.

She finished chewing. "Well, I haven't missed you," she lied and started walking to her car. "What are you doing in Old City, anyway? Looking for your next girl?"

"I already found her," he said, sliding up next to her.

"Give me a break, Haskins."

"Cut me some slack, Stella."

"No."

He stepped in front of her and she was forced to stop

walking. He took the burrito out of her hands, set it on a table nearby, and then offered her a napkin. "Salsa..." he trailed off, licking his own lips as he stared at hers.

She snatched the napkin from him, but before she could use it, he raised his hand and gently wiped the corner of her mouth with his thumb. She felt a thrill at the contact, and he smiled at her sharp intake of breath.

"I got back a few hours ago—tried you on your cell phone, but you didn't answer. So, I called Janet at the bar and she told me you sometimes stopped at the food carts on your way home. I guess I got... Lucky."

She rolled her eyes. "Listen, it's late, and I don't have time for—"

"For what?" he asked, his eyes taking on a steely glint. "For a real conversation about why you won't give us a chance?"

"No, Lucky, for a rehash of why we won't work out. We've been over it too many times already, and I don't have the energy tonight."

"Stella." She looked past Lucky at her car parked a block away. "Stella," he said again, grabbing her hands in his own and forcing her to look at him. "I can't control the paparazzi, but I can control myself. I don't know why you don't believe that about me—I've never done anything to make you doubt me. It's not my fault that I travel for my job, and it's not my fault you won't travel with me." He looked at her meaningfully, and she felt herself softening. He was right. It was a difficult life to be swarmed by photographers and cameramen at every turn. She instinctively glanced around to make sure they weren't being recorded just then.

"My car's right over there. Let's go for a ride."

She snorted and said sarcastically, "Really? You want to take me for a ride?"

He grinned back. "I sure do, Stella. All the time."

Biting her lip, she said, "I can't, Lucky. I have an early morning... thing." She felt a pang of guilt at the lie.

"Are you working on Valentine's Day?"

"Next week? I don't think so." She scrunched up her nose, trying to remember what day it fell on.

Lucky dropped one hand and took the other in both of his own to rub her fingers slowly. She felt each touch down into her toes. "Mmm. I'll plan something."

She squeezed his hand, but didn't answer, not trusting her voice. He raised her fingers to his lips, splayed them open, and without breaking eye contact, he planted a soft kiss in the center of her palm. The early flutters turned into an all-out riot in the pit of her belly.

"I'll call you, then," he said, opening her car door. Apparently, they'd been walking toward her car; she'd scarcely even noticed. "Soon," he said with another smile.

It wasn't until she was two blocks away, waiting at a stop light, that she realized she'd left her dinner on the table by the food trucks. She groaned, not wanting to chance another run-in with Lucky just to get her burrito.

She planned to call for pizza as soon as she got home, but a Post-it note stuck to her door changed everything. "Got your note, officially intrigued. I'm working late at the lab tonight. Swing by and we'll investigate."

Cheryl had written her phone number at the bottom of the small, yellow square of paper, and Stella snatched the note from her door and turned back to the parking lot. Maybe she'd finally make some sense out of Anonymous's emails.

# 8

Cones of light shone down from street lamps every ten feet where Stella was outside a nondescript building in the middle of the government district downtown. She was standing near a triangle of important city building—the police department, jail, and city hall.

She texted Cheryl, "I'm here," and waited.

After a moment, her phone pinged with a response. "Be right down."

Stella looked around with forced calm. The well-lit, deserted street could be the setting for a zombie invasion, or the perfect crime, seen by no one. She took a calming breath and reminded herself that no one would commit a crime so close to police headquarters!

Just then, an unmarked police car pulled up to the curb. To Stella's surprise, Detective Dave Gibson got out. He walked toward the crime lab, his head was bent over his phone.

When it became clear he was about to walk into her, she said, "What are you doing here?"

"What—huh?" Gibson looked up guiltily and frowned. "I'm just—I'm... wait, what are *you* doing here?"

"I thought you were having dinner with the Murphys tonight," Stella said, suddenly remembering her friend's invitation earlier that day.

"I—"

Before Gibson could say more, they heard the clunk of a lock and Cheryl pushed the door open. She looked from Stella to Gibson.

"Stella, come on in. Dave, what a nice surprise..."

All three stared silently at each other for a moment before Gibson hastily put his phone into his pocket. "I was just—just making sure Stella was okay. It's... unusual to see someone standing outside the lab at this hour. Glad everything is all right." He nodded sharply and turned back to his car.

"Goodnight, Dave!" Cheryl called.

Stella chewed her lip as they watched him drive away. Why would Gibson lie? He hadn't even noticed Stella was standing there until she'd spoken. She couldn't imagine why he was being so evasive—he had more of a right to be at the crime lab at midnight than she did.

"So, you know Gibson?" Stella asked as they walked into the building.

"Not well, but from the job, of course," Cheryl answered.

Dim security lights were all that illuminated the entryway. The room was small, and they were surrounded by bulletproof glass and a security turnstile. Stella stood, transfixed, while Cheryl ran her ID badge over a glowing light. It blinked and beeped, and she walked through. Stella hesitated—she didn't have a card.

"Um, Cheryl?"

"Yup, this way." Cheryl raised her card to another glowing light, and a door next to the turnstile clicked open, where Stella walked through. "Sorry for all the security. You can imagine that we have serious checks and balances to keep all the evidence in this building safe."

She nodded silently, wondering if she was allowed to be in here. She'd been inside the police department, in back rooms at the courthouse, inside the jail for interviews with suspects, and even in the morgue to get autopsy results, but this was her first time inside a forensics lab, and there had to be a reason for that. Before Stella could voice her concerns, Cheryl spoke.

"So, what exactly are you looking for?" They were heading down a wide hallway, and the tile floor was polished to a shine. There were no pictures on the walls, but occasional pockets of light from short, squat windows were located toward the ceiling.

"Am I allowed to be in the lab?"

"Oh, God, no—can you imagine?" Cheryl said with a laugh. She stopped at a turn in the hallway where an extra-wide set of double doors revealed the lab. Both women peered into the vast, shadowed room. Small, glowing red lights illuminated the space, shining off black soapstone countertops like beady eyes. The room was divided into several different work stations and each area had a set of tools of the trade.

As her eyes adjusted to the low light, Stella saw that the red lights were coming from different pieces of equipment on the countertops. Some she recognized, like microscopes, computers, and scales, but others were mysterious chunks of metal and glass. Everything was meticulously placed at regular intervals along the countertops.

"We're going this way," Cheryl said after a moment, leading them past the lab entrance and down another hallway. After a few closed doors, they walked into Cheryl's own small space. "Welcome to my office," she said brightly, motioning to a chair near the door. "Sorry it's so small. They keep offering me bigger areas, but I just can't fathom moving everything."

Stella looked at the bookcases bulging with technical-looking tomes and magazines and stacks of file boxes leaning dangerously toward the floor and smiled in understanding.

"So, did you bring something for me?"

"Oh, right!" She rummaged around in her bag and pulled out a 4x6 picture. "I had our graphic designers print this out. The resolution is pretty good." She set the image face-up on Cheryl's desk and watched the other woman's eyes rove over the picture.

"This is from a crime scene." It wasn't a question. "There's no doubt someone broke about a dozen different laws to send you this picture. Who sent it?"

Stella bit her lip; she wasn't about to give up her source, even if they were anonymous. Cheryl saw her hesitation and her eyes widened. "Oh, right. Sorry—not my business." She stared at the picture again, and then looked up hastily at her door. Footsteps echoed down the hallway.

A heavyset man in a white lab coat walked by, staring at some papers in a file folder. Stella thought he hadn't noticed them there, but then he muttered, "Cheryl," and nodded slightly as he passed the open door.

Cheryl hastily got up from her desk and watched him walk down the hallway. She bit her lip and said, "Hang on."

She disappeared. One minute passed and then two. Stella looked from the open door back to the picture of the dead woman on the desk. A small magnifying glass was sitting on one of Cheryl's shelves, and Stella picked it up and used it to look at the picture with greater clarity. It was still the same dead body—still those vacant eyes. With the magnification, however, Stella thought the body looked less real. It looked more like something out of a movie. She was just about to put the glass down when she noticed the newspaper loosely covering the victim. The headline read *2007 CRIME RATES DOWN*.

Her mind was making slow work of why the headline caused her pause when Cheryl walked back in the room. Her face was pale. "Stella, this probably wasn't a good idea. Jack is one of my supervisors. It's not technically against the rules to have visitors in the office, but I feel like I'm walking a fine line. I'm so sorry! We can discuss this later, if you want—back at the apartment?" Stella could feel her neighbor's angst from across the office.

"I'm sorry, Cheryl. I didn't mean to get you in trouble. I'll get out of your hair." She started gathering her things and said, "Does everyone usually work this late?"

"Jack is almost always here at night. He likes to work in the lab when it's empty; says he finds it distracting to work around other scientists. I feel the same way, so sometimes I come in after he's gone. I thought I'd miss him tonight—oops." She tried to grin.

"No worries. I'm not even sure what I thought you could find in this picture."

"Do you want to leave it for me to look at later?" she asked, holding out her hand.

"No, that's all right. I bet the graphics guys back at the station can blow it up for me—should have just done that in the first place."

Cheryl walked her out, and Stella spent the ride home thinking about the newspaper pages that covered Luanne Rockman's body. The headline referred to a crime report recently released by the FBI; Stella remembered when it came out, because it was the story she covered the day before she caught Cas Rockman's confession on camera and it had made for a great lead sentence in her story that night. "Crime stats down, but tonight, a violent shooting in the city center" was the tease she'd written for producers.

One of two things was going on. Either whoever killed Luanne Rockman did it the same day Cas supposedly shot Oliver Bennet, or the shooter had kept a pristine copy of the paper and covered her body with it a week later.

She pulled into her apartment complex and turned off the car, but sat in the driver's seat chewing on her lip. Did Cas shoot Oliver Bennet and his own mother? Could she even trust her tipster that the same man shot both people? She looked down at the crime scene picture lying on the seat next to her, but it wasn't going to give her any more answers.

She checked her phone and saw that she had a new email from Anonymous that read, *The authorities can't be trusted.* She felt a prickle of unease and her heart pounded against her chest as she reread the short email. Anonymous seemed to know exactly where she'd spent the last thirty minutes, and the thought was unsettling.

She shoved the phone into her bag and opened her car door. All of a sudden, flashing red and blue lights illuminated the parking lot. A deep voice boomed out of a bullhorn so close that her bones vibrated.

"Put your hands up where I can see them. You're under

arrest."

# 9

*Ohmigod, ohmigod, ohmigod!*

Stella swallowed back the bile that had risen in her throat and slowly stepped out of the car, raising both hands over her head. The authorities were watching, all right, from closer than she ever imagined.

She heard a commotion off to her right just before the impact of a collision sent her flying. She hit the ground with the air knocked clear out of her lungs and she stayed there, gasping for breath.

All sound ceased as she watched the feet of the man who'd hit her. They scrambled up from the ground and took off running toward the street. Two other pairs of feet quickly followed, and Stella lifted her head up a fraction to see one uniformed cop and a second man in regular clothes in hot pursuit. The cop made a leaping dive—like something you'd see on the football field—and took the runner down.

Noise roared back to Stella with the tackle. There was a grunt of pain from the officer and a yowl of rage from the man now pinned on the ground. The third man must have been an undercover cop, because he started shouting excitedly into a police radio clutched in one hand.

She was finally able to suck in a lungful of air, but she stayed on the ground, feeling safer in the shadows, hidden from the police lights and out of sight between two cars.

Before Stella could recover, a voice came from behind her. "Police, don't move. Why are you here?"

"Wha—what?" Stella looked over her shoulder and saw another undercover cop. He was holding his badge out in one hand and pointing a gun at her with the other. She was stunned into silence.

"What's your business here?"

"I—I live here," Stella stammered.

"What?" the cop asked, sounding less certain.

"I'm going to sit up now," Stella said, pushing herself up from the ground. She looked up at the officer again and he lowered the gun. He didn't change his aggressive stance, though. She stood on shaky legs and said, "I live here. I was just coming home from work, okay?"

She closed her eyes and turned her head to the side when he shined a flashlight directly into her face. When the light disappeared, she opened her eyes again in time to watch his face morph from suspicion to recognition.

"Oh, crap," he muttered, and then called out to his colleagues, "we've got a TV lady over here." He offered her his hand. "I'm Brad Stott. You okay?"

"Thank you," Stella said, grabbing onto his hand, needing the support. She took a few calming breaths before she continued, "What's going on?"

"Undercover drug buy. The guy tried to run when we moved in for the arrest."

"Drugs *here*?" she asked, dismayed.

"Drugs everywhere," he replied grimly.

They both turned to look at the suspect, who was now sporting bracelets and being escorted to the cruiser. Stella felt wobbly; the uniformed cop walked over and said something, but Stella's ears didn't seem to be working.

"What?"

"Why are you out here so late? Did someone call in a tip?" He looked around suspiciously, as if trying to identify the narc from the parking lot.

She managed a laugh. "No, I live here. I was just getting home from work."

"Why are you still holding the pretty lady's hand?" the officer said to his colleague with a smirk before heading to the cruiser. Stella looked down, surprised to see that she was still grasping Stott's hand. She unclenched her fingers and he shook his hand out.

"Sorry," she said quietly, "I think I'm in shock. It was a long day, and I was just coming home, and then this..."

"It's okay. Stella Reynolds, right?" She nodded. "It's perfectly normal to be freaked out. You just got knocked on your ass by a gun-carrying drug dealer," Stott said kindly. She smiled gratefully and grabbed her bag off the ground.

"You're friends with Detective Murphy, right?"

Stella explained her connection with Murphy's wife, and Stott nodded. He handed her his card. "Let me know if you see anything suspicious. We're here to help."

He walked her to the apartment building, and then she watched all three cruisers drive away from the safety of her living room while hugging Ole Boy close.

She let the dog out the sliding glass door and stood on the small concrete patio while he glued his nose to the ground, searching for the perfect spot to relieve himself. She noticed with surprise that Janet's cigarette stand was overflowing. The old metal coffee tin had sand in the bottom half, and usually just one or two half-smoked cigarettes were stuck inside. This evening, however, Stella noted what must have amounted to several packs of cigarettes stubbed out, smoked all the way down to the filter. Janet occasionally made noises about quitting entirely, but it seemed the pendulum had swung the other way, lately.

She sat on the patio chair and looked at her watch. It was nearly two in the morning. Ole Boy was sniffing elatedly after a squirrel at the base of a tree; Stella watched him tiredly and was just about to call him in when Janet drove up. She raised a hand in greeting, but her friend didn't see her. She was busy chewing someone out on her cell phone.

"Don't call me. Don't come to my home. I don't owe you *anything!*" She wasn't shouting, per se, but the echo of her last word clearly broke her out of her rage, and she lowered her voice. Stella could still hear her as she approached the front door to the apartment complex, though. "Don't contact me again—ever."

The door slammed behind her, and after thirty seconds, the apartment door opened. Ole Boy's head whipped up from the tree roots and he scampered in to greet Janet. Both came back outside, Ole Boy wagging his tail, Janet most definitely not.

She sat down with a huff and Stella took a good long look at her friend and roommate. She'd lost some weight— her cheek bones stood out in stark relief from the rest of her face. Her nails had been chewed down to the stub and some were even bloody, she noticed, as she took a cigarette out of her pack and raised it to her lips. The click of her lighter cut through the still air, and a flash of light met the end of her cigarette. Janet sucked in one quick breath and then a second. She finally inhaled deeply and sat back.

"God damn telemarketers," she deadpanned.

Stella forced a smile, but she was worried. Janet was obviously involved in something, and it sounded like she was in over her head. Was she in danger? Were *they* in danger?

After a moment of silence, Stella spoke. "Is there anything I can do to help?" Janet appeared to be staring out into the parking lot, but Stella didn't think she was seeing anything nearby.

Her friend shook her head, raised the cigarette to her lips once more, and inhaled deeply. She held the smoke in her lungs for what seemed like a long time, until she finally blew it out and looked at Stella.

"It'll all be over soon. This will all be behind me." She seemed to be trying to convince herself. Stella waited for her roommate to finish—to explain—but she stubbed out her cigarette, put it in the already-overflowing ashtray on the table between them, and started to stand.

"Well, then, maybe you can help me with a problem *I'm* having," Stella said, for some reason not wanting Janet to go.

The Montana native lowered herself back onto the chair and looked at her expectantly. "Shoot."

Stella quickly outlined the Bennet shooting and the Rockman homicide and explained the anonymous tipster and their certainty that the two shootings were related.

"So, what's the problem?" Janet said, finally taking her eyes off the parking lot and meeting Stella's.

"The problem is that I have no idea where to go from here."

"Well, first of all, don't trust someone who won't talk to you in person. That's what my mama always said, and I've found it to be true. You can't know this tipster's motives if you can't know the tipster. Secondly, what do you know about the two victims?"

"Well... Oliver Bennet is still in a coma." Stella rubbed her forehead, thinking. No one in town had been able to find any family members or friends willing to speak on the record about Bennet. It was unusual, but not unheard of— some people just didn't want to talk to journalists.

"So, what do you know about the other one?" Janet asked and looked at the ashtray with a grimace before getting up from her chair. Without waiting on Stella's answer, she said, "My advice is to start with the victims." With that, she nodded once and walked into the apartment.

Stella watched her fill a glass at the kitchen sink and walk straight to her bedroom. The door closed with a soft thunk that she could hear out on the patio. Ole Boy gave up on tracking the squirrel and headed into the house after Janet.

"Start with the victims," Stella muttered to herself. *Of course. It seems so obvious, now that Janet brought it up.* Stella was so wrapped up in the tipster and the crime scene photo, and Cas Rockman and his father that she hadn't been able to see the bigger picture.

She looked at her watch one more time. It was closing in on three in the morning. She didn't know how she was going to get any sleep that night, though; the adrenaline was still pumping through her veins from the undercover drug arrest she'd very nearly been a part of. She walked into her room, anyway, though, changed into her pajamas, and pushed Ole Boy off the middle of the bed.

"Pick a side, Ole Boy, any side."

She then climbed into bed and pulled the covers up to her chin to stare at the ceiling in the dark room, thinking. The neighborhood was going to hell, and Janet was involved in something dodgy. She had a picture of a dead lady in her purse and an anonymous tipster dribbling out information.

Ole Boy let out a loud snore and rolled back into the middle of the bed. His paws reached out and pushed Stella to the edge of the mattress. She grinned; at least some things hadn't changed.

# 10

"Where are you going?" Del, the nightside assignment editor, looked at Stella, her eyebrows drawn together in suspicion. Her long, black hair was piled into a bun on top of her head with random strands sticking straight out at regular intervals. She tipped her head down to look at Stella over her cat-eye glasses.

Stella had spent all of Sunday on the phone, finally securing an interview with Cas Rockman and his lawyer. It was a victory—he hadn't spoken to anyone since his mother's body had been found the week before. Despite her best efforts, her pleading, and her cajoling, it wasn't the home run she'd been hoping for.

"I have a jailhouse interview set up with Cas Rockman today. No cameras are allowed, but I'm going to ask some questions."

"No cameras? Why are we doing it?" Del looked at Stella, confused.

"Consider it prep work for another day." The woman opened her mouth to object, but Stella spoke first. "Don't worry—I already have a story shot and ready to go for today."

Del nodded slowly. "Did you clear it with Patricia?" Before she could answer, though, a tone rang out from the scanner and Del's attention shifted. Stella murmured a vague answer and backed away from the desk.

***

Twenty minutes later, she parked the news car downtown, grabbed her bag, and walked into the jail. She had to wait about half an hour for the director of the jail to meet her in the lobby and escort her through security. Eventually, she found herself sitting in a small visiting room.

Unlike on TV shows and movies, she wasn't separated from the prisoner by bulletproof glass; there was only an armed guard in the hallway and the unblinking eye of a security camera on the ceiling.

After a few more minutes of waiting, a guard escorted Cas Rockman and his lawyer into the room. Cas looked weary as he took his seat across the table from her. He had none of the bravado from their first meeting.

The bright orange prison jumpsuit hung baggy on his slight frame and his hands were cuffed together and attached by a long chain to his ankle cuffs. The entire setup looked uncomfortable and difficult to maneuver in, which, of course, was the point.

He looked thinner than when Stella had met him three weeks earlier; his face was gaunt and dark circles rimmed his eyes. The three weeks he'd spent in jail had not been good to him.

"Thanks for agreeing to see me, Cas." Stella had her notebook and pen out in a hopeful display that Cas might actually tell her something worth writing down.

"What do you want?" he asked dully.

His lawyer looked at her watch. "Stella, we don't have much time. I have to be in court on another case in about half an hour. Like we discussed on the phone, my client is pleading not guilty on all charges in court next week. Until then, we don't really have much to say."

"Not guilty?" Stella said, turning to Cas. "What happened to 'Yeah, I shot him,' from before?"

Cas stared at the wall. After a moment of silence, his lawyer said, "It's just a formality while I look into the case."

"Cas?" Stella leaned toward him, but he refused to look at her. "I have some questions about your mom. Do you know who would want to hurt her?"

He shook his head sullenly. "No idea. She was just a mom. She worked, she worked some more. She didn't have time to make enemies."

"Do you have any idea why she was shot? In that neighborhood? In that house? That wasn't her house, was it?"

"No." The single word held some kind of weight to it, but Stella couldn't figure out what.

He stared silently at her for a moment before dropping his eyes to the ground. His lips didn't move. His lawyer's cell phone rang, and she stepped to the door to answer it.

While she murmured into the handset, Stella leaned even closer to Cas, her elbows now resting on the table. She lowered her voice and said, "I'm getting some information from someone in the know. It sounds to me like you're in deep. I'm not sure anyone can help you, but I'd like to try." She let the words sink in for a moment. Cas didn't move, and after another minute of silence, she started to stand.

Cas looked up from the ground and his eyes locked with hers. "They won't let me out for the funeral. Did you know that? They're gonna bury my mother this weekend and I won't be there." He shook his head, struggling to maintain control of his emotions. "I didn't bargain for this. I didn't know... it's not something I can... I just can't." He slumped even lower in his seat and the chains binding him clinked quietly.

His eyes scanned the room until his lawyer looked up from the call. Cas bobbed his head and his lawyer nodded back. She ended the call and knocked once on the door. After a moment, a guard walked in.

"All done here?" he asked, looking at the lawyer for confirmation.

Stella's eyes were still on Cas's face. He looked upset—he looked like someone who was stuck—but he didn't look like someone who was ready to accept help. He also didn't look like he was ready to be honest with Stella—and maybe not even honest with himself—about what was going on.

She left the jail feeling certain that Cas was innocent when it came to killing his mother. He might have even been innocent of shooting Oliver Bennet. He certainly was not innocent of everything, though. The struggle now was how to prove anything without his help.

The interview had taken far less time than Stella had planned, so she took out her cell phone as soon as she got back to the news car. She punched in a series of numbers and listened to ringing on the other end.

"Coroner's office, how can I direct your call?" an official voice chirped.

"This is Stella Reynolds from CBS4 calling to get an update on the cause and time of death for Luanne Rockman."

"Please hold." Canned music came through the cell phone; Stella leaned back in the driver's seat and listened for a few minutes.

Finally, a live person answered the phone again. "Morgue," barked a voice, interrupting a soothing cannon from Beethoven.

"Hey, it's Stella from 4. Do you have a cause and time of death on the Rockman murder, yet?"

"I've got a cause, homicide. The victim was shot multiple times. We don't have time of death, yet. You'll have to call back."

Stella chewed on her lip for a moment before dialing yet another number. There was more ringing, but this time, no one answered and her call to Detective Murphy went straight to voicemail. She set her phone on the seat next to her and started up the engine. It was the fourth call Detective Murphy hadn't answered or returned since the arson last week and she wondered what was going on with him.

Before she could spend too much time worrying about her best source in Knoxville, her phone lit up and vibrated next to her. She looked down and saw that it was her old friend, Vindi, so she picked up after the second ring. "How's the hardest worker in all of San Diego?"

She and Vindi had worked together on a major story in Montana. The exclusive had propelled her friend from that tiny TV station all the way to California—a major jump, career-wise.

"Just hating all this sunshine and great weather," Vindi answered. Stella could practically hear her satisfied smile come across the line.

"What's up, Vin? Everything okay?" The two kept in touch, but usually only during weekend gab sessions. A call in the middle of the work day was rare.

"I got a weird call from the FBI about you."

"What?"

"What, what?"

"You can't just tell me the FBI called you about me without a little more explanation!"

"That's all I know. I wasn't about to call them back until I'd spoken to you. Why does the FBI want to talk about you?"

Stella stared blankly out the windshield. Was the FBI interested in Knoxville's recent shootings? Why wouldn't they just ask her, if that was the case?

She finally answered Vindi, "I honestly have no idea."

"What are you working on?"

"Murder and mayhem—you know, just like always." Vindi didn't laugh, and after a moment of silence, she said, "I swear, it must be some kind of mistake." More silence greeted that statement, and Stella searched for something to distract her friend. "You know what? Something *is* going on with my roommate."

"Something's always going on with Janet. What specifically is going on this time?"

"That's just it, I don't know. She's been arguing on the phone with someone... or multiple someones. She's definitely more stressed out than I've ever seen her, and it just occurred to me this weekend that she hasn't brought a random man home to our apartment in weeks. When I asked her about it, she said she didn't have time to date. That's when I knew that whatever's going on is serious."

She was hoping to lighten the mood, but once again, Vindi didn't laugh. "Stella, what do you really know about

Janet? Next to nothing. All we know is that she works at a hole-in-the-wall bar, dates questionable men, and brings them into your life. I don't like it."

Stella sighed. Vindi and Janet had known each other in Montana, but the two had never been friendly. "She definitely has her flaws, but she's been a friend to me over the years, Vin. That's why I'm worried. I wish there was some way I could help."

"You can help by not getting involved in whatever Janet's gotten herself into. She won't want you messing with her business any more than I do. I'm going to work on not answering my phone when the FBI calls again, and hopefully I won't have to get involved at all." Stella opened her mouth with a smart retort, but before she could say anything, Vindi said, "Be careful, Stella. Just be careful."

Vindi's warning seemed to hang in the air even as Stella started up the car and drove away.

# 11

Stella's adrenaline was pumping on her drive home from work. She'd had a great story—happy news, for once, on a military family being reunited after nine months apart— and was too pumped up after her live shot to go home. It was nearly midnight, however, and the entire city appeared to be closed for business. This was one of the few nights that made her wish she belonged to a twenty-four-hour gym. She would totally rock a treadmill, for once.

As she pulled into the apartment complex, her cell phone rang. She looked at the screen, groaned, and answered the call. "You'd better not be calling me to move that stupid RV."

Her greeting startled Janet enough that she didn't speak for a moment, but Stella could hear the chaos of the bar in the background. Glasses clanked, voices muttered, music played, and finally Janet guffawed. "Sorry, Stella. This time, I swear I forgot. If you could move it for me this one time, I promise I won't ask again."

Stella tapped her fingers against the steering wheel, sensing an opportunity. "I've got an offer for you. If I move the RV, you tell me what's been going on in your life lately."

Janet hesitated. "Dammit, Stella. Fine. I'm closing tonight, though, so it'll have to wait until tomorrow." She slammed the receiver down, but Stella was expecting it and had moved her phone away from her ear. She smiled at her small victory.

Stella looked longingly at the apartment building, which looked warm and inviting, and she debated going inside to get Ole Boy—he loved that darn RV. In the end, though, she decided to move the RV and then take Ole

Boy for a nice, long walk. Not many people would want to go for a walk at midnight, but that was the nice thing about having a giant dog—you felt pretty safe, no matter the time.

She spotted the house on wheels glowing under a street lamp about a block away. When she inserted the key into the lock and turned it, she didn't realize that there wasn't a corresponding sound of the door unlocking. She climbed up into the driver's seat and slammed the door shut. Before she could start up the engine, though, she felt something cold and hard press into the back of her neck.

"Don't move." The voice was deep and gravelly. She gasped. Despite the instructions the stranger had just given, she started to turn around. Whatever was pressed against her neck jabbed into her painfully. "I said, don't move," the man snapped.

Shivers ran down her spine as she realized that thing pressing against her body was a gun. Her eyes opened wide, and she grasped the steering wheel with both hands. Why, oh why hadn't she gone into the apartment to get Ole Boy? Surely, if she had been walking up to the RV with a hundred-pound dog, this drifter would have moved on. Now, she didn't know what was going to happen.

"Do you need money? Food? I can give you both things, just please don't hurt me." She glanced nervously into the rearview mirror, but couldn't make out anything about the stranger behind her. She eyed the door handle next to her and was rewarded with another sharp jab in her neck. "What do you want?" She heard the shakiness in her voice, but she didn't care.

"I need you to stay away from the Bennet case."

The words were so unexpected that it took her a few seconds to make sense of them. "You want me to stay away from the Bennet case?" she parroted back. Her only answer was a click from the gun behind her. "Did you just load a bullet into the chamber?" she asked in shock, recognizing the sound from movies. "Are you going to shoot me?"

She felt sick to her stomach as she eyed the door again. Would he really shoot if she took off at a run? She'd have the advantage of surprise, but of course, he'd have the gun.

"I might," he answered, as if they were discussing whether to order appetizers before dinner. "Do we have an understanding? I don't want to kill a pretty lady like you, but I will." He was surprisingly soft-spoken. Even in the back of her mind, she noted that there was no cursing and no accent. Whoever he was, he wasn't from Knoxville.

Stella took another shaky breath, but didn't answer. She raised her eyes to the rearview mirror again; the man had moved behind her and she could see that he was wearing a black face mask. It covered everything but his eyes, which were gold with flecks of black, like a tiger. She also saw the flashing glint of metal connected to her body.

"Can I go?"

"Go. Don't call the cops, don't tell your roommate, and don't investigate the Bennet shooting."

Stella pried one hand off the steering wheel, then the other, and reached out with a shaky hand for the door latch. She slid out of the RV, stumbling, and then walked quickly toward her apartment building, finally breaking out into a run when she was sure she wouldn't pass out.

Only when she was safely inside the apartment did she sink down onto the floor in a heap. Ole Boy lifted his head up, assessed the situation, and clambered off his dog bed. He walked over to Stella and lay down next to her, as if he knew she was close to the breaking point.

After a few minutes, she sat up and took some deep breaths. She had to get herself under control, so she could figure out what to do next. She took her reporter notebook out of her bag and replayed the entire incident over and over in her mind, taking notes. In the end, she was left with two major questions—questions that made her weak-kneed, confused, afraid, and a little angry.

First, how did the stranger know she had a roommate?

Second, why was he waiting for her in that roommate's RV? It appeared that Janet had a lot of explaining to do.

# 12

The next morning, Stella climbed out of bed at 8:32 after a long, restless night. After much internal debate, she had decided not to call police to report the threats from the night before—she didn't want to become the story. She was simultaneously amazed that she'd escaped the situation alive and also furious that she hadn't done more than act like a scared idiot.

She walked down the hallway to the kitchen, ready to make a cup of coffee, but stopped when she spotted Janet splayed out on the couch. Trash littered the family room. Open take-out containers were on the floor, and beer bottles were on the coffee table. She looked away from Janet and saw a note scribbled on their whiteboard. "I can't believe you didn't move the RV last night." Stella's eyes narrowed and she looked from the angry message back to her roommate and cleared her throat loudly.

Janet didn't move. Stella clenched her teeth, preparing to make more noise, when the sound of chewing caught her attention. Ole Boy was ears-deep in a white Chinese food container on the floor. She snatched it away, relieved that it didn't appear to contain anything lethal to dogs. She gathered up the other food boxes and noisily dumped them into the trashcan around the corner. Janet snorted, but slept on.

Ole Boy pawed at the side of the trashcan, whining.

"Shut up, dog," Janet muttered.

Ole Boy whined again and continued pawing the can; Stella sat in a chair to watch. After a particularly aggressive swipe, he managed to knock the can over, and it clattered to the ground like a snare drum riff.

Janet started; her head whipped up over the couch toward the noise.

"Did you get a ticket?" Stella asked from Janet's other side, startling her again.

Her roommate's face screwed up in concentration, and she turned from the trashcan to Stella. "What time is it?"

"It's morning. Did you get a ticket?"

"No," she sulked, "but I had to move that damn RV when I got home at three o'clock! I thought you were gonna move it for me—we had a deal." She tucked her head back into the pillow at the far end of the couch and closed her eyes.

"We did have a deal—" Stella started, but Janet interrupted.

"Wait, hold on. Let's not start, this morning. I actually came home last night intending to apologize. I know I've been acting crazy lately—stressed out all the time, yelling into the phone. You must think I'm on drugs."

Stella leaned forward and crossed her arms, staring at Janet with narrowed eyes. It had occurred to her that Janet was involved in something bad, and she opened her mouth to say as much when Janet peeled one eye open and held a hand out in warning.

"Let me finish. I'm always telling my customers that I don't have any right to be stressed. You're the one with the stressful job, investigating shootings and homicides! Somehow, you do all of it with ease. It makes me feel silly for getting stressed out about my life."

Stella felt her eyes narrow. "You tell your customers about me?"

"Sure," Janet said, feeling around on the table behind her for a water bottle. Her hand finally found it and she sat up to take a drink. "I brag on you all the time."

"Who, exactly, have you been bragging to?" Stella jumped off her chair, practically vibrating with nervous energy.

"Just my regulars—they're friends, Stella. Calm down! One of my regulars, Rufus Mills, was asking all about you the other day. He's definitely the strong but silent type; you can tell he could break someone half, but I don't actually think he'd hurt a fly."

Stella rolled her eyes. Janet brought home some guys who she wouldn't even want to make eye contact with on the street, let alone invite into their home. "What does Rufus look like?" she asked as she took in deep breaths through her nose and blew them out her mouth.

Janet was oblivious. She leaned back into the couch cushions and closed her eyes, picturing her friend with relish. "Well, he's tall with real broad shoulders, but it's his eyes that stand out. He has these beautiful, golden eyes. I've never seen anything like it before."

Stella's stomach dropped. There it was—the connection between the man with the gun and her roommate. "He has golden eyes? Are they, by chance, flecked with black, almost like a tiger?" She felt her face turn red with anger—Janet's chatty nature had nearly cost Stella her life.

"You know, I never would've described it that way, but yes, Rufus has tiger eyes. They are just amazing."

"What was he asking about?"

Janet smiled knowingly. "Ah-ha! I knew you wanted to date again! He was asking a lot about your job, and if you do any investigating on your own. I told him that you certainly do! You're not one of those dumb-blonde reporter types who regurgitate what cops tell you! You actually dig around on your own." She sat back and took another sip of her water. "He was pretty impressed. I bet he'd love to meet you, and I promise you'd just love him. I mean, Stella, those eyes are just amazing... you should see them."

"I'm pretty sure I already have," Stella said with a frown. She was ready to launch into an explanation of where she'd seen Rufus's eyes, but she took a few more deep breaths to steady herself, first, not wanting to launch into Janet, instead. The chime of the doorbell interrupted Stella's planned verbal attack, though.

"I'll get it," her roommate said, jumping off the couch and heading toward the door. "Did you make coffee, yet? I could really use a cup."

Stella stared after her roommate blankly. Janet had no idea of the danger she had put her in. She watched Janet reach for the door, wondering at the last minute if that was wise. Would Rufus come back in the morning with another warning? She hustled over and laid her hand on it, ready to push back if Rufus tried to push in. Instead, she almost slammed the door in the face of a flower delivery guy.

"Oh," he said, looking in surprise from Janet to Stella. "Can I come in or not?" Her roommate looked at her as if she were crazy. "Most people love the flower delivery guy!" he said with an uncertain smile.

She closed her eyes, embarrassed, and opened the door wider. "Sorry."

"I've got a delivery for Stella Reynolds. Is that one of you two ladies?" Stella nodded and he handed her the flowers.

"Valentine's Day flowers! Those are gorgeous," Janet said, snatching the card out of the holder from the vase as Stella carried it into their apartment. The arrangement was at least two feet tall and wide with flowers exploding from every side. "Can I open the card?"

Stella set the flowers in the middle of the kitchen table and turned them until they looked just right, and then took the card back from Janet. "No, you can't."

She opened the tiny envelope. *It's soon. I'm ready. Are you?* There was no signature, but Stella knew exactly who they were from.

"Well?" Janet looked like a kid on Christmas morning, and despite her lingering anger, Stella felt herself softening toward her roommate. Janet always meant well, didn't she?

"Lucky. They're from Lucky."

# 13

Despite Rufus Mills' warning—or maybe because of it—Stella wanted nothing more than to learn as much as she possibly could about Oliver Bennet. When she got into work later that day, however, the assignment editor at the station had a different plan.

"Valentine's Day?" Stella could hear the whine in her voice, but she couldn't help it. "Surely there's someone else who can cover Valentine's Day today? I've got a bigger story I want to work on."

"Really? What's the bigger story?" Del asked, pursing her lips.

"It's about the Bennet shooting—"

"Tell me, is this a story you can turn today," Del interrupted, "or is this another deep background interview that'll run in a month? I need a story *today, on* Valentine's Day, *about* Valentine's Day, and I need you to do it."

Stella went back to her desk, sulking. Valentine's Day wasn't even a real holiday—it was a Hallmark marketing ploy to get people to buy more greeting cards. There were six dayside reporters and none of them could do the dumb flower-shops-are-busy-on-Valentine's-Day angle?

She saw one of them, Hank, logging tape. Another reporter, Betsy, was putting makeup on at her desk. The other desks were all empty, as usual, with the remaining reporters out in the field, working on stories. Ernie and Laffy were messing around with something, and she stopped to take a closer look.

"It's my dad's old car phone," Laffy said, moving aside so Stella could see. The large, black case was roughly the size of a briefcase, and he pulled the double zipper open, revealing a large, black, plastic phone. It was about the same size as Stella's desk phone.

"Why do you have it?" she asked, looking between both men.

Laffy shrugged evasively. Ernie said, "You'll see."

In her bad mood, she wanted to be annoyed, but she also knew that Ernie had worked a difficult shift the day before—a sad story about a drowning. He needed to be silly and cut loose after a day like that.

She logged onto her computer, still in a funk, and saw that she was live at the top of each half-hour newscast. Grimacing, she clicked on the email icon on her screen and sat up a little straighter when she saw a message from Anonymous.

The subject line read, *Don't stop digging.* She clicked on it, expecting something good. Instead, the note simply read, *Keep at it.*

Stella glared at her screen, incensed. "Keep at it," she muttered through her gritted teeth. She punched the delete key with enough force to erase the email from the entire universe and not just her computer.

"Stella," her boss called to her from across the newsroom. "I've got you set up at this cute, little boutique florist. I thought we'd take a slightly different angle than usual. This shop serves Knoxville's wealthiest—you know, your basic local celebs. They invited us to come in and look at their expensive floral arrangements—none of those $49.99 specials you find online." Stella tried to fix a smile on her face and nodded like she was thrilled. Her news director continued, "We're planning on you interviewing the owner at five, just a straight live shot at five thirty, and I want a package with a live wrap for the six. Have fun." She bustled off around the newsroom, talking with the two other reporters as she made her way to the producer's pod.

"You ready to go?" Melissa was filling her many pockets with different news-gathering equipment. Double-A batteries for the wireless microphone went in one pocket and the microphone, itself, followed into another. She was standing near Stella's desk at the photographers' station with her camera bag open. It, too, was stuffed full of equipment for the evening live shots.

Stella nodded, logged out of her computer, and followed Melissa out the door. Clouds were moving in, and during the ride, a slight rain started falling. They drove in relative silence for about twenty minutes, until they finally arrived at Mercer Florist. The shop was at the outskirts of Knoxville; there was one delivery van in the parking lot, but slots for five more, and Stella wondered how many employees were working that day.

As they walked inside, it looked like a flowery war zone. Broken stems littered the ground, crushed flowers were discarded underfoot, and there was barely an open stretch of ground to walk on. There were full vases sitting on every available surface; tables, shelves, and even the floor appeared to be sectioned off by some unknown system.

The arrangements were like stunning pieces of artwork—nothing like your typical flowers shoved into a vase. Stella's eyes went wide in wonder. They were masterpieces, reminding her of her own floral delivery from that very morning. Melissa coughed as Stella bent down to look at one lovely vase. A riot of red roses stood at least two feet tall, surrounded by twists of paper and unique flowers. There was more coughing, and then an unfortunate sounding snort combined with a sneeze had Stella looking around with concern. Melissa's eyes were watering and her nose was red and running.

Melissa grimaced. "Allergies," she said taking a tissue from a pocket and blowing her nose.

"Why didn't you tell Del? They could've sent me with someone else!" Stella exclaimed. She hated to think that Melissa was going to be miserable for the next three hours.

"I was going to do just that, but the only other photographer free for the evening live shot was Jim. I just couldn't do that to you, Stella—not on Valentine's Day."

Stella smiled gratefully and then bit her lip when Melissa sneezed again.

The owner of the shop came out to greet them. Sallie Mae Mercer seemed to vacillate between being thrilled that they were there and being irritated that they were in the way. This was by far the busiest day of the year for them, though, and in the end, the value of free press won out for the owner.

"Try to stay out of the way until the live shot," Sallie Mae said, pointing to one corner with empty floor space. "I've instructed all my designers to tell you if they don't have time to talk. You understand, I'm sure." With that, she bustled out to the front room to meet a customer.

They got video for their stories and interviewed several designers and delivery drivers as they hustled in and out of the store. Stella pulled the hood of her jacket up against the misting rain as they walked back to the truck to edit their stories together for the night. When they were half-way across the pavement, yet another delivery truck pulled up. The driver hopped out and Stella stopped in her tracks, making Melissa bump into her from behind.

"Whoa! Sorry, Stella. Everything okay?" she said, wiping her nose. "Darn! That's my last tissue."

"Oh, I'm fine. Sorry," Stella said, moving toward the truck again. She'd recognized the driver from her delivery that morning and a warm, fuzzy feeling filled her chest, knowing that Lucky had bought her flowers from such a fancy place. In the scheme of his financial situation, spending a couple hundred dollars on an arrangement was like her buying a piece of gum, but she was still pleased to know that he cared.

With everything that had been going on, she'd forgotten he'd asked her the week before if she had plans for Valentine's Day. Her face wrinkled in distaste—he hadn't called about doing anything in the end, so maybe he'd forgotten, too. Perhaps he was busy with someone else. That thought was still bumping around in her head when another sneeze ricocheted around the van; Melissa's eyes were almost swollen shut, her nose dripped like a faucet, and her breathing had developed a certain wheeze. Stella realized they had to make a change.

"Melissa, you can't go back in there. You're having an allergic reaction."

The woman opened her mouth to respond, but she sneezed three times in a row, instead. She looked miserable. "I think you're right, Stella. It's never been this bad before, but I've never been in a room with so many flowers before, either."

She looked at the dashboard in the van. It was only four o'clock, so there was plenty of time for the station to send out someone else. Even if it had to be Jim, surely he couldn't screw up running the camera for her live shots.

Stella made the call and Del put the new plan into place. All too soon, Jim Blunt was pulling up to the scene in a news car, and Melissa shot her a sympathetic glance before she headed out.

"So, what's the plan, Stella?" Jim asked.

"Live interview with the owner at five, straight live shot at five thirty, and then we'll roll the package that Melissa edited for the six o'clock news."

Jim nodded and started pulling cables for the live shot.

By ten minutes to five, they were ready to go. As they stood around, waiting for the newscast to begin, Stella watched a florist create an arrangement that looked like a living sculpture. More than two dozen long-stem roses floated out of the vase, and as Stella watched, he nestled a final flower into the arrangement, twisted it thirty degrees to the right, and then stood back to admire his work.

He lifted the vase and walked it over to an already-crowded corner of the room. It was only after he placed on the floor that Stella realized it was sitting next to eleven exact replicas. In fact, the longer she looked at the arrangements, the more she realized that they closely resembled her own flowers from that morning. She watched a delivery driver gather the identical arrangements onto a rolling cart and head toward the door.

After touching the florist lightly on the arm and nodding after the delivery driver, she said, "Those flowers are gorgeous." His cheeks warmed with the praise. "Are they all headed to the same place—some kind of Valentine's Day wedding reception?" The longer she looked at the identical arrangements, the more she realized that they might be centerpieces. Wouldn't that be a great thing to mention for her love story for the news that night?

The florist shook his head. "Can you keep a secret?" Stella nodded and the florist went on. "Lucky Haskins—you know, that famous NASCAR driver who lives here in Knoxville? Well, he ordered thirteen of the same arrangements. I guess he's got a whole harem of women to keep happy today."

# 14

It took Stella a moment to realize that she was staring open-mouthed at the door after the flowers. Her stomach had seemed to drop right out of her body. At first, she felt nothing but shock. As the seconds ticked by, though, her shock gave way to a very real anger burning from deep within her belly. Was she one of Lucky's *harem?* Did he have the gall to send flower arrangements to thirteen different women on the National Goddamn Day of Love?

"Standby, Stella. The show starts in one minute. We're live off the top, right after the cold open." Jim was standing behind the camera with no idea that Stella's world had just been rocked. She nodded to let him know that she'd heard and realized nearly thirty seconds later that she was still nodding.

She shook herself. *Keep it together,* she thought sternly. She didn't even want to date him, after all, but a slow-burning rage was simmering just under the surface, and Stella was worried it might spill over during the live shot. She whipped out her cell phone and sent a quick text to Lucky. "Watch me. Live @ 5." Her fingers were shaking to the point that she hit the ampersand and then the quote symbol before finally touching the correct one, but she hit send and tossed her phone into her bag by Jim's feet.

"Coming to you in ten seconds, Stella."

Through her earpiece, she heard the anchors begin to read the intro to her story.

**Chet**
**Good evening, everyone, and happy Valentine's Day!**
**We begin this evening at Mercer Florist on the outskirts**
**of Knoxville.**
**Andrea**

**That's where we find our own Stella Reynolds, live
with more on the busiest day of the year for flower
shops everywhere. Stella?**

**Stella**

**Chet, Andrea, we are here at the very exclusive Mer-
cer Florist, where many of the rich and wealthy, and
even some celebrities, in the Knoxville area do their
shopping.**

At the word "celebrities," she felt her smile fade. She
glared at an arrangement of flowers near her before continuing.

**Discretion here is key, but I can tell you—without di-
vulging any names, of course—that we just saw twelve
identical arrangements head out the door, all sent from
one man. You'd hate to think what a dozen women
would do if they knew one man was trying to woo them
all on Valentine's Day!**

She laughed lightly, she thought, and then recoiled
when she heard it reverberate angrily around the room.
The silence pressed in around her, and she turned to find
that all activity behind her had ceased. Half a dozen flo-
rists were staring at her, agog.

She turned to the owner of the shop, and Sallie Mae
looked back at her with a bit of panic visible around the
edges of her eyes. Stella cleared her throat.

**It is the holiday of love, after all, so maybe they'd just
be happy with the flowers.**

She tried to focus on her live shot, but she couldn't believe Lucky had thirteen women in his life! *"Trust me,"
he'd said.* Sure.

**You know, not every woman would stay with that
man. I wouldn't put up with that, of course, so then he'd
be down one woman, wouldn't he? No more baker's
dozen for him!**

Jim moved his face away from the camera and
mouthed, "Baker's dozen?"

The funny expression on his face was enough to startle

her out of her anger.

**Ah. Anyway, joining us now is the owner of this lovely shop, Sallie Mae Mercer. Sallie Mae, some really beautiful, unique arrangements have been coming out of your shop today. Talk to me about how you ramp up for the massive scale of production on Valentine's Day.**

It took Sallie Mae a few seconds to recover from the shock of Stella's introduction, but she did her best to keep the interview lighthearted and tried to focus on the festiveness of the occasion.

"Clear," Jim said after what felt like an hour, even though her watch assured her that only two minutes had passed. He unhooked the camera from the tripod and set it down on the floor, having no idea of the stress Stella was under. Sallie Mae appeared to be sweating, but she gave her at tenuous smile before getting back to work.

Her cell phone buzzed in her purse and she wanted to take it out and smash it with her heel. Instead, she ignored it completely, which is exactly what she planned to do to Lucky for the rest of her life.

***

It was an extraordinarily long night. The news director was so happy with her live shots that she had to stay at the florist for the eleven o'clock newscast.

"I thought you were going to out me there," the handsome florist from earlier said to Stella as he cleaned his workstation from the day.

"I didn't mean to make you sweat," she said, forcing a rueful smile. "I guess I got a little nervous," she lied. "I started rambling a bit, huh?" He smiled, and she walked outside to the live truck feeling like she'd eaten something rotten.

The misting rain from earlier was changing over to snow, and tiny snowflakes dotted the ground, turning the slushy puddles to shining, icy slicks.

After she signed off at the last time at 11:03 p.m., she helped Jim tear down the live shot and thanked Sallie Mae for keeping the shop open for them. As she and Jim went to the live truck, Stella thought she'd never been so glad to be done with work for the day.

After sitting in the passenger's seat for fifteen minutes, though, she realized she wasn't going anywhere fast. Jim was still messing around with the control panel in the back of the van, trying to get the mast down.

A giant, steel, twenty-foot antenna telescoped up from the middle of the van, beaming video and audio from their live shot back to the station via a microwave link. A transmitter at the top of the mast rotated three hundred and sixty degrees, until it connected with the receiver back at the station.

A simple switch on the control panel usually raised and lowered the mast with ease. Tonight, however, the wet that had turned freezing rain and snow had frozen the mast in place. Jim toggled the switch back and forth, but nothing happened. The twenty-foot pole remained fully extended. Jim scratched his head and tried the switch again.

Stella turned around. "You know what you have to do, right?" Jim shrugged. "You have to climb on top of the van and pull the mast down. You know, grab the handles?" She'd seen Melissa do it a dozen times. It didn't seem like the safest thing to do, but it was what needed to happen to get them on their way.

Jim looked at her like she'd grown a second head. "Climb on top of the van in the snow? I could slip and fall—no way."

Stella stepped out of the van. "So, what do you suggest we do? Sit out here until morning? Wait until the spring thaw? I'd like to get home tonight!" They stood facing each other, arms crossed and glaring. Jim wasn't moved by her anger. "Are you going up?" she asked, pointing to the sky.

Jim ignored her completely. He tried the switch again, and then he picked up his cell phone and dialed the station. After another discussion that lasted less than two minutes, he hung up.

"Well? What did engineering say?"

"They said I have to climb on top of the van and pull the mast down by the handles."

Stella looked at him triumphantly, but noted with a frown that he still wasn't moving. "Well," she asked, impatiently, "are you going to do that?"

He jutted his chin out defiantly. "No. I told them they had to send someone out to do it. I'm not going up there in this weather."

"That could take hours!" Stella wanted to stamp her foot in frustration. Instead, she said, "Give me your shoes."

She kicked off her heels and put her feet into Jim's too big, too warm, and too smelly black sneakers. She tied the laces tightly and started climbing the ladder on the back of the van. Stella had never been afraid of heights, but if she'd been in her right mind, she probably would have been afraid of the ice. She wasn't in her right mind that night, though; she was mad as hell.

She marched across the top of the van and grabbed the handle that rose five feet above the roof, along the widest part of the extended mast. It was icy, cold, and slick with frozen rain and snow. When she pulled on the bar, nothing happened. She pulled again, this time with all her might, but it didn't budge.

Stella stepped back and glared at the steel tube. It couldn't be this difficult—she'd seen Melissa do it before without breaking a sweat. After pushing her sleeves back and reaching up with both hands, she grasped the handle that circled the base of the mast, pulled herself up in a perfect chin-up, and used her body weight to bounce up and down, until she felt the mast give. She let go and watched it sink slowly toward her, bouncing every few feet on its hydraulics. Eventually, it went low enough that they would be able to lock it down and safely drive away.

Stella climbed off the roof and gave the sneakers back to Jim. "Why are you wearing my heels?" she asked, her face screwed up in distaste before he handed her the black wedges.

"Well, you had my shoes on, so I thought..." Jim trailed off, his face the color of the dozens of roses they'd seen that day.

"Sure. Makes sense," Stella said, not making eye contact. She didn't really understand anything about her day, and she was ready for it to end.

# 15

It took at least an hour to get back to the station. The roads were slick, and Jim drove slowly, narrowly avoiding two crashes and a slide-off on the way. After Stella entered her story information into the news program on her computer, she finally got in her car to head home for the night.

She felt her anger growing exponentially with each passing minute. Her phone buzzed at least a half-dozen times, but she refused to even look at the screen, lest she be tempted to answer and scream at Lucky. She wasn't going to give him the satisfaction of even acknowledging his duplicity. He knew what he did, and that was enough for now.

She'd only been driving for a few blocks when she realized something was amiss. A black Escalade with dark, tinted windows had been following her since she'd turned out of the news station's parking lot. The streets were mostly deserted at midnight on Monday, and the Escalade was just one or two car lengths behind her. They drove several blocks together, the Escalade staying with Stella, even when she slowed to a crawl and moved to the far right lane. She couldn't make out who was inside, but she wondered if Rufus was planning another "talk."

The thought only fueled her rage; she wasn't going to let Rufus Mills scare her at her house. If something was going down, it was going to happen right here, in the middle of Knoxville!

She stopped for a red light at a major intersection and sensed her opportunity. After slamming the gearshift into park, Stella threw her door open and stalked back to the Escalade. She knocked sharply on the driver's side window and waited for it to roll down.

Behind her, the red glow of the stoplight turned green, but she didn't move from the double yellow lines on the pavement. Finally, the window rolled down, revealing not Rufus, as she'd suspected, but two men in business suits. It was unusual enough at midnight, but it didn't stop Stella's simmering anger from boiling over.

"Can I help you?" she snapped.

The driver was a solidly-built man. His dark brown hair, flecked liberally with gray, was cut short, and his face was smooth and pale, save for two blotches of red at his cheeks. He opened his mouth to speak, but the smirk on his face pushed her over the edge.

"Are you kidding me, right now? Is there something funny about the fact that you two are following me when I'm driving home alone after midnight? What is wrong with you?"

The man in the passenger's seat, also solidly-built with dark brown hair and no facial hair, held out a hand in supplication. "I was going to apologize if we frightened you, but the last thing you seem is scared."

"I'm not scared, I'm pissed off. What's going on?"

"That seems like a fair question. I'm Special Agent Thomas Jones with the FBI, and this is my partner, Special Agent Harry Roberts. We'd like to ask you some questions."

"What?" That amazing proclamation jarred Stella enough that she felt her anger start to dissipate. Curiosity moved in as Stella crossed her arms and looked at both men inside the Escalade. "I'd like to see some ID."

By then, the light at the intersection had cycled through several times, but not a single other car had passed. Both men took their wallets off the console between the front seats and flipped them open. The badges looked official, but what did Stella know? She'd never seen an FBI badge before.

"Are you based here, in Knoxville?

Special Agent Jones, the one in the passenger's seat, had taken over the role of spokesperson. He was leaning into his partner's space, so he could see Stella out the driver's side window.

"No, ma'am, we're out of Washington, D.C. We're doing background on someone, but we're having trouble getting through to the right person."

"Well, I guess you are, especially if you're calling California for information," she said slowly, remembering Vindi's call the other day. "Who is the background check for?" Stella asked, now genuinely curious.

"Sampson Foster."

"I've never heard of him," she said, feeling a bit disappointed. This whole thing had been starting to feel like a James Bond movie, but now Stella was certain the agents had the wrong girl.

Special Agent Roberts nodded. "We figured. We're actually trying to get in touch with Janet Black. She keeps giving us the slip, though, so we thought we'd start with you and work our way back to her."

"What do you mean 'start with me?'"

"You know, talk to the roommate."

Special Agent Jones smiled enigmatically, which was infuriating.

"You're telling me that two professional, seasoned agents like yourselves can't find Janet?" Special Agent Roberts touched his gray sideburns self-consciously, and she threw her head back and laughed. "Oh, that's just great. Good luck, gentlemen," she called over her shoulder, already headed for her car.

Special Agent Roberts called after her, "It'd be pretty uncomfortable for you if we started poking around your business. We can do that, if you don't help."

Stella froze with one foot in front of the other. Her simmering rage had died down, but that comment had struck a nerve. She pivoted and marched back to the Escalade. "What did you say?"

His partner was already distancing himself physically

from Special Agent Roberts. Jones opened his mouth, but Roberts spoke first. "I said that we could make things difficult for you, if you don't help us."

Stella rested her forearms on the open driver's side window. She narrowed her eyes and glared at the agent in front of her. "I don't know who you're used to dealing with, but you can't talk to me like that. I know exactly where your rights end and mine begin, and I have friends here—friends who won't like folks from Washington, D.C., coming in and threatening me. You got me?" Roberts's face was turning a deeper shade of purple with every word she uttered, but she wasn't done. "If you have legitimate business with me, then you may contact me at my office during regular business hours. Don't follow me at midnight when I'm alone and think you're going to scare me into narcing on my roommate."

Her eyes were locked on the man in front of her, and she opened her mouth to speak again, but was startled to feel a light touch on her arm. She spun around to see Special Agent Jones at her side. In her anger, she hadn't even heard him get out of the car.

"Ms. Reynolds, my apologies. We're not here to investigate you," he shot his partner a sour look through the window and then turned his gaze back to Stella, "but we would like your help talking to Ms. Black. That's all we want to do. Just talk. Here's my card. Call if you think you can help."

Stella turned and walked stiffly to her car, slipped behind the wheel and started driving. Much to her chagrin, the Escalade continued to follow her. She assumed that they already knew where she lived, but just in case they didn't, she wasn't going to be the one who led them back to their apartment—their empty apartment.

Now that she was alone in her car, with adrenaline pushing through her veins from confronting two strangers in the middle of a deserted street, she realized what an idiot she had been. *Thank God those were FBI guys. What if it had been Rufus Mills?*

She shook herself; she had to think. She didn't want to go back to the empty apartment, knowing two agents from the FBI would be outside, watching. How creepy. Where else could she go, however, at 12:03 on a Tuesday night—scratch that—on a Wednesday morning?

The answer was as obvious as if someone had written it in the dust on her car's dashboard. There was only one other person she knew who would still be awake and winding down from a day at the office. He might even be happy to see her. She did a U-turn in the middle of the deserted street and headed toward John's apartment.

# 16

She couldn't tell if the Escalade was still following her when she pulled into the parking lot at John's apartment complex, but she didn't spend too much time checking. After throwing her car in park, Stella grabbed her bag and raced into the building, only looking behind her as the doors closed, when she was safely inside.

A pair of headlights shone into the window, and then turned off with the low running lights still visible. She wrinkled her nose in distaste. *Being followed by the FBI. What next?*

John lived in a nice building in a neighborhood that wasn't so much up-and-coming as it was already arrived. She took the elevator to the third floor and headed to his apartment. The plan that had sounded so good just minutes earlier now seemed to have as many holes as a colander.

It was 12:32 in the morning; Valentine's Day had technically just ended, but if anyone was celebrating, they might still be. She cringed at that. Was John busy inside with Katie? She gulped, raised a hand, and knocked tentatively.

After hearing some shuffling and seeing a flicker of light through the security lens, the door opened. John was still wearing his button-down shirt and dress slacks, and she saw his tie crumpled on a chair behind him. There was no sign of Katie. She grinned, feeling slightly triumphant that he apparently didn't have plans with his girlfriend.

"Stella?" he asked with a smile. "Did we have plans? I'm pretty sure I'd remember, but... well, I don't remember."

"No, we didn't have plans. Sorry to barge in, but I kinda need your help."

John held a sandwich in one hand and his other rested on top of the door. He pulled it open, inviting her in. Stella quickly explained the FBI situation, and John's face morphed from intrigued to horrified.

"Sampson Foster? Why does that name sound familiar?"

"Do you think so? I have no idea who he is."

"How does Janet know him?"

"I'm going to ask her, except, uh... she's not answering her phone."

"Of course not. Of *course* she's going to put all of this on you." He shook his head in disgust. "That woman is going to get you killed, someday," he added. Stella grimaced, thinking about Rufus Mills holding a gun to her head in Janet's RV. John might have been right. "So, let me get this straight. You didn't want to lead the FBI to your place, so you led them to mine?"

John seemed to be flickering between anger with Janet and amusement at the way Stella was handling things. They locked eyes and smiled. A laugh died on her lips when a sharp knock echoed through the apartment, though, and she and John turned to the door.

"Who's there?" John asked. When there was no answer, he motioned for Stella to go into the kitchen. Instead, she moved next to him. He stepped in front of her, putting himself between her and the door, and she stepped up, so they were next to each other again.

He shot her a glare and said again, "Who's there?"

"Dude," came the response.

John's shoulders relaxed. "Pearler, what do you want? It's almost one in the morning."

"Dude, open the door."

John looked at Stella and explained, "My stoner neighbor." He pulled the door open, but didn't invite Pearler in.

She peered around John and saw a short, round man wearing cargo shorts that came down well past his knees and an open Hawaiian shirt over a dirty white undershirt.

His shaved head was overdue for another round with the razor, and he had an unlit cigarette hanging out of his mouth.

"Dude, my supplier is nowhere to be found. You got any weed?"

John started to close the door. "Goodnight, Pearler."

"Wait, stop, seriously. I'm totally out. Like, not even the little leftover bits at the bottom of the Ziplock—just totes out."

"Pearler, I don't smoke pot, so I have less than you do."

Stella ducked under John's arm. "Pearler, is your supplier usually so unreliable?" She ignored John's confused look and smiled at his neighbor.

"Whoa, bro. I didn't know you had company. Nice," he said, nodding in appreciation. "Does that mean Katie's fair game, because I've been thinking wicked thoughts about that—" John's silent glare was loud enough to stop him mid-sentence, and Stella took the opportunity to ask her question again. "Uh, no, man. We meet once a week, like, you know... clockwork? He's been MIA for the last three, though. I'm high and dry, dude. It's awful." After a pause, he chortled. "Actually, I'm not *high* and dry. That's the problem."

"Have you known him a long time?"

"Uh, are you a cop? I'm not like that, man. I'd never—"

"No, I'm just worried about your, uh, your friend."

He laughed, relieved. "Okay, cool. Truth be told, I'm worried, too. We usually meet real regular-like. I'm just—I guess I don't know what to do."

"What's his name?"

"His name?"

Despite the fact that talking to Pearler was like trying to communicate with a bird, Stella worked hard to keep the friendly smile on her face. She smelled a story; she'd just watched a guy get arrested in an undercover drug buy at her apartment complex, and now this guy's dealer was missing. Did Knoxville have a drug problem? Had there been a new push—a new mandate—to combat the problem, or were the events isolated and unrelated? She might as well ask a few questions while she had Pearler right in front of her.

"I was just thinking that maybe we could check the jail or the morgue and make sure he hasn't had some kind of accident. Maybe he needs your help."

Pearler looked shocked by the thought. "The morgue? Dude, that's intense, man, that's real intense... but I see where you're going with this." He nodded, staring over Stella's head while he thought. Finally, he said, "Yeah, sure. We should check. His name is Scarecrow."

She heard John sigh behind her, but she continued, "That can't be his *real* name."

"Might be hard to find him, huh?" He shot one more hopeful look at John. "Got any beer?"

"Go home, Pearler!"

"Okay, then. Thanks, anyway, dude. I'll see y'around."

John closed the door. "What was that all about?"

"Nothing. It seems like there are drugs everywhere. I'm just trying to get a handle on... things." He gave her a look, but she didn't elaborate.

"Why do I get the feeling that you're working on something big—and that, whatever it is, you're going to leave all of us in your dust... again." He smiled as he said it, but she sensed an underlying edge to his voice. They were competitors, after all, no matter their personal history.

Before she could say anything, though, her phone buzzed inside her bag. She frowned to see that it was stupid Lucky.

"You were on the Valentine's Day beat today, eh?" John said with practiced indifference as he walked into the kitchen to fill up a glass of water. He was trying to be casual, but she noticed him watching her out of the corner of his eye.

"Well, somebody has to cover it every year. I guess it was my turn." John's after work snack was sitting half-eaten on the coffee table; she sat on the couch and helped herself to a pretzel. "I see *you're* not celebrating tonight," she added slyly, keeping her eyes on her pretzel.

There was a pause, and then John said, "Well, Katie has a big paper due tomorrow." He cleared his throat as he came back into the room. "Her program is pretty intense." Stella thoroughly chewed her pretzel as the silence hung heavy between them. "Anyway, I saw your five o'clock live shot. What was going on?"

Her mouth was full and she took a moment to decide whether to tell John the truth. He handed her his glass of water and she took a sip, finally ready to relay the story about the flowers. John's open, curious face took on a knowing look by the end of her tale.

She felt tears spring up, and surprised by the emotion, she jumped up and paced to the window. Looking out into the dark parking lot, she tried to clear her mind. John gave her a minute to collect herself, but soon she felt him behind her. She turned, and he took both her hands in his own. He looked exhausted, too.

"Why did you come here tonight, Stella?"

She looked past him at the door. "I guess I need to borrow your car, so I can go see Janet at the bar without leading the FBI there."

He squeezed her hands until she met his eyes. "Do you even hear yourself? You're not Jack Ryan or Jack Reacher. You're not even Jack Tripper." Stella smiled at the *Three's Company* reference, but John wasn't laughing. "I don't know what you think you're playing at, but it doesn't sound safe. I'm mad as hell at Janet for putting you in this situation in the first place." Stella looked up at John and saw nothing but concern and a little bit of hurt in his eyes. She gave his hands a squeeze.

"I know, John, and that's why I want to go talk to her. I have to tell her that this has to stop. She has to talk to the agents, so I don't have to." He nodded once, and she continued, "So, can I borrow your car?" He nodded again, and she started to pull away.

"There's something else, Stella—something we have to

talk about." He pulled her close again, and she felt the heat rising between them. It was late, she was stressed from her night, and he looked delicious in his rumpled shirt.

They heard a noise from behind the bedroom door just then, and John dropped Stella's hands. He blew out a breath and shook his head. "Katie has a big paper due in the morning," he said again, avoiding Stella's eyes.

"What?"

He started to repeat Katie's schedule, but Stella interrupted. "No, what do we have to talk about?"

He ran a hand through his hair, still looking at the bedroom door before he turned back to her. "Nothing, Stella. Just be careful, okay? I don't want to cover your funeral."

She bit her lip and smiled reassuringly. "Don't worry, you won't. I'd never be buried here, in Knoxville."

John frowned at her joke. "I'm serious, Stella. I couldn't take it." He handed her his keys and turned away from her angrily.

She nodded at his back, put her car keys on the coffee table, and left his apartment without another word.

# 17

In the hallway outside John's apartment, Stella leaned against the wall. John was right, she was no spy. Then again, the men following her weren't that special, either. They were on background check detail, which had to be kind of low-ranking work at the agency.

She squared her shoulders and headed down the hall. When she was on the main level again, she peered out the front windows, scanning the parking lot for John's ride. Finally, she had a bit of luck. John's ancient, wood-paneled station wagon was on the opposite side of the parking lot from the FBI agents. She stared at the Escalade. Its engine was running, and low blue lights from the men's phones lit up the interior of the vehicle.

If Stella walked out the main door to the apartment complex, she would be on full display. After a quick glance around the lobby, though, she followed a maze of hallways and finally came to a side door close to John's car.

She grasped the key and waited, watching the parking lot like a hawk. Finally, it happened—a distraction. A stretch Hummer limousine pulled up to the main doors, and a bachelorette party tumbled out. Even from inside the building, she could hear the drunk screams and raucous laughter. She sauntered out to John's car, shaking her head in wonder. A bachelorette party on a Tuesday night? That was hard core.

Stella left the parking lot and took a circuitous route to Janet's bar, doubling back and taking unexpected turns. She didn't think she was being followed, but what did she know? Finally, after twenty minutes of what should've been a five-minute trip, she was there.

Janet's bar was called The Spot, and it most certainly

was, that night. The lot in front of the bar was packed, and Stella had to park on a street several blocks away. She took her suit jacket off, left her pearl earrings in the glove box, and switched out her slingback heels for a pair of flip-flops she'd found in the backseat. They were about her size, and she made a face when she realized that they must have belonged to Katie.

John's old car fit in perfectly, but she felt drastically out of place. The swish of her dress pants and her beige camisole seemed to glow along the dark street. She found herself glancing over her shoulder every few moments—not for the FBI, but for Rufus or someone like him. This wasn't exactly the kind of neighborhood a woman wanted to be walking around in alone at night, so she walked a little faster. When she got close to The Spot's main entrance, she saw why it was so crowded that evening.

An inexpensive sign was propped up on the sidewalk, proclaiming the special for the evening—half-price drinks until closing. She slipped into the bar, hugging the inside wall, and took a moment to get her bearings. There were scantily clad women and men with hungry eyes, dim lighting, and loud music. In other words, it was your typical dive. Stella spotted her roommate behind the bar pouring drinks as quickly as they were ordered.

Janet was in her element. With exposed skin at her belly and a plunging neckline, she blended right in with the customers. Tonight, she wore heavy eye makeup and dozens of bracelets on each arm. Her hair was piled into a messy ponytail, and tight jeans showed off her every curve. Stella stood back and looked at her with new eyes. She'd never understood why Janet wanted to work at this place, but now it made a little more sense. Janet fit in.

No, it was more than that. She didn't *just* fit in, but she was king of the castle. She called out the customers by their names, smiled at their jokes, and cracked some of her own. She looked more at home here, in the bar, than she ever had in their apartment.

When one customer got a little too friendly and grabbed her hand, Stella watched in awe as Janet bent his fingers back painfully. He sat down on a barstool with a thump, and the other patrons howled with laughter. The man who'd overstepped his bounds smiled ruefully and shook his head. Janet poured him a shot, they clinked glasses, tossed them back, and all was well.

Stella's smile faded as a slight pounding started behind her right eye. She needed to talk to Janet and get home. After pushing her way through the crowd toward the bar, she finally rested her elbows on the countertop two or three people down from Janet. Another bartender was working that night, moving at about half the speed as her roommate. He was in the middle of helping someone when he caught Stella's eye and leaned in.

"How can I help you, little lady?" he asked her, his drawl thick and his eyes roving.

"I'm actually waiting for my friend over there," Stella said, nodding at Janet with her chin.

His face split into a wide grin, and he turned to Janet. A wolf whistle cut through the noisy din. "You swinging both ways, Janet?" he called across the bar to her.

Her roommate finished pouring a drink, but Stella saw her eyes narrow in distaste at her coworker's tone. "Screw you, Chalmers," she said without even looking his way, again making the people around her laugh. Janet's eyes scanned the customers lining the bar three deep, looking for whatever had caught the other bartender's attention. Her gaze slid right over Stella, but soon her brain caught up with her eyes, and she called out, "Shots for everyone, on the house."

Stella shook her head, but smiled in spite of herself. Before she could move away from the bar, though, someone shoved a small glass in her hand and the countdown began.

"Three, two, one!"

All around the bar, heads tilted back, eyes watered, and people cheered. Stella locked eyes with Janet, who handed her a lemon wedge. "When in Rome, Stella."

Janet's head tilted back, and Stella shrugged. Why not? She raised the glass to her lips, tipped it back, and then slammed the tiny glass onto the bar.

"That is *not* top-shelf vodka!" she exclaimed, doing her best not to cough as the liquor burned down her throat uncomfortably. Janet cackled and poured someone else a drink. "I need to talk to you. Now."

Janet's eyes swept the bar. "It's a little busy right now, hon. Can't it wait?"

"It's about Sampson Foster." The name had the same effect as a gunshot on Janet's countenance, and her open, happy face shut down immediately.

"Who've you been talking to?" Her angry glare was meant to silence Stella, but her hands trembled as she handed someone a glass of beer.

She stepped up on a brass-tone foot rail that ran the length of the bar and leaned across the countertop. "I was stopped by two FBI agents on my way home from work tonight. I didn't tell them anything, but now you need to tell me everything." Her glare matched Janet's, and the two women were locked in a silent, but furious, staring contest.

Janet was the first to blink. "Chalmers," she shouted off to her left, "I'm taking a break. Be back in five."

She untied her half apron, balled it up, and threw it in a cubbyhole under the bar top. After she motioned for Stella to follow her, they wound their way into a back room, leaving the noise, chaos, and smoke behind.

Janet led the way into what appeared to be the manager's office, although there was no manager nearby, as far as Stella could tell. The cinderblock room had one grubby window overlooking the parking lot. An old office desk, chipped and watermarked, was pushed against one wall, along with two folding chairs and a safe that appeared to be bolted to the floor.

"What happened?" Janet asked, taking one seat and gesturing to the other.

"I had two guys following me on my way home from work. When I confronted them, they told me they were FBI agents trying to do a background check on Sampson Foster. They say you've been giving them the slip, so they decided to talk to me." Janet's clenched jaw seemed to clinch tighter at the name. Stella paused, waiting for Janet to explain, but there was only silence. "Janet, who's this Foster guy, and why does the FBI want to talk to you about him? Are you in some kind of trouble?"

Janet snorted. "I've been in some kind of trouble since I was born." She fell silent again and gazed out the window for a moment, collecting her thoughts.

"He's someone... from another lifetime."

"That other lifetime just caught up with you, so why don't you tell me about it, okay? We'll figure this out together."

Janet glared at the floor. "You know, that's the difference between you and me, Stella. You want to come up with a plan to make it better, and I want to outrun it for good."

She looked uncertainly at her roommate. "You can't outrun the FBI, Janet—not from our apartment, at least."

Janet slid down her seat so her head was resting on the back of the metal chair. She crossed her arms protectively around herself and nodded at the ceiling. "You're right."

"Thank you! Finally, you're listening to reason!"

"No," Janet said, sitting back up with a look of triumph on her face. "I can't outrun the FBI from our apartment, but I can from my RV! I knew I was holding onto it for a reason! Don't you see, Stella? It's the perfect way to stay under the radar!"

Stella felt like screaming—and kicking and shouting. Maybe combined, it would knock some sense into her roommate. There was no way she could out-crazy Janet, though, so she needed to find a different approach.

"Then you need to talk to the FBI for *me*." Janet looked surprised, but she continued, "I can't have them following me around, and I don't want to feel like I'm responsible for keeping them away from our apartment or this bar. More important, I don't want you to be on the run! You belong with me, in Knoxville."

Janet bit her lip and nodded slowly. "I'm sorry. You're right. It's not fair."

Stella stared at Janet expectantly, but her roommate remained silent. "So?"

Janet looked up expectantly. "So what?"

She groaned. "So, who is Sampson Foster?"

The words had barely left her mouth when a huge commotion from the bar made both women jump out of their chairs. Janet grabbed a baseball bat in the corner of the room.

"Goddamn maniacs!" she shouted as she raced out the door.

Stella stood in the office, unsure of which way to go. Should she race toward the problem, or away from it? After a moment's hesitation, she walked purposefully toward the chaos.

# 18

It was like walking into a fight scene from a bad roadhouse movie. She edged along the back wall of the room, trying to locate Janet in the chaos and not believing that her roommate worked here, in such a dangerous place! The friendly drunks, who minutes ago had been smiling and laughing with Janet, were now locked in ugly, violent fights around the bar.

A group of people closest to the door were involved in a knock-down, drag-out fight; fists flew, and through the shouting, she heard beer bottles break with deafening pops. As she took another step, someone unplugged the jukebox and the popular country-western song that had been playing at top volume was cut off mid-lyric.

Next, two things happened simultaneously. First, someone flipped a switch, changing the dim nighttime lighting inside the bar to full, fluorescent daylight. Second, Janet leaped onto the bar, waving the baseball bat threateningly in one hand.

In a powerful, commanding voice that Stella had never heard her roommate use before, Janet shouted, "I just called the cops! Clear out if you don't want to see them in the next two minutes!" She swung the bat across her body, and it slammed into a support beam with a resounding crack.

Whether it was the sudden light, Janet's booming voice, or the threat of cops arriving, the crowd thinned almost immediately. Stella slumped back against the wall, feeling relieved. Janet leaped lightly off the bar and picked up the pieces of a broken beer bottle from the ground. Before Stella could move to help, though, something caught her eye—actually, someone.

He was a mountain of a man, wading untouched through the dwindling crowd, and he moved with purpose from the front door to a stool at the bar. He reached behind the counter, took a beer from an ice bucket, and twisted off the cap. Stella realized with awe that he was drinking a Heineken—they didn't have twist-off caps. He casually raised the bottle to his lips and took a slow, steady sip. Something about him was familiar, but not in a good way. She froze against the wall as his eyes swept the room. They were gold flecked with black.

Rufus Mills—Tiger Eyes—didn't notice her standing in the shadows in the back corner, and she blew out a relieved sigh when he turned and said something to Janet, making her laugh.

She slid into a booth as far from the bar as possible, and out of the corner of her eye, she watched Janet quickly cleaning the worst of the trash left behind by the near riot. Tiger Eyes chatted with Janet while she worked; they looked to be friendly. The man who had threatened her life was friends with her roommate. She sat in the booth, holding her head in her hands, too stunned to know what to do next.

There were two ways out of this bar. The main entrance was right behind Tiger Eyes, so that way wouldn't work. The other exit was through the manager's office, and she would need Janet's help to get back in there. She was trapped; she shouldn't have come here tonight.

The slight throbbing behind her right eye from earlier in the evening was pounding out a steady beat of pain. She took out her cell phone and dialed Janet's number, and after a few moments, she saw Janet take the phone out of her pocket.

"Are you afraid of the cops, too, hon? Did you run out on me?" she asked with a smile, still sweeping shards of glass toward a dustbin.

Tiger Eyes' golden orbs made another slow, deliberate sweep of the bar, and Stella ducked behind her booth, out of sight. "Don't say my name—just say yes or no. That man sitting at the bar near you threatened me inside your RV the other night *with a gun.* Is he the man who was asking about my job?" She kept her head down hoping, like a toddler, that if she couldn't see anyone, no one could see her. Her body was tense, like piano strings about to pop. "Well?" she prompted when Janet didn't answer.

"Yes," Janet drew the single syllable out for a few seconds.

"Did he happen to know that I was going to move your RV last night?"

She gave another long, snake-like response in confirmation, and then added, "Where are you?"

"I'm hiding in a booth by the office, because that man you're so casually talking to told me he'd kill me if I continued investigating the Bennet shooting. I wasn't supposed to tell you about it, either, but now I need you to get me out of here... or get *him* out of here. I'd love to know why he wants me dead, but first I want to get out of your bar alive."

There was another long pause while Janet processed Stella's words. Finally, she said, "Yes, hon, it's another late night, but don't worry. I'll still make it to church with you tomorrow."

Janet disconnected the phone and Stella resisted the urge to peek over the booth to glare at her roommate. No explanation? No whispered plan? What was she supposed to do now?

She rested her head on her folded hands on the tabletop and took a moment to collect her thoughts. What was Tiger Eyes going to do, anyway? Surely he wouldn't shoot her in the middle of the bar—the mostly deserted bar, she realized with dismay. Maybe that's exactly what he would do. She guessed that she could wait them out; she had nowhere else to be until two o'clock the next day, when her shift at work started, anyway.

When the lights in the bar dimmed again, she was startled, but she immediately felt less exposed and realized

Janet was enacting some sort of plan. Soon, the jukebox started back up with some country-rock song that had her foot tapping, despite her rising panic.

Finally, Stella heard a bell ring out and Janet calling, "Shots on the house, y'all. Thanks for staying to help clean up!"

Stella chanced a glance over the booth and saw Janet pouring alcohol into a stainless steel shaker. She gave the alcohol and ice a vigorous attack before doling out a dozen different shots onto a tray. She plopped one down in front of Tiger Eyes and made her way around the bar, passing out shots as she went.

The other bartender was gone; Stella smiled in spite of herself when she realized that he had apparently been among the many there that night who hadn't wanted to chance a run-in with the cops.

A tiny glass landed in front of Stella, and Janet, without slowing her stride, said, "I just unlocked the office door. When you see an opening, you head out."

Stella nodded and slammed the shot back. This time, she reveled in the fiery drink that burned down her throat, appreciating the liquid courage she would need to escape unnoticed. Janet finished her lap around the bar and stopped between Tiger Eyes and the front door. He swiveled on his barstool to chat with her, and Stella made her move.

She squeezed out from the booth and hurried to the office door without looking back. After twisting the handle and pushing the door open, she slipped inside. Stella closed the door, quickly turned the deadbolt, and blew out a breath. She felt safe for the first time in twenty minutes.

Taking a moment to stand still in the dark space, she allowed her heart rate to slow. As she looked out the big window to the parking lot, she could barely make out John's car parked a few blocks away.

"Just a couple of streets to freedom," she said to herself in the quiet office.

After rubbing her forehead and taking a deep breath, Stella left the sanctuary of the room and headed out into the cold night air. Her breath left puffs of white steam behind her, and within minutes, she was sitting safely behind the steering wheel with cold sweat edging her forehead, as if she'd just run a mile. She started up the engine and sat, lost in thought, while the heater warmed up. She could go home to her apartment, or she could be proactive about her situation.

She turned the heat down, as her body was already warming with her plan, and dug her cell phone out of her bag to dial the same numbers as before.

"Hello?"

"I want to know everything about Rufus Mills. I want to know where he lives, what he does, and who he hangs out with. Can you get somewhere you can talk?"

There was a pause as Janet considered Stella's words. Finally, she said, "Let me check the office, sweetie, and see if you left your coat in there earlier today." When she came back on the line, it was much easier to hear her.

"Listen, Stella, ever since you asked about Rufus and his tiger eyes earlier this week, I've been doing some reconnaissance—real stealth-like, asking questions. Here's what I found out. He's not the nice guy I thought he was." Stella snorted, but her roommate continued. "I guess he's in some kind of drug gang and pretty high up. Word on the street is they're as mean as snakes and they kinda run things in Knoxville, as far as drug traffic goes."

"The question is, why does the drug gang care if I'm doing a story on a shooting?" It must have been drug-related, but what could Stella possibly uncover? Reporters did stories on shootings all the time; what was different about this one?

"I don't know, but that is a dangerous man, Stella."

"Why do you sound more interested in Rufus now than you did earlier this week?"

"He just sounds kind of exciting, don't you think?" she asked. Before Stella could answer, she muttered, "Oh, great, I think he left. Yup, that's him walking to his car—I can see him through the office window. At least we can breathe a sigh of relief for tonight. Maybe tomorrow we can figure out what to do." Stella felt her heart rate accelerate. She had an idea. It was a bad one, but she was tired of waiting for things to happen to her. "Stella?" Janet asked, suspicious.

"I'm thinking about seeing where Rufus Mills lives."

"That's a bad idea, Stella. I just told you he's a drug dealer! Don't follow him; you'll stick out like a sore thumb."

"You haven't seen the car I'm driving. If anything, I'll blend in."

"Don't do it, Stella. Just go home. We'll figure something out tomorrow."

"Oh, tomorrow?" she asked angrily, not hiding the irritation in her voice. "No. Tomorrow, you have other fish to fry, Janet—you need to talk to the FBI and tell them everything you know about Sampson Foster."

There was only silence on the other end of the line. From her spot along the street two blocks away, Stella saw a pair of headlights slowly sweep the road as the car turned out of the bar parking lot and drove away.

"I've got to go." She put her car into drive, pulled away from the curb, and followed Rufus Mills down the road.

# 19

"Do not follow him!" Janet was still at the bar, but her screech was so loud as it came through the cell phone that it sounded like she was sitting right next to Stella in the passenger's seat.

She carefully spun the wheel with one hand. She was a few blocks behind Rufus, but at this hour, there wasn't much traffic and she didn't want to blow her cover. She was busy concentrating on the road and didn't answer Janet, but she didn't hang up, either, needing the courage of another person, even if they were getting farther away by the minute.

"I am serious, Stella! Do not follow him. You think you're stealthier than the FBI?" she asked. Without waiting for a reply, she answered herself, "No, you're not—and you saw them following you right away tonight!"

"Yes, but they were trying to be seen," Stella muttered, changing lanes. She glanced in the rearview mirror, looking for cops—the last thing she wanted was to get pulled over for failing to use her turn signal.

"Where are you?"

"Right now? I'm on Fourth Avenue, headed west."

"Where is Rufus?" Janet asked suspiciously.

"He is also on Fourth Avenue, headed west."

There was a pause while her roommate crafted her argument. "This is ridiculous, Stella. I'm hanging up the phone. First, I just want to say that you're supposed to be the calm one who uses her head. I'm the one who makes last-minute decisions without thinking them through. So, you just think about what you're supposed to be doing."

"That's just it, though, isn't it, Janet?" she replied, hitting the steering wheel in frustration. "My way hasn't been working out, lately, so I'm gonna try your way. Your bud-dy, Rufus, thinks he can follow me around and threaten me at my own house? I figure I at least deserve to know where he lives."

Rufus had turned off Fourth and was heading into a neighborhood Stella had never been in before. The houses were smaller and shoved closer together. Lawns were nonexistent and more dirt and trash than grass, and an oc-casional bright orange flag or curtain was all that broke the dull, barren landscape in this part of the city.

Before too long, Rufus turned into one of the many en-trances to a set of long, low-slung row houses that snaked down the road. She slowed to watch. Each unit had park-ing spots directly in front of the main door, leaving no room for grass or rocking chairs. It was a very unfriendly look, and Stella thought it matched Rufus perfectly.

He pulled into a spot and his headlights cut off as Stella rolled slowly past, lost in thought. Heavy breathing in her ear reminded her that Janet was still on the line.

"Janet, what do you know about the Wingate Hills Row Houses?" she asked, remembering the sign as she first drove up.

"I've never even heard of it."

"Where are you? There's a lot we need to go over."

"I'm closing up. You better get home right now, Stella; I'll be there as soon as I can!"

She disconnected the call and turned her car in the di-rection of their apartment. Rufus Mills must have been making good money with his position, but he was living in what appeared to be public housing, or close to it. Maybe it wasn't a full-time thing. Maybe dealing drugs was some-thing he did part-time? She shook her head—gang life probably wasn't an on-the-side kind of gig.

Stella shuddered as she thought about feeling the cold metal of his gun pressed into her neck. He'd seemed pret-ty full-time when he was threatening her life. She couldn't imagine him at a desk job at the bank.

She was exhausted. After an emotional day at work, the adrenaline-packed evening was catching up with her. Before pulling into her own apartment complex, she circled the block to make sure she was alone. It seemed that all the bad guys—and likely the good guys, too—had called it a night, and Stella wished she could do the same. First, however, she needed answers from Janet.

It was hard to believe that the Valentine's Day flower debacle had happened only hours ago. She was still angry with Lucky, but with everything else that had happened that night, the anger seemed further away and less intense.

As she walked in the main door to the apartment building, she was greeted by a heady floral scent. It was a nice change from the usual antiseptic cleaning aroma mixed with Indian food from an apartment one floor above.

Stella inhaled a lungful of it and turned toward her own apartment. The floral smell only got stronger, and after four more steps down the hallway, she came to an abrupt halt. There were a dozen gorgeous floral arrangements lined up on either side of her doorway. They were identical vases with identical, lovely flowers spilling out in every direction. She froze, not wanting to get closer; a sinking feeling in her stomach had her reexamining her live shot from that evening.

She snatched the card off the first arrangement she came to. "To my one and only." The next read, "One delivery just wasn't enough." Another said, "So I sent a dozen more." After that, "My number may be 13." On the next, "But you're my lucky charm." On it went with each card having a thoughtful, sweet message from Lucky.

A hand flew to her throat as she stared, speechless, at the flowers. It appeared that she'd jumped to conclusions at the florist. Still standing in the hallway, she pressed her phone to her ear and listened to the first of several messages that Lucky had left that night. The first came in before she'd texted him from the flower shop.

"Stella, I thought you were off today—I have some deliveries going to your house. I should have sent them to your office, I guess. Happy Valentine's Day. Enjoy."

Next, there was a barrage of calls after her text and ensuing live shot.

"Stella, you've got the wrong idea. Call me."

"Stella, God dang it, call me. It's not what you think!"

"Stella, come to my house. Or go home—you'll understand."

"Well, now I'm getting pissed. You better call me, girl. I'm accepting apologies until midnight."

It was well past midnight, but Stella hit a button and listened to the phone ring once, twice, and three times. There was no answer, though. She was gearing up to leave a message when Lucky finally came on the line. "Did you figure it out, super sleuth? Finally git yer reportin' done?" Through the thicker-than-usual southern accent, Stella also sensed a bit of slurring.

"Are you drinking alone, Lucky Haskins?" she asked, trying not to smile.

"You would, too, if yer Valentine's Day went to hell in a band hasket... a hand basket."

She winced. "I feel so foolish for jumping to conclusions, Lucky. I'm sorry—so sorry. The flowers are gorgeous." He harrumphed on his end of the line, and Stella heard him take a gulp of something. "But you have to admit, seeing all those arrangements going out the door at the same time was like, well, a smoking gun," Stella said, biting her lip.

"Smoking gun? I've got a smoking gun for you," Lucky said, letting out a garish chuckle that made Stella blush.

"Come over," he drawled.

"I can't. I have to—there's a situation with Janet," Stella said, not up to explaining the whole thing. "Tomorrow?"

"Oh, are you gonna set up a date with me, now? What is this, feeling guilty? Is this a pity date?" Lucky slurred.

"No. I just—I'm sorry," Stella searched for the right words. She wasn't ready to be exclusive with him, but maybe an occasional date would be okay.

"Can't. I'm leaving."

"Oh," Stella said, taken aback. "Where are you headed, this time?"

"Bristol."

"Are you visiting your rental properties or something?" she asked, smiling wistfully as she thought about her old apartment and friends at the station near the Tennessee-Virginia border.

"No, no, Bristol, Connecticut. I have a thing happening on ESPN."

"Oh."

After a silence that stretched for minutes, she heard Lucky sigh. "I'll be gone till the weekend. You still got my code?" he asked.

Stella nodded and then realized he couldn't see her. "Yup," she said aloud.

"Come on by the house whenever you need to. You're the only one with the code," he added. "Well, you know, you and my dozen other girlfriends, anyway."

"Lucky, I—"

"I'm ready, Stella—ready to try us again, or ready to move on. Which one are you ready for?" He disconnected, and Stella stood in the hallway, alone with her thoughts and one hundred and forty-four roses.

***

"What the hell?" Janet asked as she edged inside the apartment. Stella could just see the top of her head as she passed between the door and the table. Roses, greenery, and vases obstructed her view from the couch.

"Exactly," Stella said, jumping up. She'd had half an hour to think about Lucky and John, and that had been twenty-five minutes too long. She was ready for a new topic. "There's so much we need to talk about, Janet." It was now just past three in the morning, but Stella was wired as she paced the apartment with a bottle of water grasped tightly in her hands.

Janet continued to stare at the flowers surrounding her, her mouth half-open in wonder. "Seriously, Stella, what the—"

"Janet! Focus! Rufus Mills, the FBI, Sampson Foster. There is so much to talk about that doesn't involve flowers!"

Her roommate seemed to shake herself. "Okay," she said, drawing the last syllable out for several seconds. She picked her way through the greenery and stood next to Stella.

"Before we talk about Sampson Foster—" At the look on Janet's face, she cut herself off. "Oh, we're going to talk about him, Janet, so you just get ready. First, though, I want to talk about Rufus. I want to hear every single thing you know about him—no detail is too small." Janet shook her head silently, so she continued. "The more I think about it, the more it just doesn't make any sense. I've been reporting in this town for two years and I've never heard of a gang problem. Where did they come from?"

"I bet cops aren't too worried about it. The newspaper even said that crime is down and arrests are up. What do they care if there's a small gang running around Knoxville?"

"Yeah, but how small is small?"

Her friend wrinkled her nose. "I would definitely say less than one hundred, but more than ten."

Stella snorted. "It's so nice to have specifics." She set the water down on the end table and ran her hands through her hair.

She was glad they lived on the first floor, so she didn't have to worry about a neighbor below. At this hour, she even felt guilty for keeping Ole Boy awake; he was in the corner on his dog bed, watching them with alert eyes. Every once in a while, he'd huff out a sigh and change positions, but his eyes never left them.

She rubbed her temples, trying to think. "Last I heard, the Knoxville Police Department severely cut back their drug crimes unit a few years ago because crime rates had gotten so low. They couldn't justify the expense in the annual city budget."

Janet sat up. "Sounds like you've got somewhere to start. Who's left? I bet they'd have a lot to tell you."

Stella's eyes widened. She didn't know why it surprised her, anymore, but Janet often had very illuminating things to say at just the right time, and this morning was no different. "That's brilliant! Thank you." She nodded, happy to have made a contribution. The smiles faded off both women's faces at almost exactly the same time, though. "Sampson Foster," Stella said, keeping her eyes on her roommate. She wanted to take in any tiny facial expressions or shifting of her body. "Start talking."

It was Janet's turn to pace the room. "I don't even know where to start," she said solemnly before disappearing into the kitchen. She came back out moments later with a glass of ice water and took a sip. While looking at Stella, she opened her mouth, abruptly closed it, and started pacing again.

"Why don't you tell me who he is," Stella said, looking at her with concern. "After that, you can tell me what he's done wrong and why the FBI is investigating him." There wasn't a single name in her life that could elicit such a strong response, and Janet's nerves were transferring to Stella the longer she didn't answer.

"Sampson Foster..." Janet barked out a humorless laugh before recovering, "Sampson Foster is my father."

She set her glass on the kitchen table with such force that it shattered, sending ice, water, and shards of glass across the table and onto the floor. Stella stared soundlessly at the mess, wondering what alternate reality she'd just entered.

# 20

"He's your father?" Stella asked, recovering from her shock. "You told me your father was dead!"

"To me, he is."

"Is he in some kind of trouble, because I know people at the local FBI and prosecutor's office; we can make sure that he's at least treated fairly, no matter what he's accused of—"

Janet interrupted. "He's not in trouble. I think he's running for office."

Stella stared at back Janet, confused. "Huh?"

"He's been the attorney general of North Dakota for the last six years. When this term is up, he'll probably be ready for the big leagues—some kind of national appointment out of D.C., I'd guess."

"What?" Stella stared incredulously at her roommate, not sure if she believed Janet or if this was all some sort of elaborate joke.

"Don't you recognize his name? I know you were only out west for a short time, but surely it came up during one of your stories."

Stella shook her head slowly. "Maybe... I don't know. I guess we covered mostly Montana issues." It would explain why John had thought the name sounded familiar— he had worked in Bozeman, too. She looked back at Janet with new eyes. "It just doesn't seem possible. You're telling me that *your* father is the attorney general of North Dakota?"

"Don't look so surprised. What were you picturing, that I was born and raised in a trailer?"

Stella felt her cheeks color. "No, of course not, I just, I..." she stammered. After turning away from Janet to get the dustbin and broom, she swept up the shards of glass. Janet got a towel from the kitchen and sopped up the water that had spilled minutes earlier.

When the flurry of activity was over, Stella looked up to find Janet staring at her. She looked back down at the floor, and finally, her roommate snorted.

"Well, if it makes you feel any better, I *was* raised in a trailer. I didn't even know who my father was for the first fifteen years of my life, and my mom gave me her last name when I was born. Now, I guess he wants to cross me off a list of questions for his background check, and I want nothing to do with him."

"That extends to giving the FBI the slip? It seems to me like the best way forward is to answer their questions so both they and you can move on."

Janet shook her head. "I'm not gonna do anything to help that son of a bitch. If that means giving the slip to the FBI, that's what I'm gonna do." Stella cleared her throat and gave her roommate a pointed look. "*Was*," she said hastily. "That's what I *was* going to do, but I'll come up with a new plan."

She leaned forward, her eyes narrowed in distrust. "What do you mean 'a new plan?' Operation RV Runaway doesn't sound too grown-up to me." Janet made a face. "Why can't you just talk to him? What did he do?"

Janet huffed out a sigh, threw herself into a chair, and laid an arm over her eyes. "It's not what he did—it's what he didn't do. He left my mom before I was even born. My dad left us high and dry.

"We did everything on our own. My mom worked two jobs and we both cleaned houses for as long as I can remember—we needed every cent just to make ends meet. Montana isn't cheap; the damn tourists drive the cost of living up to the point that the locals can't even survive." Her calm demeanor was quickly giving way to an angry fervor. "He came waltzing into our place when I was in high school, like a God damn superhero, telling me he's my father and he's ready to get to know me!" She was practically shouting now as she leaned forward in the chair, daring her roommate to disagree. Stella stared back, wide-eyed, not sure what to say.

Janet seemed to remember herself and sat back in the chair. The fire left her eyes slowly as she continued, "Well, I didn't give a shit who he was and I still don't. My mom died three years ago, and I'm not going to dishonor her memory by getting to know the man who left her on her own when she was pregnant—no way! So, he can take his job and shove it."

"What did your mom have to say about him?"

Janet slouched in the seat and stared at the ceiling. "Nothing. She would never speak of him—at least, not to me."

After a silence that stretched for minutes, Stella spoke, choosing her words carefully. "Have you ever considered that you'll always be running from him, unless you confront him and what he did to you and your mom?" Janet only grunted in response. "It seems like you've been dating these completely unsavory characters because you don't have any trouble keeping them at arm's length... and if you don't let anyone get in close, no one can hurt you like your father did."

"You're one to talk, Stella!" she snapped and was out of the chair, eyes smoldering. "You're over there, mooning on and on about John and Lucky. The only reason Lucky is on the back burner is because you've allowed John to stay in the picture. He has a girlfriend, Stella—a woman he moved across the county for—but you keep him close just to have a reason to keep Lucky away. Do Lucky the courtesy of telling him that, okay? I'm tired of looking at his sad face when he looks at you—it's pathetic." Janet stormed out of the room and Stella jumped seconds later when her roommate's door slammed shut.

She heard a low whine from the corner of the room and got off the chair. "It's okay, buddy. Everything is just fine," she crooned to the dog. He stretched one paw toward Stella and rolled onto his side, and she sat next to him and gave his belly a rub.

She sensed that there was a kernel of truth to what Janet had said, but she was too exhausted to think about it. It had been a long day both emotionally and hour-wise, and she was ready to call it a night. She took the dog out one last time, and as they walked back inside their apartment minutes later, she heard her phone ringing.

After picking it up, she checked the time before answering. It was 3:34 in the morning, and she didn't recognize the number.

"Hello?" She was half-expecting a butt dial.

"Stella, it's Murphy."

"What phone are you calling me from? I don't recognize this number."

"My work phone is dead—this is my personal cell. I just wanted to let you know that our shooting investigation just turned into a homicide."

"What?"

"Oliver Bennet is dead. He died a couple hours ago in the ICU at the hospital. He never regained consciousness."

"When will prosecutors upgrade the charges against Cas Rockman?"

"They'll file the papers when court opens."

"Thanks for the call. I've been wondering what's—"

"Just wanted to make sure you guys had that for the morning news," he interrupted gruffly and hung up without waiting for her response.

"Thanks," she said to the empty room.

She huffed out a frustrated breath and immediately called the tip into the newsroom. After giving the overnight producer all the details, she tried to settle down to bed.

Her body might have been ready to rest, but her mind refused to shut off. The leader of a local drug gang had gone to the trouble of threatening her against investigating the Oliver Bennet shooting, and now Oliver Bennet was dead. It was time to start digging a little deeper.

She rolled over, feeling surprisingly calm about her decision. So what if Rufus Mills found out? She essentially had an FBI detail following her until Janet made nice with her father. *Just let Rufus try to get to me with the Feds watching.*

# 21

The next day, Stella set up her story from home. The mayor was holding a press conference about Oliver Bennet's death, and Stella would cover the meeting before going live for the early evening news from City Hall. When she called in her plan to the assignment desk, however, Danielle just laughed.

"Boss says you have to come in. The corporate consultant is here today and tomorrow, and he wants to meet you before your shift."

Stella groaned inwardly before hanging up; a critique by a corporate consultant sounded painful. She took a deep breath and tried to clear her mind of negativity. Maybe this would be a good thing. Maybe a consultant would coach her on her writing—make it tighter and improve her story pacing. Her two-year contract in Knoxville was almost up, and the critiquing might help her get a job in a top market down the line.

By the time she got into work, she had convinced herself that talking to a corporate consultant was going to be the best thing that had ever happened to her. After all, she hadn't really had any training since her last college class. What a great company to spend the time and money on their reporters like that.

She waved to Ernie and Laffy huddled together in the photographers' corner and walked over to her desk. Before she could sit, though, Patricia flagged her down.

"Hey, boss, what's up?"

"I have you meeting with the consultant for thirty minutes. His name is Matthew Mason. He's highly respected in the field and we're lucky to have him in town for a few days. You'll be in conference room B."

Stella nodded, set her bags down, and logged into her computer. She had just enough time to check her email and the rundown for the evening newscasts.

Ernie walked by while she was working; she opened her mouth to say hello, but he caught her eye and signaled that she should be quiet. The subtle grin on his face meant he was up to no good, and she sat back to watch. As he walked closer, she noticed that he had Laffy's dad's old car phone clipped to his belt. It was zipped into the black leather case and hung from his belt loops down to his knee. He slowed as he got close to a dayside reporter's desk. Hank was relatively new, and as far as Stella could tell, he didn't have a sense of humor.

As she watched, Ernie nonchalantly cruised past his desk. The antique phone on his hip rang, which was impossible, since it couldn't have been in working order for at least ten years. Ernie gamely unzipped the leather case and unlatched the phone from its console, using two hands to grab the handset to emphasize how large the receiver was. As soon as he picked it up, the phone stopped ringing.

"Hello?" After a pause he said, "No, I didn't order a pizza. You must have the wrong number." He shrugged at Hank and then clipped the car phone back into its giant case, zipped it closed, and walked away without another word.

Hank scratched his head and looked around the newsroom for a few seconds before going back to his computer, and Stella stifled a laugh as she scanned the office. She finally found Laffy crouched by the photographers' lockers with his cell phone in one hand. He high-fived Ernie, who pulled his iPhone out of his pocket, and they looked around for their next target. They saw Del and started their joke over again.

Stella tried to turn back to her work, but she instead watched Ernie and Laffy pull their prank four more times. Each time, she found it sillier than before. She was still smiling when Patricia waved her over, and she grabbed a notebook and pen and headed toward the conference room.

Stella took one look at the man sitting at the conference room table and faltered. Matthew Mason was an overly-tanned, overly-coiffed, overly-exuberant man with a smile affixed to his face. His silvery-white hair was styled into a perfectly puffy pouf, and when she sat in the chair as he instructed, she realized with a start that he was wearing makeup.

It wasn't unusual to see men in the newsroom wearing makeup—they were on TV, after all, and to look normal on TV, you had to wear makeup. It was unusual, however, to see someone not on-air wearing pressed powder. They shook hands, and Matthew Mason got right down to business.

"Stella Reynolds." She leaned forward expectantly in her seat, but he appeared to be done. When she smiled and nodded encouragingly, he started up again. "I've been wanting to get my hands on you for almost a year and a half." He smiled and paused, almost as if waiting for her to thank him, but she remained silent. "Let's take a look at your story from yesterday."

Stella turned her eyes to the TV monitor in the corner of the room. Maybe she'd been right about Mason. Maybe she was going to get some constructive feedback on her work. That hopeful thought was dashed, however, as soon as Matthew Mason opened his mouth again.

"Love the story, love the writing, and love the pacing. Don't love the necklace, don't love the hairstyle, and definitely don't love the makeup."

So began the next sixty-five minutes of Stella's life. Matthew Mason declared her hopeless and pushed his appointment with Piper back by thirty minutes, so he could have extra time to tell her how to fix herself. When she finally left his office, she had a bag full of makeup samples, instructions on what color of clothing to wear on air, several insightful tips on where to get the best blowout in town, appropriate nail colors for newscasters, and a business card for a professional stylist.

She couldn't get out of the building fast enough.

***

There was a buzz of excitement downtown. Thursday marked the unofficial start of the weekend in this college town, and several businesses had already rolled out their orange window decorations and drink specials.

Inside the city building, she found a podium set up in the lobby. She nodded to Melissa, who was set up with the other photographers at the back of the room, and took a seat in the front row. All three local TV stations were there, along with the newspaper and talk radio stations.

At a few minutes past three, the mayor filed into the room, along with half a dozen command staff on the police department, the county prosecutor, and the coroner.

The mayor wasted no time getting down to business. "I called you here today to discuss crime. Despite the recent spate of violence in our city, numbers released by the FBI show that Knoxville has never been safer. Our crime rate is at the lowest in recent history, and arrests and prosecution rates have never been higher. That means that, if you commit a crime in our great city, you will be arrested, you will be prosecuted, and you will go to jail."

Stella heard the whirring of cameras in the background. Flashbulbs from the still photographer at the local paper occasionally illuminated the mayor's face as he continued talking.

"Recently, two Knoxville citizens were viciously murdered. Our police force immediately made an arrest in the Bennet shooting, but now that it's become a homicide, the suspect, Cas Rockman, will face aggravated homicide charges. We're asking for the public's help with the other shooting. In the Luanne Rockman homicide, as of today, we have no suspects, no leads, and no evidence tied to any suspects. That's going to change, though. I'm joined by the prosecutor, now, who tells me that he will ask for the death penalty against Cas Rockman. We will not tolerate such violence against our citizens."

There was a murmur from the crowd—the death penalty was an unusually harsh punishment. Hands shot up around the room.

"Why the death penalty?"

"Has his lawyer been told?"

Stella stood up. "What was the last death penalty case in Knox County?"

The county prosecutor, Raymond Fazer, held his hand out. "Calm down, everyone. We haven't had a death penalty case in years—not since 1998, in fact. Police have uncovered aggravating factors in this case that make it death penalty eligible. As we are still in the discovery phase, it would be inappropriate for me to comment further. I promise it will all come out during the trial."

Fazer had been in his position for nearly thirty years, and the younger prosecutors surrounding him made him seem older, grayer, and even more stooped than usual.

As he turned his remarks to less-controversial details about the case, Stella's focus shifted to the other people in the room. Homicide was well represented with both Murphy and Gibson in the crowd. The coroner, Grace Bailey, stood a little apart from the others.

After the press conference, Stella caught her eye from across the room and held up a finger, asking her to wait. Bailey nodded and continued her conversation with the mayor, and Stella flagged down Detective Murphy.

"Hey, Murph. Time for a quick interview?" Melissa hitched the camera on her shoulder. Murphy started edging away, but Stella flipped on the microphone and blocked his path. "Detective, what can you tell me about Oliver Bennet? I haven't been able to find any friends or relatives of the victim."

Murphy nodded. "It doesn't surprise me. Bennet's not from around here—he's kind of a lone wolf."

Stella waited for more, but Murphy was done. "Any arrest history?"

Murphy shook his head. "Not that we know of."

So, he was gonna play hardball. She mentally rolled up her sleeves. "Do you have a motive for the shooting? Why would Cas Rockman want Oliver Bennet dead?"

Murphy looked at Stella evenly. "We have solid evidence from the scene of the shooting tying Rockman to the crime. For now, I have no comment on the motive."

She looked down at her notes; there wasn't a lot to go on for a story. She ran through the facts in her mind, thinking of one final question. "Do you have any work history on the victim?"

Murphy gave her a funny look and seemed to consider his answer carefully. "Oliver Bennet was a forensic scientist here, in Knoxville. He was downsized about six months ago, and no one had heard anything from him since then, until he wound up shot."

Stella pounced. "Did he take a different job?"

His face remained blank. "He was unemployed at the time of the shooting."

"Do you have any suspects, yet, on the Luanne Rockman homicide?"

"Nope."

She got the feeling that she was missing something important, but she had run out of questions. After thanking Murphy, she waved the coroner over. Even though the focus of the press conference was the Oliver Bennet homicide, her story tonight would incorporate both recent murders.

The next interview was much more informational. "Dr. Bailey, thanks for your time. I know you're busy, so let's get right down to it. Does your office have a cause of death for Oliver Bennet?"

"Bennet was shot multiple times at close range. He was on life support for several weeks and succumbed to his injuries overnight."

"Luanne Rockman was also killed by multiple gunshot wounds. Last week, your office couldn't release the time of death, but is that available now?"

Bailey nodded, but took her time answering. "I don't have my notes in front of me on this case, but I can tell you that we believe her body had been lying in the vacant house for up to a week before she was discovered by fire-fighters."

Stella looked up in surprise, quickly counting in her head. "You're saying Luanne Rockman was shot the same day as Oliver Bennet?"

"I can't say with certainty that it happened on the same day, but it was close—quite close."

Stella thanked Grace Bailey and looked around the room in wonder. Her anonymous tipster had said weeks ago that there was one shooter and two victims. Was that right? More important, was her anonymous source here? Obviously, someone in-the-know was trying to get her on the right track in this investigation, but why couldn't they ask the questions? Why did they need Stella to do the digging?

Her eyes flitted over the mayor, Detective Murphy, a group of prosecutors, and the head of the jail before they landed on Detective Gibson. He was glaring at her, and she wrinkled her nose before looking away.

One shooter, two victims. She needed more information on Bennet. Her neighbor, Cheryl, could help with that—they must have worked together at the crime lab. She picked up her phone, but the call went straight to voicemail.

Later, as she sat in the live truck writing her story, she couldn't help circling back to one thing. If there was one shooter, it wasn't Cas Rockman. When she'd spoken to him at the jail last week, it was clear that he revered his mother. So, if he didn't kill Luanne, then her tipster was saying he also didn't shoot Oliver Bennet. If that was the case, though, who did?

# 22

"I don't know. Are you sure that's how it's supposed to look?" Melissa was looking at Stella with healthy dose of skepticism mixed with a tiny bit of disgust.

She looked down at herself and shifted her feet again. "Is it the outfit, the hair, or the makeup?"

"Hmm. I think it's just..." she waved her hand in a loose circle that seemed to include all of Stella.

They were interrupted by a cue from the producer back at the station, who spoke to Stella through her earpiece. "Standby, thirty sec—Holy shhh... what happened to you?"

"I, uh—"

"Never mind. Twenty-five seconds."

Stella tried to clear her mind; it was too late to make any changes, now. She quickly read the bullet points she'd jotted down for her live shot, but she jumped slightly when she caught her reflection in the camera lens.

Her hand slid up to touch her hair, but stopped when it met the resistance of a thirty-second "spritz" of hairspray. Instead of her usual soft, sleek locks, her auburn hair felt like sticky concrete.

Earlier that afternoon, when she was about halfway through writing her story, Matthew Mason had pulled up to the scene in a shiny, black Mercedes. When he climbed out of the car, his hands were full of bags.

"Let the fashion rescue begin!" he'd said, a broad smile revealing gleaming, white teeth.

Stella's surprise had quickly given way to concern as she watched him unpack his bags. He had a curling iron powered by an 8-volt plug-in, a giant, forty-eight ounce can of White Rain aerosol hairspray—plus a smaller, trav-el-size can he tucked right into her coat pocket—and a palette of makeup colors that would have left Barbie blushing. He spent nearly fifteen minutes talking to her about why he chose an aerosol hairspray instead of a pump bottle. "The finer mist gives you good hold, Stella, without making the style rigid!"

Now she found herself standing beside the live truck in the middle of downtown Knoxville feeling a bit like someone from one of those old '80s movies.

Her hair was teased so high that it startled her if she moved too quickly. She felt like a fluffy dandelion, ready to blow away with a stiff gust of wind, which is why Matthew Mason used so much aerosol hairspray, she guessed. Her peach-colored eye shadow mingled menacingly with the violet eyeliner Matthew swore would bring out the green in her eyes, and a line of blush cut across her face so starkly that she was concerned it looked like some kind of injury suffered at the hands of a fashionista.

Matthew Mason had left just moments ago, claiming he wanted to watch the big reveal on TV, himself. Based on the way Melissa was staring at her, Stella wanted to see it, too.

She tried to find her inner Zen. The weather had warmed considerably from the week before, and Stella turned her face to the sun, letting the bright, happy rays sink through her eyelids. Within seconds, she felt better—until she tried to open her eyes. Several coats of mascara had glued them partially shut.

"Anchor intro in five," Melissa announced, not even attempting to quash her grin as Stella pried her lashes apart with her fingers.

**CHET**
**Switching gears now to a follow-up. An aggravated assault has become a homicide investigation as the victim loses his fight for life overnight. Stella Reynolds is live at the jail downtown with the latest on the Oliver Bennet homicide. Stella?**
**STELLA**

Chet, a lot of new information is coming down from police and the coroner's office today about the Bennet homicide and how it might be more closely related to another crime that happened not long ago.

Through her earpiece, she heard the package that she wrote play back over the airwaves. She had included soundbites from the mayor, Detective Murphy, and the coroner in her report. She wasn't able to link the two shootings today, but she did mention that they might have happened on the same day all those weeks ago.

"Standby, Stella. Back to you in ten," Melissa said.

**STELLA**

No one has been officially charged, yet, in the Luanne Rockman homicide. In fact, police tell me that they have no suspects in the case. Of course, if anyone watching tonight has information, please call Knoxville Police.

Reporting live, I'm Stella Reynolds. Back to you.

She stared at the camera for five extra seconds to make sure she was clear, but looking at reflection in the camera lens got to be too much. She started to take her earpiece out when the producer back at the station interrupted her.

"What happened out there?"

"What do you mean?" Stella asked, wondering if there was a problem with her story.

"I mean, what's wrong with your face?"

Stella flinched. "Oh, uh... it's something that consultant guy wanted to try out. It's good?" she asked, looking hopefully at the camera.

There was a pause while the producer tried to figure out how to respond. Finally, she said, "It's, uh... it's definitely eye-catching."

Stella barked out a laugh. "I'm not sure, but maybe that's what we were going for." She disconnected her IFB cord from the box and set her microphone on the ground. They would be live again during the six o'clock newscast, so she and Melissa had about forty-five minutes to work on a new version of their story.

As they walked back to the live truck, however, someone sitting on a bench nearby lifted his hand in greeting. Stella squinted through the mascara and her eyes widened in surprise. It was Harrison Keys, Cas Rockman's father. She had been trying to get in touch with him for weeks, but had been unable to find a phone number or address for him. He was obviously the type of person who got in touch with you, not the other way around.

She walked to the bench. "You're a difficult man to find."

Harrison nodded. "You would be, too, if you'd spent twenty years in prison for murder." There wasn't any anger in his voice, but Stella picked up a strained sadness.

She sat next to him. "I'm glad you're here."

"That's the first time someone's said that to me in a long time."

They sat in silence for a while. Stella expected him to explain why he was there, but he didn't speak. Eventually, she said, "I think you're right about your son, but I'm going to need a lot of help proving it—especially when Cas, himself, is still claiming that he's guilty."

Harrison leaned forward, rested his elbows on his knees, and spoke without looking at her. "That will all change," he said with his now-familiar, formal way of speaking. "With the death penalty on the table, Cas is going to have quite a lot to think about in that jail cell—twenty-three hours a day to think. I suspect he will be ready to tell the truth soon. I just hope the truth will still be an option."

"What do you mean?" Stella asked. "Is he being threatened?"

"Not yet," he said, measuring his words, "but it will start. Everybody knows the stakes are higher now. He was willing to do time for a shooting, but that would only be six or eight years, and Cas would be out in four for good behavior. A death penalty murder case is a whole different hell, though, and he knows that—they know that."

"Who?" she asked, perplexed. "I don't really know who

all the players are. Enough games. Tell me where to start."

"Start with the gang. Did you know there is only one gang operating in the city of Knoxville? They have total control of the streets. I have never seen anything like it," he said, scratching his head in wonder. "Back in my day, you had rival gangs controlling different turf. There were different areas everyone was allowed to be in. Things are different, now, though. One gang controls everything."

*Rufus Mills*, Stella thought grimly. She held up a hand. "Why haven't I heard anything about this gang before this case? It seems like, if there was gang trouble in the City of Knoxville, we would've been reporting on it for years."

Harrison stared at her through narrowed eyes and didn't say anything for a while. "That is probably a story for another time." Stella looked down at her notebook and blew out a frustrated breath. He continued, "I am not saying Cas is a great person. I was not there when he was younger. His mom did her best, but in truth, she was not there, either. She worked three jobs to keep them in an apartment. When he got off track, well, it is the shit that happens to any kid in his situation."

The swear word sounded oddly at home in his formal diction, and Stella nodded, understanding how easy it would be take the wrong path in life under those circumstances.

"He got into the gang and sold drugs—easy money. Somehow, though, he got behind on payments with no way out. He came to me about a month ago with the problem." He took a deep breath and paused. When he was sure he had Stella's full attention, he continued, "The gang wanted him to kill somebody, and if he did it, his debts would be cleared—no more trouble. He agreed, but when it came down to it, he could not pull the trigger. He let Oliver Bennet walk away."

Harrison leaned forward, resting his head in his hands. He rubbed his head and finally sat up in frustration. "Cas was going to stay with me for a while. I have a place, and no one knows where it is. It is... removed from society.

Cas would have been safe." Stella was rapidly jotting down notes, but she looked up when Harrison stopped talking and raised her eyebrows in question. "He left," he said with a sigh. "The only thing worse for a young man than being in trouble is being bored. He had nothing to do, so he left. It wasn't twelve hours later that I met you for the first time, right here, on this very bench."

"The day Cas was arrested?" Stella asked.

"The day Cas was arrested," he agreed. Harrison turned sideways on the bench to look directly at her for the first time. "You see the situation Cas is in, now? If he tells the truth—that he did not shoot Oliver Bennet—he will find trouble with the gang. If he stays quiet, though, he is in trouble with the law."

"Which one is worse?" Stella asked.

"I don't know," he replied. "Up to this point, I felt like he was safe in the jail. But, with the death penalty hanging over him, I worry about insiders at the jail getting him, first. I think he's in trouble, either way."

"The coroner's office says Cas's mom was killed on or about the same day that Oliver Bennet was shot. Isn't it possible that whoever shot Bennet also killed Luanne to, I don't know, send a message to Cas?"

"It has been keeping me up at night, wondering the same thing. I just do not know. If that is the case, Cas is next, no matter where he is."

"Mr. Keys, what do you want me to do with all of this information? It sounds to me like, if I dig into this and find the truth, Cas might be in more trouble than he's in now."

"The truth is always the best option. I want you to find the truth."

"Do you have a phone number? An address? Some way I can get in touch?"

Harrison was already walking away, but he paused and turned back. "I'll email you."

Stella had already packed away her notebook, but she hurried to take it back out of her bag. "That's a great idea,

Harrison," she called, diving back into her bag for a pen. "Let's exchange email addresses. That way, we can stay in touch." She looked up, ready to write down his address, but he was gone.

She stared at the bench where he'd been sitting just moments ago. Could Harrison Keys be her anonymous emailer? If so, where was he getting his insider information?

# 23

In truth, her first mistake was checking her email. She had finished her six o'clock live shot and helped Melissa tear down the equipment before she packed up her bag and took out her phone. She had a few minutes to wait as the mast slowly bounced back down to the live truck, and she should have known better, but with one small click, it was done. Her email account was open, and it was a disaster.

At first, she thought the twenty new messages in her inbox was some kind of mistake. At second glance, however, they appeared to be from viewers. They were all bluntly... constructive in their criticism.

"You look like a whore on a Sunday morning."

"Must need glasses, if you think that looks good."

"Not right in the head. Actually worried for your mental health. You should go see a doctor."

The comments went on and on, and those were just the ones that were fit to print.

Stella swiveled the side view mirror on the live truck around for the first time since Matthew Mason had arrived at the courthouse and took a good, hard look at her face. She smiled—she grimaced. She said the first line from her live shot, and she had to admit it. She agreed with the viewers. What a mess.

She dug around in her bag, finally finding a pouch of makeup-removing wipes. She rubbed one roughly across her face to take off the most offensive colors. Smears of peach, purple, and black quickly filled the small, white square. The chemicals burned her eyes slightly, but she didn't care—in the end, it was worth it to be free of that ridiculous makeup. She turned away from the mirror and saw a bag in the back of the live truck.

"Is that yours?" she asked Melissa.

Melissa looked away from the switch she was holding and shrugged. "Nope."

Stella opened the bag and groaned. Matthew Mason left the makeup, the curling iron, and the offending can of hairspray. She picked it up and marched it over to a near-by trash bin, ready to throw the entire thing inside. Before she could, though, Detective Gibson came walking out of the police department.

"Ho-oh!" he exclaimed when he caught sight of her, a wicked grin splitting his face. "What happened to you, Reynolds?"

She squared her shoulders and flicked her hand. "Just trying out your mom's hairstyle, Gibson," she said as she pivoted toward the live truck, still grasping the offensive bag of makeup.

"Hey, wait up. I actually wanted to talk to you about your pet project."

"What are you talking about?"

"I heard you asking questions about Cas Rockman. What's your interest in the case?"

Ignoring her better judgement, she stopped. "It's a death penalty case, Gibson—I doubt I'm the only one interested in it."

"Yeah, but you're the only one Rockman has talked to from jail. I just saw you chatting it up with his dad over there," he pointed to the bench, "so I'm guessing you're a bit more invested in Rockman than the other reporters."

It was too much, his condescending tone and the makeover from hell—she'd had enough. "Gibson, do you have a point? I'm just trying to do my job, okay? If you have something related to the case to tell me, then by all means, share. Otherwise, just... just... ah!" He picked up a section of her cemented hair and rubbed it between his fingers, and she batted his hand away.

"Calm down, Reynolds. I do have some information for you. It's off-the-record, and if anyone asks, you didn't hear it from me."

"I'm familiar with what off-the-record means, Gibson."

He raised an eyebrow. "Do you want to hear it or not?"

She sighed. "Fine. What?"

"Your boy, Cas, is on the line for another murder—a cold case out of Nashville. We got a DNA hit in the CODIS system after he was booked into jail. His DNA was left at a murder scene five years ago. It looks like Cas isn't new to killing. I just thought you should know who you're going to bat for, ya know?" He shoved some papers into her hands. "It's all in there—that's the fax we got from Nashville."

As he turned away, Stella thought she heard him whistle as he unlocked his car door.

She couldn't move. "CODIS" was the acronym for the Combined DNA Index System. Forensics labs all over the country entered DNA information collected from crime scenes into the program, and DNA swabs from people booked into jail on unrelated crimes could be matched to unsolved crimes across the country.

Could Gibson have been telling the truth?

She looked down at the papers and her stomach sank. It was a request for more information from Nashville Police. As she skimmed the report, she saw that the victim had been just eighteen years old and caught in the crossfire of a shootout as she walked her little brother to school one morning. She tried to keep reading, but her eyes couldn't focus on the lines in front of her.

Even though Gibson's information didn't change anything about the Bennet homicide and Cas's possible innocence, it certainly put a damper on her feelings about the case. Was she going to risk her life for a killer, even if he was innocent of his current charges? If he'd gotten away with one murder, it didn't seem a great injustice that he was charged with a different one he may not have actually committed. Her journalism ethics class in college had never covered anything like this.

"Hey, let's go! I'm on the clock, Reynolds. Dinner

time," Melissa called from the live truck.

Stella nodded numbly and walked over. On the ride back, the only thought to break through the shock of new information had to do with Gibson. Why did he go out of his way to tell her about the DNA hit? He'd never been one to tip her off to a story before, so why now?

Back at the office, Stella saw another reporter, Betsy, scrubbing similarly awful makeup off her face. They exchanged grimaces. Her lovely, dark hair was curled and frizzy, and teal eyeshadow radiated from her eyelids, even as she wiped them clean. Stella shook her head and sat at her computer, momentarily distracted from the news about Cas. Apparently, it had been a tough night for everyone.

She hated to log onto the computer, worried about more emails, but she had to write up her story for the station's website. After avoiding her inbox as long as she could, Stella finally succumbed to curiosity and opened the program to see forty-eight new messages. A quick glance told her that they were all from viewers who had something to say about her new look. She deleted them all without reading them and logged off the computer.

After grabbing her bag, she called across the newsroom. "Hey, Del, I'm going to grab a quick dinner. I'll be back to front the story for the eleven o'clock news." Del nodded, never taking her eyes off the computer screen, and Stella walked out of the newsroom.

Twenty minutes later, she was walking into her apartment complex, deciding between heating up last night's spaghetti or nuking a can of soup. She rounded the corner to her hallway, and a tiny scream escaped her when she looked up to see a man standing in front of her door. He quickly held up a hand in greeting, but Stella was already stumbling back down the hall. Was this one of Rufus' henchmen?

Before she could turn and run to safety, he said, "I'm so sorry. I didn't mean to startle you. I'm looking for Janet

Black—I'm her father."

# 24

Stella was still backing away, although slower now, as she tried to figure out what to do. She finally bumped into the door that led to the lobby and stopped. Her eyes narrowed as she took in the man in front of her. He was tall and bald, but it wasn't the kind of baldness that looked like he'd lost the battle with a receding hairline. Instead, it looked like precise work with a razor to keep his head neat.

His shoulders were broad, and he had a bit of a paunch at his midsection. He might have been in his fifties, making it possible for him to be Janet's father. He took a few slow, careful steps toward her, and as he got closer, she looked into his hazel eyes—Janet's hazel eyes—and knew, without a doubt, that he was telling the truth.

"I don't think she wants to talk to you." She laughed a little, knowing what an understatement that was.

"I know she doesn't," he said with a sigh, "but I have some things she needs to hear."

"I don't need to hear anything you have to say." The voice came from behind them both, and Stella looked past Sampson in surprise to see her roommate.

"I knew you were in there," her father said, tilting his head to one side. "I could practically hear your bad attitude through the door."

Stella looked at Sampson Foster with new eyes. This obviously wasn't some apologetic father, hoping for a second chance. He had some steel in his backbone, and she realized that she was going to be in for quite a show.

"Well, that's fitting," Janet said, crossing her arms in front of her chest, "because, despite the fact that you were knocking on the door to come in, I could already imagine what it would be like when you were gone—because that's all I know."

The two stared at each other with such similar sour faces that Stella rubbed her eyes to make sure she wasn't imagining the whole thing; it was like looking in a fun-house mirror. After her night, she couldn't take it.

"No need to have this family reunion out in the hall-way. You either take it inside or outside." Janet turned her glare on Stella, but she shrugged, unperturbed. "Don't look at me." After walking past Sampson, she started to push past Janet into the apartment.

"I actually can't take my eyes off of you," Janet said, reaching out to rub some strands of Stella's stiff hair between her fingers. "What's happening here?" She gingerly sniffed her head. "Is that White Rain hairspray? I haven't smelled that since high school."

Stella shrugged by her and headed straight into the kitchen. She opened the cabinet above the refrigerator and pulled out her emergency bag of mini Snickers. What a day! First, there'd been the makeover, the news about Cas, and now, finally, the shock of a stranger at her door. She needed chocolate.

Janet gave her a suspicious look as she unwrapped one and popped it into her mouth. Before she could ask any questions, though, her father spoke from the doorway.

"We need to talk, Janet. I don't want the FBI following you around—I don't want the FBI following your room-mate around. They just need to ask you a few questions about me for what's supposed to be a very standard back-ground check and then they'll get out of your life."

"Well, they can take lessons on how to do that from you, can't they?" Janet snapped.

"God damn it, Janet, if you'd just give me five minutes to explain..."

Stella snorted and popped another mini candy bar into her mouth. It was amazing—Sampson Foster had no part in raising Janet, but the two spoke like carbon copies of one another. She grabbed a soda out of the fridge and sloshed some into a glass.

Distracted by the noise, Janet turned away from her father again and looked at Stella. She opened her mouth, but Sampson spoke, instead.

"Do you know when I found out that you even existed?" Janet looked at her father through narrowed eyes, and the two stared at each other for what seemed like forever. Finally, Janet shook her head. It was barely perceptible, but Sampson nodded triumphantly. "I found out about you ten hours before we met for the first time. Do you remember? We were standing in the middle of that... living room... in the place you and your mom called home."

"Liar." Janet glared at her father. "I don't believe you."

"I was in Williston, North Dakota, when I found out. I sat in shock for two hours and spent six hours driving to Bozeman. I waited outside your house for two hours until you came home."

"Mom said you left her the minute you found out she was pregnant. She said you'd have outrun a moose, you took off so fast."

Stella snorted again and Janet turned to her once more. "A moose? Really?" she asked.

Janet nodded. "That's the exact phrase I heard her use a dozen times growing up."

"It's just not true, Janet." Sampson sat down heavily on a chair by the sliding glass door. Stella looked over and thought that he'd aged ten years in the last ten minutes. "Your mother broke up with me and it broke me. She wouldn't take my calls and wouldn't tell me why she ended things. After a couple months with no word from your mom, I realized I couldn't stay in Bozeman. That's when I moved to Bismarck, finished law school, and opened my law practice." His words and the pain behind them had a raw edge of truth that was hard for even Janet to ignore.

"It was only years later that I found out you were alive. My sister was still living in Bozeman and she saw a news clip about you—some small article in the local paper about Janet Black. It was for the Honor Society inductions your junior year. Do you remember? My sister would've missed it, except for a quote from your mom. She said, 'I've never been more proud—'"

"'Of my amazing daughter. The world is your oyster.'" Janet finished. She looked at Sampson uncertainly, as if her mind couldn't shift to this new reality so quickly.

Neither could Stella's. *Honor Society?* It's like there was a whole other Janet that she hadn't even met.

"My sister did the math and went to your field hockey game to be sure. As soon as she saw you, she knew. She called me, and I've never been the same."

"Why would Mom lie about that? It doesn't make any sense."

No, it didn't. Stella couldn't imagine her roommate wearing a preppy field hockey kilt and shin guards. When had she changed so dramatically?

"I wish we could be having this conversation with your mom, because I'd like some answers, too. I missed out on your whole life. Your whole life," he repeated, his face ashen. He leaned forward in his seat and got his wallet out of his back pocket. After opening it, he pulled out a small newspaper clipping, creased and worn with age. He held it out to Janet with trembling hands.

She walked over, and if Stella didn't know her so well, she would've thought Janet was unaffected by what was going on. Her step was sure and steady and her hand didn't shake  as she reached for the clipping. Sampson Foster was staring at the article, but Stella saw Janet's eyes darting around the room.

Sampson was delving too deeply into his daughter's long-held convictions, dredging up too many memories of her mother and her old life, and she was desperate for a way out.

Stella decided to cut her shaken roommate a break. "Hey, Janet, can you take Ole Boy out for me, please?"

Janet passed the newspaper clipping back to her father and looked at her. "Oh, great God damn timing, Stella. Fine," she snarled. Janet shot her a thankful look, though, as she grabbed his leash from closet by the door. She was out of the apartment and pulling the dog behind her in thirty seconds flat.

The room was quiet for a few moments. Stella found a bendy-straw at the bottom of the silverware drawer and used it to slurp up half a can of caffeinated soda. The drink, combined with the healthy dose of sugar from the candy made her feel a bit loopy. Janet's father had recovered himself, and he now stared at her shrewdly.

"You've been good for Janet. I don't know her well, but I can see that. So, for that, I thank you."

She rolled her eyes. "Nice try." At Sampson's surprised look, she wagged her finger at him. "You're not gonna win the roommate over and have her help you get to your daughter. Janet's my friend, first; you're just a nobody to me."

A smile tipped the corners of Sampson's lips, almost in spite of himself. "I like the sound of that. She needs some loyal friends, like you."

"Nope. Not gonna work," she said, unwrapping another Snickers. Curiosity got the best of her, though. "Why didn't you track her down before now? She moved out of her mom's place years ago. Why didn't you try to talk to her about this then?"

Sampson blew out a sigh. "I tried, but I could never find her—no tax information and no lease information. I even hired a P.I. who found nothing."

Stella chewed on her straw, thinking. When she'd met Janet, she had been living in a hotel and getting paid under the table at her bartending job. Sampson Foster was probably telling the truth.

"Well, how'd you find her, this time?"

"Parking tickets."

Stella smiled. It always came back to the RV. She felt herself softening toward the older man, and she purposefully turned her back on him. As she cleared off the wrappers from the counter, she thought of how funny it was that she'd never pick up a full-size candy bar, but eating a dozen mini-bars left her guilt-free. She studiously ignored Sampson until Janet made it back inside. She could tell her roommate had also steeled herself in the hallway, but before she could send her father packing, Stella interjected.

"Janet and I were talking earlier, Sampson Foster," she said archly, "about how she would like to get this interview with the FBI out of the way." Janet shot her a glare and her angst radiated across the room.

Stella decided to let the two of them duke things out without an audience. "You know what? It's been a long day." She plucked up two mini-candy bars with one hand and grabbed two more with her other. "A long freaking day, and it's not even done, yet." The thought was depressing.

Instead of grabbing an additional handful of candy, she took the entire bag off the counter and tucked it under her arm. The nuts were protein—she could easily call this dinner. When she looked up, both Janet and Sampson were shooting identical amused looks her way.

She looked down her nose at the pair. "I can see I'm no longer needed here, and surely you two can figure out this last piece of the puzzle without me. Let me know the plan tomorrow, okay?" She headed to her room, planning on taking a few minutes to gather her thoughts before returning back to work.

She lay on top of her covers, fully-clothed, ate some more Snickers, and made a decision. She was going to stop investigating whether Cas Rockman was innocent in the Bennet homicide. He could rot in jail, for all she cared—it was apparently where he belonged. She had a hot exclusive for that evening, and she'd just need to confirm it with someone in Nashville. The decision left her feeling slightly guilty as she thought about Harrison Keys' reaction, but she shoved those feelings aside, feeling betrayed by his son's history.

As she geared up to head back to work, she couldn't help but think that Janet's father had been trying to help her for a long while, even though she'd refused to see it. Sometimes, kids had a way of sticking their heads in the sand, unwilling or unable to hear the truth of the matter.

Despite her disappointment with Cas, she wondered if that was the case with him, too. His dad seemed to have good advice and a good handle on what was happening, but Cas either couldn't or wouldn't see the big picture. She wondered if he would be able to change. She wondered if he had time. Most of all, she wondered why she still cared.

# 25

Stella's sugar buzz had given way to a slight headache, and she sat up and groaned when she saw the clock. Her dinner break had run long; it was time to get back to work and make some calls on the Nashville cold case. She was going to have a hard time finding anyone to answer the phone this late at night.

A sudden flurry of shouting had Stella off the bed, and she opened the door to see Janet and her father locked in an angry battle of words, their faces mere inches apart.

"Don't you dare talk about my mother that way," Janet snarled. Her face was as red as her low-cut, V-neck sweater.

Sampson wasn't going to take orders from his own daughter, though, no matter how little he knew her. Now he was shouting, too. "I'll say what needs to be said. She never told me she was pregnant. I would have stayed, but she never gave me a chance to be a father and she never gave you a chance to have one. She did a disservice to both of us, and the fact that she's dead doesn't change that. It only makes it more infuriating for me!"

"Shut up!" Janet shouted, her voice taut with emotion. "Shut up! It's not about you—it's about me and my life!"

Sampson seemed to remember himself, and he took a step back, slowed his breathing, and nodded. "Exactly, Janet," he said quietly. "It is about you!"

Janet stared at him open-mouthed for a moment. She took a shaky breath and raised a hand toward the door. "I think you'd better leave."

Sampson took a few steps to the door before turning back. "I'm not walking out on you—you're kicking me out. I hope you'll remember the distinction when I come back tomorrow." The door closed with a soft thump.

Stella was still standing by her bedroom, unsure of what to do. She had to go, but Janet was crying—actual *tears* falling out of her eyes as she stood in the middle of the apartment. She didn't feel like she could leave her roommate in such a state.

After clearing her throat, Janet hastily wiped her face with the sleeve of her sweater. She still didn't turn around, though. "Things took a turn for the worse out here, huh?" Stella asked.

Janet laughed without humor. After a few deep breaths, she squared her shoulders and turned around. "Why all the candy tonight?"

"Huh?"

"You eat candy like that when you're stressed. What's going on?"

"Oh, nothing. Don't worry about me. I'm worried about you! What happened?"

"Honestly, I'd rather worry about you. I need a break from me. So, what's the problem?"

"Uh..." Stella needed a moment to regroup. She glanced at her watch. She was already late, so what did a few more minutes matter? She filled Janet in on the Nashville cold case and the DNA match. "So, basically, he's a murderer and I'm not wasting any more of my time on it."

"That doesn't make any sense."

"I know, right?" she said, glad Janet agreed. "I knew he wasn't a Boy Scout, but I thought he had some redeeming qualities. To find out he's involved in another murder, though, it's just—"

"No, I mean it doesn't make any sense that you're just quitting on Oliver Bennet. His family, wherever they are, deserve to know that his killer was brought to justice—not just a killer, but his killer. If you quit this story now, you're essentially saying it's okay that Oliver Bennet is dead."

"No, I'm not, I—"

"Stella," her roommate took a few steps toward her

with a fevered expression on her face. "You have to keep digging and asking questions. It's your job!"

She shook her head. "Listen, Janet, it'd be one thing, if—"

"Stella, I need you to do this." She seemed to have shifted the focus of her anger from her father to her friend. "I need you to do the right thing. I have to be able to count on you. What are you saying, here? Cas Rockman doesn't count, because he screwed up in the past? He's trying to do the right thing, now, though. Doesn't that matter?"

"He's not trying to do the right thing, Janet—that's just it! He's not telling the truth! He's still saying that he shot Oliver Bennet. If he's not even going to help himself, how am I supposed to—"

Janet cut her off again, "It's your job! Do your job!"

Stella felt her own temperature rising at her roommate's increasingly accusing tone.

"What are we talking about? Cas Rockman and Oliver Bennet, or you and your dad? I am trying to do my job, just like your dad is trying to do his. Don't blame him for a decision your mother made!"

"Don't talk about my mother, Stella!"

"She's not here to talk some sense into you, so I will! Your dad didn't know about you because your mom never told him anything. Why are you making him out to be the bad guy?" Janet spluttered, but she didn't or couldn't speak. "I'll tell you why. Because it's easier than blaming your mom. At least admit to yourself what you're doing."

Stella stormed past Janet and stalked out of the house, slamming the door behind her. She was furious. How dare Janet accuse her of not doing her job! She'd done more than most reporters would, especially after having her life threatened!

Scanning the lot for her car, she realized it wasn't there--she still had John's crappy station wagon. She marched over and shoved the key in the lock, turning it with such force that she managed to rip the top of her fingernail off.

"Damn it!"

She threw herself behind the wheel and slammed the car into gear. She'd only been driving for a couple of blocks when she noticed it—the black Escalade driven by the two FBI agents. She knew what they were doing, and if it wasn't for the day she'd had, she probably would have ignored them. After the dozens of mean emails, the scare of seeing someone outside her apartment door, and getting yelled at by Janet, though, she couldn't take it.

At a stoplight—the same stoplight as the first time she'd met the FBI agents, she realized with a grim smile—she threw John's car into park and stalked down the street.

With several startled drivers giving her funny looks, she marched past the two cars between hers and the Escalade and knocked on the driver's side window. She had some choice words for the agents for following her again and she couldn't wait to lay into them. They chose the wrong day to mess with her. Stella threw her hands on her hips and watched the window finally roll down. She was struck silent by what she saw.

"What are you doing?" the man in the driver's seat, a stranger, said with a glare. Stella stepped back in surprise, first at the driver's anger and then again when she took in the gun being trained on her from the passenger's seat.

"You're not... you're not the FBI!" Stella was barely able to say, as the words had almost gotten stuck in her throat.

"What are you, some kind of comedian?" the driver snarled. His glare reduced his eyes to barely-visible, tiny slits.

"I—I'm so sorry," she stammered, wondering if her day could get any worse. "I thought you were following me. I've obviously got this all wrong." She started to back away slowly as the traffic moved on either side of her. Several honks sounded as drivers tried to maneuver around her to get through the green light.

"We were following you—we just didn't expect to have

this conversation in the middle of the intersection. It works for us." The man in the passenger's seat was talking now, his gun held low, so passing cars couldn't see it. From her higher angle, though, Stella couldn't take her eyes off it.

"What do you—what do you mean?" she stammered, now thoroughly confused.

"We wanted to tell you to stay away from the Bennet case. Maybe you didn't get the first message, but we were serious. No more stories and no more questions, or no more life."

Stella's jaw dropped and she couldn't seem to find any words. They apparently weren't planning a discussion, though, because as soon as the man with the gun stopped speaking, the Escalade peeled away with a squeal. She had to jump back, so the side-view mirror didn't hit as the SUV flew past.

The sound of metal crushing metal made her flinch, and she looked up in time to see the side mirror of John's car fly into the air, struck by the Escalade as it screamed through the intersection. "Well, crap."

She stood in the middle of the street for several moments, collecting herself, and only moved when another car honked. The woman yelled out the window, "You crazy idiot, get off the street! You're going to get yourself killed!"

Stella shook herself. *Don't I know it.*

She hurried to John's car on shaky legs, got behind the wheel, and slowly pulled out, only to screech to a halt again when several more horns blared. The light was no longer green; she'd almost driven headlong into the intersection full of traffic.

She shook herself again and muttered, "Get it together, Stella."

After making her mind go blank, she focused only on the task of driving to her apartment. Green light. Lift foot off brake. Press down lightly on gas pedal. Engage blinker. It was like that the whole way home. When she finally pulled into the parking lot, she was glad to see that the apartment looked dark.

Cautiously, she unlocked the door, not looking forward to another screaming match with Janet. With a sigh, she realized that everyone was asleep. In the corner of the main room, Ole Boy barely lifted one eyelid to check who'd come in before rolling back over on his dog bed with a snore.

Stella went straight for the kitchen again; this time, she bypassed the remaining emergency bag of candy bars, reaching instead for the bottle of vodka.

The liquid glugged into a glass. What had she gotten involved in? A second threat on her life over the Oliver Bennet shooting. Her hand shook as she raised the clear liquid to her lips and swallowed.

This second threat—so brazen, so open—caused her to rethink things completely, but not in the way the man with the gun likely intended. Stella now knew without a doubt that she had to be close to something big for so many people to go out of their way to try to kill the story.

Who was behind it all, though? She was certain she'd met some of Rufus Mills' friends that night, but the gang was working with someone in-the-know. Detective Gibson's uncharacteristic tip had almost caused her to walk away, and Detective Murphy was no longer answering her calls.

She took another gulp and her hand was steady once again. The story of who shot Oliver Bennet needed to be told and she was the one who had to do it. As she came to a decision, she felt relieved. She set her glass down, no longer needing it. Before long, she heard movement behind her.

"I'm sorry." Janet was in pajamas. Her hair was pulled back into a ponytail and her face was scrubbed clean of makeup. She looked calm and almost resigned.

"No," Stella said, turning around, "I'm sorry. You were right. I need to keep digging. Not for Cas, but for Oliver."

Janet nodded. "You were right, too. I shouldn't be blaming my father. It's just hard to change my way of thinking after all these years." She walked closer. "Jesus, you look like crap. What happened to you? Why are you home so early?"

"Wait," Stella said, holding up a finger. She marched to the phone on the hall table and dialed the station. After a brief conversation with Del in which she called off work for the night, she turned back to Janet and filled her roommate in on what happened on the road.

"This is crazy. You must be close to something for that kind of reaction."

"That's exactly what I was thinking. The men tonight couldn't have known about the tip I just got on the Nashville case. That means they're only concerned about making sure Cas takes the blame in the Bennet homicide. It all but confirms that he's innocent. So, who's guilty?"

Janet chewed her lower lip. "The police don't seem interested in digging into the case, prosecutors don't seem worried about the lack of evidence, and the mayor seems pretty happy with an arrest. They all look guilty to me."

"I know," Stella said slowly, reaching into the cabinet for a Milky Way. "I know."

# 26

Stella awoke the next morning with a dry mouth, a splitting headache, and a sick feeling in her stomach. It turned out several slugs of vodka, a half-bag of candy, and no real food was a terrible combination.

She stumbled out of her bedroom, determined to find a cup of strong coffee. When she rounded the corner into the kitchen, she practically wept with relief. Janet was sitting at the table, and at the seat next to her, she had lined up a cup of coffee and enough Tylenol to tranquilize an elephant.

"God bless you, Janet," Stella croaked. She guzzled down the medicine with two sips of coffee, wincing as the hot liquid burned her tongue.

"So, what's the plan?" her roommate asked, surveying her over her cup. She looked worried, and Stella was glad they were back on friendly terms.

She took another long sip of her coffee, realizing she didn't have one. "I don't know, but I'll need to tread lightly. I can't be asking too many questions. It's going to be difficult." She pressed her fingertips against her forehead, feeling like she was staring up at a giant mountain, looking for the path to the top. "What about you? Your dad said he's coming back today. Are you ready?"

Janet nodded. "I called him last night after you went to bed. We're going to try lunch today. It turns out that he's up for a federal judge spot," she said with a hint of pride in her voice. "Oh, and he's setting me up with the FBI. I guess they're just trying to vet him for the position and make sure there aren't any surprises."

Stella looked up from her coffee and waited until her roommate met her eyes. Both women burst out laughing.

"You're just about the definition of surprise, aren't you?" Stella said when she could finally speak again.

They sipped their coffees in silence for a few more minutes before Janet cleared her throat. "You just be careful, Stella. Keep your cameraman close, okay?"

***

By the time Stella walked out of the apartment for work, the sun was shining angrily and her head was pounding with each step. She had already reached the limit for Tylenol for the day and wasn't sure how she would make it through her shift.

It was the kind of day Stella would have loved to cover spot news—something easy, like a robbery. She'd be able to knock out all the interviews in one spot and have time to focus on the real story of interest for the day—who killed Oliver Bennet. She planned to get someone from Nashville on the phone as soon as she walked into the office. Instead, when she got into the newsroom, her boss delivered a blow.

"You'll be speaking to a class of first-graders about what it's like to be a news reporter," Patricia said, looking at her computer over the top of her reading glasses. "It was supposed to be just one class, but all three of the first grade teachers at the school thought their students would love to hear from you, so you'll be talking to about sixty-five six- and seven-year-olds."

Stella's eyes bulged. That did not sound like the cure for a hangover. In fact, it sounded like a punishment for over-indulging the night before.

"Do you feel all right today, Stella? How's your car?"

"My car?" she asked, almost forgetting that she'd called off the night before and used John's car as an excuse. "Oh, it's fine. I used Gorilla Glue to reattach the mirror..." She fell silent, distracted by the headline of the paper on her boss's desk. It read *Police Chief Wright is So Wrong, Search for New Chief Underway*. She asked, "Chief Wright was fired? When did that happen?"

"The paper got a press release last night. They were supposed to embargo the news until today, but there you go," Patricia said, scowling at the headline before turning back to her computer.

"Well, who's covering it for us? I should head downtown, talk to my contacts, and see what—"

"Not a chance, Reynolds. We're covered—Barger's already down there—but nice try." She smiled without taking her eyes off her computer screen. Don Barger was a dayside reporter and had probably been working the story since he got in at nine o'clock that morning.

"What?" Stella asked, innocently.

"You're going to the elementary school." She looked up from her computer with a smile. "How about Matthew Mason, eh? He thought the new makeup looked amazing last night!" Stella spluttered, but couldn't come up with a single polite thing to say. Patricia took her silence as agreement. "I know. Some people say he's over the top, but I think he's at the top of his game, and he'll help us get there, too. Well done!" The phone rang, and Patricia dismissed Stella with a nod toward her office door. Stella grumbled all the way back to her desk.

An hour later, she walked wearily toward a single-story, long, brick building. It was cold, but not viciously so, and she could almost taste spring in the air. The sun was still out, although it didn't seem quite as painfully bright as it had when she'd left her apartment.

Inside, Stella felt like a giant. The hallways were wide and the ceiling was tall enough, but everything was hung lower than usual. She had to bend to read the notices clipped to bulletin boards about a fundraiser, spirit day announcements, and posters urging fellow students to vote in an upcoming class election. Stella walked past it all on her way to the office where she signed in and met with a very happy principal.

"We are so thrilled you're here, Ms. Reynolds," the woman said. She had bright red hair that might have been natural when she was younger, but now clearly came out of a bottle. "I'm Mrs. Stevens. When Mrs. Warren told us you were coming, it was everything I could do to limit it to the first grade classes. Did you bring a photographer?" She looked eagerly behind Stella, as if a photographer might materialize out of thin air.

"No, unfortunately they couldn't spare a videographer today. That, however, leaves us lots of time for any questions the kids might have." Stella tried to ignore her mild headache and smiled as pleasantly as she could at the other woman while she waited for her next instruction.

"Right you are, my dear. Follow me. We were just going to be in Mrs. Warren's room, but with so many students, we decided to move to the multipurpose room." Mrs. Stevens led the way out of the office, down a labyrinth of hallways, and finally came to a stop outside some double doors. "I'll just say a few words to introduce you, and then you can take the stage."

They walked into the room and Stella was greeted by a din of noise that didn't seem to match the crowd inside. Tiny bodies were in perpetual motion, and each child was making more sound than any five adults combined. Mrs. Stevens took the stage and started clapping out a strange beat. It had a magical effect on the children, who clapped back and were sitting quietly within seconds.

Stella's surprise must have shown on her face, because Mrs. Stevens said, "Ms. Reynolds has obviously never seen the Allen Elementary way. Well done, first graders!"

She couldn't help but smile broadly as Mrs. Stevens continued the introduction. When it was Stella's turn to talk, she took the microphone off the stand and stood in front of the students. She had a few minutes of speech prepared from similar appearances she'd made over the years and she talked about all the different people she worked with every day, from homicide detectives and the mayor to criminals and celebrities.

Speaking to younger kids like this was always interesting. Half of them were still thinking about what their moms forgot to pack for lunch that day, while the other half were wondering if they were going to get to go to the ice cream shop after school. Stella kept it short and opened the floor to questions.

Afterward, the kids gave her a standing ovation, and the teachers kindly shook her hand. Mrs. Stevens led her out of the multipurpose room and down the hall toward the front door. Instead of heading out, though, Mrs. Stevens took a left turn into the school library.

"I thought you might appreciate this," she said, bustling between rows of books to a back wall. She bent and ran a finger along the spines of dozens of books, finally pulling one off the shelf. "You mentioned Detective Murphy with the police department being someone you work closely with. I wondered if you knew that he went to school here?" Mrs. Stevens smiled proudly. "It was a long time ago." Stella now saw that she had taken a yearbook from the shelf, which she placed on top of the stacks and fanned through the pages, looking for something. "Ah, here he is. He's a good egg. It's nice to know that so many of our alumni have gone on to do great things."

"Mrs. Stevens," a voice broke in, "you're wanted back in the office. Something about an EpiPen situation?"

"Thank you, Mr. Cardoza. Can you see that Ms. Reynolds makes it back out of the building, please?" She buzzed out of the room for the office and whatever medical crisis was happening nearby.

"We all wear a lot of hats, these days—there's not enough money in the budget for a school nurse, anymore. The allergic reaction scares are always the worst." At Stella's look, he stuck out one hand. "I'm Anthony Cardoza, school librarian and—and probably the next job on the chopping block, if you want to know the truth," he added honestly.

Stella grimaced. "I feel your pain," she said. "Broadcast news is always cutting corners. I sometimes worry if they're going to do away with reporters, altogether, and just have the photographer shoot video over the anchors talking."

She took one last glance of the photo of her friend's husband as a kid. She looked at the cover and saw that it was the yearbook from 1974. She and Annie hadn't even been born, yet, and here was a little Murph. "Already a hell-raiser, it looks like." She looked up, expecting a smile, but Anthony was now scowling at the yearbook. When he looked up, he made an effort to smooth out his expression. "Do you know Brian Murphy?" Stella asked.

Anthony shook his head, a small smile now on his face. "It's silly, isn't it, to still hold grudges from so long ago? I try to remind myself that we were all just kids back then, but you know what they say. Old grudges die hard." At Stella's look, he elaborated, "We went to school together. Let's just say that Murphy's motto wasn't always to protect and serve." He reached across her and flipped through more pages in the yearbook. He found the one he was looking for and pointed to a picture. "This was Murphy and his gang. Man, did they used to make my life tough! I was shocked to find out he became a cop. I guess we all change over time, though."

Stella tilted her head. "Have you changed over the years?"

"Well... no, not really, but I'm sure he and his crew did. Lots of kids grow out of mean streaks," he added without conviction.

She glanced at her watch. "I've got to go back to the station, but it was so nice to meet you." As she took one last look at the picture Anthony was still pointing to, she realized that Annie would get a kick out of this old snapshot of her husband.

"Can I have a copy of this?"

He shrugged and took the book to a photocopy machine in the corner. A minute after punching in a code, Stella was holding a warm sheet of paper with the black and white image.

Anthony folded the book shut with a thump and placed

it back on the shelf. "That book belongs right there, in the past," he said with a self-conscious smile.

Stella grimaced. "Was elementary school that bad for you? You seem so normal and well-adjusted." She winked, and he laughed.

"Let's just say I had a growth spurt in middle school and people stopped messing with me. After that, it was smooth sailing."

"Ah, yes, middle school is known everywhere for being so easy to navigate." They both laughed at that, and Anthony saw Stella to the front door.

She sat in her car for a moment, looking at the picture. Ten-year-old Murphy was standing with two other boys with their arms around each other, grinning. The longer she looked at it, the more familiar all three boys looked. She scratched her head, wondering if she knew the other two, but after staring at it for a few more minutes, she gave up, unable to place them.

She started up the engine, then rooted around in her bag. She needed to take a page out of Murphy's book and rely on an old friend for this mystery. Finally finding her cell phone, she picked a number from her contact list.

"Annie, are you free tomorrow? Let's meet for coffee."

# 27

By eleven-thirty that night, Stella's head was swimming. The talk at the elementary school had only been the beginning of a long and busy shift. She'd gotten her robbery story, followed by a shooting and then a stabbing. She and Bob had been on the run all night, and she was finally logging off her computer, ready to head home, when the ping of an incoming email caught her attention.

Anonymous was finally back with another message. *Be careful. Don't trust anyone, but keep digging. This story needs to be told.* She glared at the screen and reread the message before she noticed a post script at the bottom of the screen. *Trash the new makeup.*

Her jaw dropped and her eyes skittered around the newsroom. Seriously? Now her tipster had the gall to weigh in on her eyeshadow color? Unbelievable.

She logged off her computer and gathered up her bags. In John's car, she caught sight of herself in the rearview mirror. Her boss had convinced her to continue with a more muted version of the consultant's new look. Her hair was back to normal, but her makeup colors were again the unusual blend of peach and violet. Anonymous was right about one thing, at least. This new look was terrible. She remembered the last time she'd listened to a consultant and ended up wearing fake glasses on air. She should have learned her lesson.

Stella knew exactly who she was and what she stood for, and she didn't need anyone to "fix" her or tell her what she should and shouldn't wear, say, or do. She glared at the road and felt a shift in her mindset. She wouldn't let herself be bullied around—not by thugs with a gun, and certainly not by a super-smiley consultant.

As she drove down the road in her ex-boyfriend's car, she came to another conclusion. She didn't need to be jealous of John and his girlfriend. She didn't want what they had, so why was she spending any time worrying about them? She wanted to have fun with someone she enjoyed spending time with, but without having to stress about if she'd be married in five years or if she'd have to sacrifice her career to make the relationship work.

She wound her way through town on auto-pilot and was halfway there before she really realized where she was headed. Lucky lived in a lovely area of Knoxville. The houses were spread out across an old horse farm, tucked into valleys and hidden behind hills without the need of special landscaping or obnoxious gates to keep the curious away. You had to know where you were going to get there, and luckily, Stella did.

She pulled into the driveway to find that the house was dark. Lucky wasn't supposed to get back from Connecticut until the weekend, but she craved the peace and quiet of the empty home.

After disarming the security system, she walked in through the garage door and headed to the master bedroom upstairs. Past the giant bed, sitting area, and enormous walk-in closet, Stella headed straight for the master bath.

The floor underfoot was deliciously warm when she kicked off her shoes—the heated tiles Lucky had installed when he bought the house were definitely worth it. She sauntered to the Jacuzzi and cranked up the faucets, smiling as the sound of rushing water echoed through the room. While the tub was filling, she took a wipe out of her bag and scrubbed her face until all traces of peach and violet were gone.

She slipped out of her clothes, leaving them in a pile on the floor, and when she sank into the hot water, a long sigh escaped her. What a treat. At five-foot-nine, in a normal tub, she had to decide whether she wanted the lower or upper half of her body underwater. In Lucky's extra deep and long Jacuzzi, however, she could almost lie flat.

After a good, long soak—long enough that her fingers had turned wrinkly and the water had grown cold—she climbed out, wrapped herself in a ridiculously luxurious white robe, and towel-dried her hair. She walked loose-limbed to Lucky's monstrous bed, crawled under the covers, and fell into a deep, dreamless sleep.

***

"Stella."

The voice seemed to float in the air, unattached, and she ignored it. She'd slept like the dead. The stiffness in her back let her know she probably hadn't moved in twelve hours. Slowly stretching out her legs and rolling onto her back, she barely opened her eyes against the brightness in the room. Her hair streaked across the pillow next to her, the auburn color cutting a sharp contrast against the stark white pillowcase. She closed her eyes again and guessed it was past noon; wiggling her fingers and toes with a smile on her face, she felt amazing.

"Stella?"

Her eyes flew open and she rolled onto her side toward the voice. When she saw who was there, she quickly sat up. "Lucky? What are you doing here?" The lopsided smile on his lips made Stella blush. "I—I mean, I thought you didn't get back until later," she stammered, suddenly embarrassed.

He ran a hand through his blond hair and Stella watched his eyes take in her loosely-tied robe. He looked away guiltily and took a step back from the bed. "I caught an earlier flight. Something told me I had to get home."

He inched forward again, almost as if by accident, and picked up a lock of her hair to let it run through his fingers. They both watched it fall soundlessly to Stella's shoulder, and when she looked up, their eyes met.

She licked her lips, unable to look away. The silence between them seemed to spike, grow, and heat up until it was scorching. He tilted his head with a confused look on his face, but Stella pounced before he could speak.

She launched into him, ripping his shirt off in one rough movement, and the ping of buttons as they bounced off the bedside table and lamp was the only thing that broke the silence. Lucky's surprise quickly gave way to lust, and soon his hands were as greedy as hers. The ties on her robe got stuck, and Lucky growled in frustration as he pulled at the fabric.

Batting his hands away, she undid the belt, herself, and let the robe fall away from her shoulders. Within seconds, he was on her, his hands exploring her skin. It was too slow, though—too reserved—so she climbed up his body until she was standing on the bed, pushing him down onto the mattress. He pulled her down with him, and soon, it was all hands and sighs, bodies entwined, and heads forgotten.

It wasn't until after, when they lay together, panting, that Stella realized not a word had been spoken between them since shortly after she'd woken up. She turned to him with a grin on her face. "God, I needed that."

He chuckled, rolled her on top of him, and drew lazy circles on her back. "Me, too, but, uh... well, what happened? Last I heard, you didn't even miss me. You thought I was dating a dozen other women. You didn't trust—"

She put a finger to his lips, silencing him. He shot her an annoyed look, but fell quiet. "I realized that... well, that it's okay to be with you and not get swallowed up by you. Maybe we can try dating. Nothing life or death involved this time, and, I don't know, we can see how that goes."

"Officially?"

"Well..." Stella wrinkled her nose, "I don't want to be known as Lucky Haskins's girlfriend. I want to be me and date you."

"Is that what's been holding you back?" She nodded. "Why didn't you just tell me that?"

"I don't think I knew it until just now."

His eyes crinkled around the corners and he made a humming sound deep in his throat. She took her finger away from his lips and he grinned. "I can work with that," he said, nipping her finger. She squealed, and he added, "I can work with that right now, as a matter of fact." He scooped her up in his arms and headed for the bathroom.

Twenty minutes later, she surveyed the puddles of water near the huge walk-in shower. They had made good use of Lucky's various lotions and potions, and she was now back in the tub, leaning against one end and looking at Lucky who leaned against the other end.

She'd just explained what was going on with the murders, and he was staring at her quizzically. "So, what's next?" he asked. "You've decided to ignore this violent gang's warnings?" His words were measured, but she could see what he thought of her plan by his expression, which was concerned with a touch of astonishment and anger mixed in.

"Not ignore them, but I'm not going to let them dictate what stories I cover. I'll be careful—don't worry," she added hastily when he opened his mouth to argue. He clamped his lips shut and nodded, and before he could say anything else, she changed the subject. "What's your schedule like? More travel?"

He blew out a breath and shook his head. "Stella Reynolds, girl, you're crazy. I guess that's one of the things I like about you." After another moment during which he clearly had to swallow his better judgement, the smile made its way back onto his face. "The season starts next weekend, so life'll get crazy." Stella smiled. This was going to be great. She'd be dating Lucky, but there would be no pressure to get too serious, as he'd be out of the state more than he was in it until the fall. "What?" he asked, looking at her suspiciously.

"Nothing, Lucky. I'm just glad we're doing this, is all," she said, poking him in the ribs with her toes. That was all she said for the next hour.

# 28

It wasn't until the following Thursday that Stella could get time on Annie's schedule to meet. It was especially tricky, because she had switched shifts with another reporter, which meant she was working a normal dayside shift that day. The coffee date with Annie fell over her lunch break after her noon live shot, but before an early afternoon budget meeting at City Hall.

She still had John's car. They'd been playing phone tag for a week, and Stella wasn't sure when they'd reconnect and switch cars again.

She sipped her coffee while waiting at a small, round table inside the Starbucks in Knoxville's Warehouse District. She waved as Annie walked into the store. A few minutes later, with a drink in her hand, her friend sat across from her with a smile.

"I just signed up for this hot yoga class. I think you should come to the next one with me."

Stella wrinkled her nose. "Those classes with super-heated rooms for the workout?" Annie nodded. "No, thank you," she shuddered. "It actually sounds like my worst nightmare. Heat, sweat, and no fans anywhere? Not an open window anywhere nearby to catch a cool breeze?"

Annie shook her head, laughing, and the tinkling sound caused people at a table nearby to turn and smile at them. "What's up? You sounded kind of stressed out the other day."

"Work has just been kind of crazy lately. I think I need a vacation."

"I hear ya," Annie said, leaning back in her seat and resting her hands on the armrests. "I was just saying the same thing to Brian and he agreed. He booked us a trip immediately." At Stella's look, she continued. "We're gonna do another cruise! It's a nice reason to overindulge in everything," she said with a laugh.

"Nice!" Stella leaned forward, her hands warming on either side of her coffee cup. "Speaking of your husband, I just had a fun time at his old elementary school. The principal there dug out the yearbook from when Murph was in fifth grade—can you believe he was ever this small?" She pulled out the picture, now creased and wrinkled from being in her bag all week.

Annie's face brightened and a delighted grin turned up the corners of her lips. "Aww, look at my honey!" she crowed. "I'll have to tell him. He'd get a kick out of that. He's mentioned that old principal before—I think he went back to speak to some students there a couple years ago and she was sweet on him, even then."

"Do you know who those other two boys are? For some reason, they look familiar."

Annie leaned over the picture and squinted. The black and white copy wasn't the best, and the image was a little blurred. "I'd bet my double mocha latte that's Kevin Lewis," Annie said, "but I don't recognize that last boy. Hard to tell so many years later, isn't it?"

"Kevin Lewis, as in the mayor? Murphy grew up with the mayor?" No wonder the boy in the picture looked familiar.

"It's a small town, and don't you forget it," Annie said, still looking at the picture. "If I recall correctly, they practically lived next door to each other," she said, taking a sip of her coffee. "Their neighborhood was rough. Not like rough neighborhoods today, but rough just the same. There weren't many dads around, and Brian barely made it through high school to tell the story. He got a real roughneck job after graduating, and that's where he met Dave. That only lasted a couple of years before they found their true calling."

"When did they decide to become cops?"

"I think you only have to work in a manual labor job for a short time to know it's not gonna be the job for you for life. Brian had the good sense to know his body wouldn't hold up to that kind of work for long. I think Dave was harder to convince, but eventually he bought into the idea."

"Were they always such do-gooders?" Stella asked, fishing for information. She thought back to the librarian's comments about Murphy being mean and wondered if Annie knew anything about that.

"Do-gooders?" Annie asked with a laugh. "I think they were anything but when they were younger." She grew serious—contemplative—and took another sip of coffee. "In fact, when Dave talked about it, it sounded like they were both headed down the wrong path in life. They had too much time on their hands and were making too much money for eighteen-year-olds. It's easy to make the wrong choices when you're young."

Stella thought about what Cas Rockman's dad had said just the other day—that Cas had been destined to wind up in jail. Not enough supervision as a kid and too many bad influences around him enticing him into making bad choices—choices that had led him to jail. Somehow, Gibson and Murphy had been able to avoid that life.

"I wonder what made the difference for them." Stella said.

"I ask myself the same thing almost every night," Annie said. "Brian talks about it, himself, when he arrests these young guys who have their whole lives ahead of them. They make one wrong choice after another. It really eats at him."

"How long have they been cops, now?" Stella asked, trying to do the math in her head.

"Almost twenty-five years."

"This shake-up at the top of the department—could it be good for them?" She had not been assigned to cover the story that week, but she'd certainly been following it closely from both her station's reports and the newspaper stories. Annie's face shut down almost imperceptibly, and Stella spoke quickly. "Sorry, sorry—I didn't mean to pry. I wasn't asking as a reporter, or for any kind of news story." Stella laughed lightly and was happy to see Annie relax.

"Well, just between you and me, Brian's being considered for the position of chief!" Her face glowed. "He's done such a great job at homicide, and the city council has really taken note. He's made it through two rounds of interviews, already, and we're just waiting on Kevin to make a decision."

"Wow, that'd be huge!" Stella said, but her mind was reeling. It didn't feel right having the mayor put an old childhood friend into such a powerful position. If it was illegal, however, she didn't know. It wasn't exactly cronyism, but... She pushed the thought from her mind for the time being.

The women finished their drinks and hugged goodbye. Both had things to do. Stella had to finish her workday and Annie was off to the spa for a nail appointment.

Back in her car, Stella couldn't stop thinking about her conversation with Annie. It was certainly a glowing and rosy picture of Murphy and Gibson with a rough start to life, but deciding to become the good guys. Is that what they had become, though?

The department had a better arrest and prosecution record than almost any in the country, according to FBI stats, but something marred that happy story. She was convinced a man was sitting in a jail cell charged with a homicide he didn't commit, and the detectives didn't seem to have any interest in digging deeper into the case. She did—she just had to figure out where to put the shovel.

# 29

Stella's mind was so full of conspiracy theories and police chief hiring issues that she messed up both of her live shots that evening and couldn't wait to get home. When she pulled into the parking lot, however, she realized that home didn't really have the same feeling it had a few weeks ago. Home now meant potential danger, surveillance, guns drawn, and threats made.

Janet was closing at the bar and Lucky was out of town, on his way to Daytona for the first race of the season. She considered going to his house to spend the night, knowing he had a top-notch security system that would make her feel safe, but she stood outside of her car, keys in hand, feeling indecisive.

While she was still waffling, Cheryl came out into the parking lot. She walked over when she noticed Stella and looked her over from head to toe. "You look like you need a beer."

Stella tilted her head. "I think you're right."

"I've got just the event for you. My boyfriend is having a cookout. Totally low-key with lots of beer and lots of burgers."

Stella hesitated. Her one meeting with Cheryl's boyfriend had not been pleasant, and she remembered back to Ole Boy knocking Cheryl over and her boyfriend's angry response.

Cheryl seemed to be remembering the same occasion. "Tim feels terrible about his behavior when you met for the first time. He's invited you over several times, but I've never been able to extend the invite. He'd love to see you and to apologize in person."

"Should I bring the dog?" Stella deadpanned.

Cheryl threw her head back and laughed. "I think Ole Boy should stay here, and we'll be fine."

Stella laughed, too. After letting said pet out for a potty break, she climbed into the passenger's seat of Cheryl's car.

They drove in silence for a few blocks before Stella remembered she'd had a question for her neighbor for weeks. "I keep thinking about texting you, and then something comes up at work. I wanted to ask you if you knew Oliver Bennet."

Cheryl's grip tightened on the steering wheel, but her face remained neutral. "I didn't know him well," she said. Stella waited for her to say more, but she was silent.

"Did you work with him?"

"Yes and no. We were both forensic scientists for the city, but I hardly ever saw him in the lab."

She waited again, but the woman's lips were clamped shut. "Well, I'm sorry for your loss. It's difficult to know anyone who's passed away so suddenly." She remembered her own turmoil when she thought someone she knew had died years before. She had firsthand knowledge of how difficult it could be to process your feelings about such an event.

They were getting close to John's apartment, and Stella realized she didn't know where they were headed. "Where does your boyfriend live, anyway?"

"Just a few miles up the road here," Cheryl answered, turning on the radio.

They listened to a song for a few minutes. The silence was comfortable, but Stella felt bad for bringing up the murder. "How did you meet Tim, anyway?" she asked, hoping for a happier conversation.

Cheryl looked at her sideways. "You mean because he's so much older than me?"

She felt her cheeks color—this just wasn't her day. "No! No, I—I mean I'm just always interested in how people meet other people these days," she stammered. "Online, through friends, or good, old-fashioned bumped into him over apples at the grocery store?"

"Are you in the market for a boyfriend?" Cheryl asked, taking her eyes off the road to glance at Stella.

"God, no. I've got my hands full at the moment, thank you."

She smiled. "I'm just giving you a hard time. Tim is definitely older, thank God. I can't handle men our age; they all seem like babies, to me. No one wants to work—no one wants to be an adult—and that's not a problem with Tim."

"What do you mean?" Stella asked.

"Tim runs his own business, so he's all-in. He knows what it means to work hard and be rewarded for doing a good job."

"What business is he in?"

"He owns a roofing company. Actually, he owns the biggest roofing company in all of Knoxville." Cheryl added with a smile.

"Would I recognize the name?" Stella wondered. She thought about all the commercials that played on her station during newscasts. One jingle came immediately to mind. "Call Tim Tingle when you need new shingles. Tingle Roofing, the company you can trust," she sang to a laughing Cheryl. She nodded, and Stella felt her face scrunch up in confusion. "The guy in all the commercials—I would have recognized him at our apartment."

"They hired an actor—they wanted someone with a friendlier face."

Stella snorted. "How did Tim take that news? It's kind of hard to learn you're not friendly-looking." Although, truth be told, she agreed with whoever made that decision.

Cheryl bit her lip. "The marketing guy who told him that got fired. After Tim cooled off, though, he saw the wisdom in the idea—especially now that the company has taken off. I think he likes having the anonymity."

Stella certainly understood that. It was annoying to feel like you had to shower and put on makeup just to run to the grocery store for milk. Inevitably, the one time you didn't, you ran into twelve viewers who all wanted to take a picture with you.

"Whatever happened to that crime scene picture you wanted my help with? Did you figure out the clue?"

Stella shrugged. "Work has been so crazy that I haven't really had time to delve into it, yet."

They turned off the main road. "Well, here we are."

There was no guard, but an empty security shack with beautiful siding and a shaker roof sat between the divided boulevard for show. The homes had wide, green lawns, and the houses sat back, away from the road.

They wound through the neighborhood, and when they finally pulled up to Tim's house, Stella mentioned with a grin that the roof was gorgeous. "Tim has his crew redo it every few years to make sure it's perfect. He says the best advertising is to make sure his own home is in order."

They bypassed the front door and walked around the side of the house to the backyard. The space was landscaped beautifully. Beds of mulch curved around the perimeter, huge pine trees provided nice privacy between Tim's house and his neighbors, and several heating towers were set out in the backyard to take the chill out of the cool, night air.

Stella looked at Cheryl inquisitively. "You said lowkey."

She smiled. "Well, this is low-key for Tim."

They walked over to a small cluster of talking men, and Tim extracted himself from the others to face them with a rueful smile. "Stella, I'm so glad you could join us. I've felt awful about our first meeting, and I hope we can put it behind us."

Stella was taken aback by Tim's sincerity. She smiled, and nodded. "Of course, Tim. I've been working with Ole Boy on manners ever since."

He handed Stella a beer, got one for Cheryl, and then assessed Stella with a smile. "So, are we good?" he asked.

She nodded. He smiled at the women and was off to get

the burgers ready. The two took seats by one of the heaters and Stella blew out a breath, happy to have a cold beer in her hand and warm air blowing on her face.

"Are you guys affected at all by the change at the police department?" she asked.

"Not really," Cheryl answered. "We collect evidence from crime scenes no matter who's in charge over there."

Stella nodded. They sat in silence for a bit, and she realized they actually had very little in common—no mutual friends and no common interests.

Cheryl must have been feeling the same pressure to find something to chat about, because she finally said in a low voice, "You know, I heard that your friend, Detective Murphy, is up for a promotion."

"Huh, really?" Stella took a sip of her beer. She didn't want to break Annie's confidence by confirming anything, so she tried to change the subject.

"I've been thinking about a human interest piece at the crime lab. People would be so interested in what you do every day, don't you think?"

"Probably not. It's not as glamorous as they think from the TV shows."

"Oh, I'm sure it's more interesting than you think." Cheryl shrugged and Stella searched for something to say.

"What kind of oversight do you guys have at the lab?"

Cheryl looked up sharply. "What do you mean?"

"I'm just wondering about checks and balances," she said, trying to make conversation. "If you test a piece of evidence, does anyone else look over your work, or is your word final?"

The other woman shrugged again and took a sip of her beer before answering. "We follow the standard practices recommended for every forensics lab in the country, so of course, we have checks and balances. In each case, the defense is certainly allowed to do their own testing of the evidence."

"Do they ever get the first crack at the evidence, or has it always been touched by someone in your lab, first?"

She felt Cheryl staring at her, and turned to smile brightly back. She didn't know anything about how the crime lab worked, and she was simply curious.

Cheryl assessed her neighbor neutrally over her drink. She finally took a deep breath and said, "No, we always get it first, but we know how paramount it is to remain neutral in the investigation and to treat the evidence with respect. You know, Stella," she said, wiping her mouth with a small cocktail napkin, "if you're wondering if we can fake evidence, create it when it's not there, or plant it, that's much harder to do than you might think—especially with all the new technology that exists. Pictures are taken at the crime scene, so the evidence we test has to have been there from the beginning."

Stella mulled over that information, and the two women sat in silence for a few minutes, watching the party around them.

"Plus, I mean, you guys are scientists," Stella reasoned out loud. "Not a lot of emotion involved in what you're doing, right? Why would you care who's charged with a crime? You just test the evidence."

She didn't say anything for a while, and Stella was content to sit quietly, feeling like she had done her part to fill the silence, but then Cheryl spoke.

"I'll tell you what, though. It's so frustrating when defense attorneys get their clients off on technicalities." Her face took on a contemplative look. "Too many jurors watch *Law and Order*—they think there needs to be a smoking gun, a bloody fingerprint, and a glove that fits. Usually just one of those is enough to prove beyond a reasonable doubt that the suspect is guilty. Get them off the streets, and honestly, everyone's safer, even if that means you sometimes snare an innocent person. Chances are that they've probably done something wrong along the way, anyway, you know? Nobody's totally innocent, Stella."

She shifted in her chair, at a loss for words. Before she could ask Cheryl about her explosive statement, Tim walked over.

"Cher, I want you to meet a friend of mine. Stella, do you need another beer?"

Cheryl smiled up at him, and the two walked away. All of a sudden, Stella realized that there was nowhere she would rather be than home. She tried to tell herself that her neighbor must have been kidding, but she couldn't discount her serious expression. She hadn't had the slightest trace of a smile or a laugh; her face had been intense and full of conviction as she spoke of sending an innocent person to jail.

# 30

The next morning Stella lay in bed for far longer than usual. It had been weeks since Cas Rockman was first arrested and she'd made no headway in the case. Instead of narrowing down a list of guilty people, the number of people she thought might be involved was growing at an alarming rate.

If Cas Rockman was innocent in the death of Oliver Bennet, then Murphy or Gibson—or Murphy and Gibson—weren't. They couldn't put the wrong guy behind bars without help, though—help from someone at forensics. Why, though? What would a scientist gain by helping convict the wrong person? If Cheryl was involved, it didn't seem like she was getting paid for her part—she lived in the same crappy apartment complex as Stella and didn't drive a fancy car or take extravagant vacations.

Where did the drug gang come in, then? They had to have a stake in making sure Cas took the fall for the murder. It didn't make any sense. She jumped out of bed and threw on some clothes, stopping only to pour herself a quick cup of coffee in a to-go mug. It was time to ask some point-blank questions to the people on her list.

She opened the door and came face-to-face with a stranger. Her first impression was that he was clean-cut and handsome, but on second glance, she saw a kind of raw sex appeal that wasn't squeaky clean, at all. They faced each other wordlessly for a moment.

He finally spoke with an apologetic look on his face. "Sorry, you look like you're in a hurry, but man, that coffee could fix me up right. Is there any extra?"

Stella stared at him in wonder. Who was this hot, friendly stranger with a slight twang, asking for caffeine?

Before she could say anything, she heard Janet's voice. "I don't care what anyone else says, J, that video was H-O-T, hot. Oh, morning, Stella—didn't think you'd be up, yet."

They pushed past Stella into the apartment, and she stared after them wordlessly. "Where were you?" she finally got out.

"We slept in the RV. More privacy," Janet said matter-of-factly.

"And better shocks," the man added wolfishly. Stella snorted. "I'm Jason," he said, offering his hand. He smiled at her warmly as they shook hands, and she looked past him uncertainly at Janet's back.

Stella hadn't seen her roommate since she'd reconnected with her dad the week before. Different shifts and long hours meant only a few phone conversations over the last week. When her roommate turned around, Stella nearly gasped. Janet looked, well, kind of normal. Her face was clean of makeup and clear of obvious signs of hangover. She looked younger and more carefree than she had ever seen her.

She finally unstuck her tongue from the roof of her mouth. "Jason, do you need a ride anywhere? I was just heading out..." she asked, fishing for information. Janet winked at her.

"No, thanks—my car's out back. Anyway, I think we're going to get some breakfast, right?"

Janet nodded and a blush spread across her cheeks. "Yup, at that little place downtown."

Stella's eyebrows practically raised right off her forehead, and Janet smacked her when Jason ducked into the fridge to get the milk.

"Oof," Stella exclaimed, rubbing her arm. She tilted her head to check out Janet's new man. Colorful tattoos were visible at his wrist as he poured milk into two mugs—he already knew how Janet took her coffee. When had that happened?

He caught her staring and she said, "Well, enjoy the

morning. Jason, it was so very nice to meet you." She looked at Janet, her eyebrows still raised. Her roommate smiled widely back before pushing her out the door and following her into the hallway.

"Well?" She stared quizzically at Stella.

"Well what?"

"What do you think of Jason?"

"Oh. Well, I mean, I just met him, but he seems really nice." Janet nodded happily. "Kind of... different from all the others, you know?" Stella added diplomatically.

Janet guffawed. "I'll say. I met him at his job, so there's one point in his favor. He has a job!"

Stella joined her laughter. "You seem different, too—really happy. I'm so glad!"

"I've been getting to know my dad. We hashed out our differences, and I think he's an okay guy, ya know?" Stella nodded, and she continued. "I wish my mom was here to really explain things, but I think it's good. It's nice to not feel so alone, you know?"

"So, it all worked out?"

"Yeah, I think so," Janet said.

"Well, that's really great. I'm glad you have him."

Janet opened the door to the apartment, but she turned back at the last minute. "Oh, yeah, he told the FBI to give it a rest, so you shouldn't have any more problems from them."

She nodded and watched her walk back into their apartment. After the door closed, she heard a crash, laughter, and then moaning. She pivoted and jogged out of the building before she heard something she couldn't un-hear.

Stella hurried to her car; she didn't want to lose any of her resolve from first light. She was going to go straight to Annie's house to ask Detective Murphy flat-out if there was something illegal going on. There would be no more waffling or indecision for her.

She knew she'd be able to tell in his answer if he was being honest or not, and she pulled up to the gorgeous house and cut the engine. When she stepped onto the street, she nearly ran into Murphy's partner.

Gibson shot her a disgusted look and growled, "What are you doing here?"

"I came here to talk to Murphy. What are you doing here?" Stella bristled. She was tired of Gibson's crappy attitude.

"About what?" He stepped back to take in Stella's agitated state.

"None of your business." She went to push past him, but he grabbed her shoulders, stopping her in her tracks.

"I say what my business is. Start talking."

"Fine," Stella snapped. "I'd like to ask you the same questions, actually. I want to know why an innocent man is behind bars when it seems like the Bennet homicide is related to the Luanne Rockman homicide and it's clear that Cas had nothing to do with his own mother's death. I want to know what's going on with Cas Rockman!"

She stepped back and crossed her arms, looking at Gibson accusingly. Chances were that he was just as involved in this cover-up as Murphy was. She wanted to read his expression as he processed her words. If she expected him to look contrite, surprised, or even angry, though, she was disappointed.

"Jesus Christ, Stella," he said, pinching the bridge of his nose. He finally opened his eyes and glared at her before quickly glancing back at the house. "If you go marching up there, asking about that, you might blow a two-year undercover investigation that's already resulted in one informant's death. So, keep your mouth shut, for once."

Her mouth dropped open in surprise and it took her a few seconds to process his final words. When she did, she clamped her mouth shut and glared at him. "What are you saying?" she snapped. "You're investigating your partner?"

Gibson grabbed her by the shoulders again and propelled her toward his Jeep, which she only now noticed was parked at the end of Murphy's long driveway. He pushed her into the passenger's seat, walked around the car, and got behind the wheel. She thought he was going to explain things in the privacy of his car, but instead, he started up the engine and pulled away from the curb.

"Where are we going?" Stella asked, looking at Gibson's hands. They were gripping the wheel so hard that his knuckles had turned white.

"I can't answer those questions in front of the prime suspect's house." He made a turn too fast, and she slammed against the car door. She steadied herself and shot another glare at Gibson. He didn't take his eyes off the road, but he continued smiling blandly, and Stella felt her anger boil over.

"Now that we're in your car, you'd better start talking. I've got a lot of information, and to be honest, I don't mind ruining your two-year investigation. Now that I know that police are involved, it sounds like a pretty great news story right now," Stella snarled, breathing hard.

Gibson slowed the car, finally pulling into the parking lot of a small strip mall. "Do you like ice cream?"

The question seemed so out of place that she snapped out of her anger. "What?"

He was already out of the car, though. She crossed her arms, determined to sit there until he was ready to talk. Instead, her door opened, and Gibson held out a hand.

"The eating area outside the ice cream parlor is a good place to talk," he said, speaking to her without glaring for the first time maybe ever.

She looked up and saw that he was assessing her, too. She nodded, climbed into the sunlight, and followed him into the ice cream shop at just after ten in the morning.

Five minutes later, she was sitting at a wrought-iron table with a cup of cookies-n-cream ice cream in front of her, waiting for Dave to start talking. He wolfed down a few bites of his caramel chocolate swirl, and Stella got the impression that he was deciding what to say—or how much to share with her. Finally, he spoke.

"I'll be honest with you. We're stuck, trying to figure out the link at forensics. We need to know who's involved with Murphy before we can move in. We think it's your buddy, Cheryl, and up until this morning, when you came marching up to Murphy's house, we thought you might have been involved, too."

# 31

"What?" Stella said, practically spitting out her ice cream. She felt outraged, but she tried to stay calm. Maybe this was all part of his plan to keep her off-balance.

"Listen, you're connected to Murphy. You're always getting tips from him, and you're friendly with his wife. I've seen you chatting it up with Cheryl a few times, too, including a late-night rendezvous at the crime lab."

She flicked her hand, brushing away his comments. After all, his being at the lab that night was just as suspicious to her.

"You showed up at that undercover drug buy, and my guys were convinced you were the buyer." Gibson took another two bites of ice cream. "It made sense to me, but the cop you spoke with that night, Brad Stott, said you were either an amazing actor or not involved. I was on the fence until just a few minutes ago, when the look on your face told me you weren't part of it."

"I lived there! That drug buy happened right outside my apartment!" Stella stared at him, trying to sort out what was going on. Finally, she gave up. "So, you're going to have to explain things from the beginning. I've figured out a few things, but it sounds like there's more to this than even I imagined."

He shook his head. "No dice. You tell me what you know and I'll tell you if you're right or wrong." At her look, he continued. "I'm not going to blow up the last two years of my life for a news story. I'm going to see this thing through until someone's in jail—or multiple someones, if that's how it goes down."

Stella didn't trust him, but the fact that he didn't seem to trust her was a major point in his favor. She chewed her lip and finally realized that, if she wanted to learn anything, she'd have to open up—at least a little.

"Here's what I know. I've been threatened twice—at gunpoint—by men warning me to stay away from the Bennet investigation. So, there's something shady going on there. I have reason to believe that the same person shot both Bennet and Luanne Rockman and that Cas Rockman certainly didn't shoot and kill his own mother. That makes me think he's innocent in the Bennet homicide, as well, despite what he's telling you, me, and the judge." She paused and waited for Gibson's reaction. He swallowed his ice cream and nodded once, and Stella continued. "I know that Rockman is innocent—"

"Innocent of these murders," Gibson interjected, "but don't forget Nashville."

"Okay, innocent in this case, and I know that Murphy—and you—haven't done anything to clear him. So, then I wonder how this is happening—who else is involved and who benefits from Cas going to jail."

Gibson stared thoughtfully at the parking lot and the street beyond. "You've gotta think bigger," he finally said.

"Bigger?"

"Yes. Who benefits from any criminal going to jail?"

"Well, the whole city," Stella answered, not understanding his point.

"Think more specifically," he said with an infuriating, know-it-all tone.

"You're telling me to think bigger, but more specifically?" She sat back, irritated and looked around for a drinking fountain. When she spotted one inside the shop, she excused herself, filled up a tiny cone-shaped cup, and walked back outside. Gibson had finished his scoop by then, and the table in front of him was clear.

"The mayor," she said triumphantly. "He's been getting elected off these great crime stats the FBI compiles every year."

"Mmhm. Who else?"

Stella sat down with a thump. "What? You're saying the mayor's involved?"

"No, I'm asking who else has benefitted from Cas' arrest—from any criminal's arrest?"

"Um, okay. Prosecutors? It's another feather in the prosecutor's cap to put away a supposed bad guy."

"Keep going."

She laid the empty cone cup on the table and leaned forward, resting her elbows on the table. After dropping her head and pressed her fingertips to her forehead, she said, "I don't know, other criminals? There's one less person for them to compete with?" She threw it out on a lark, thinking Gibson would laugh. He didn't, though, and she looked up to find him staring at her pointedly. "What?"

"That's what you need to focus on. The criminals. They're one of the many parties benefitting from Cas' arrest and others who've been arrested over the years."

"Come on. The mayor's working with criminals? Why?"

"Not the mayor—he just benefits. Murphy. Dig into Murphy's past. He wasn't always focused on doing good, okay?"

Gibson took her back to her car without another word, except to say that he'd already said too much.

"How much time do I have?" she asked.

They were back in Murphy's driveway, and he ran a hand over his head as he stared over the roofline. He finally blew out a breath, as if he'd come to some kind of internal decision. With a penetrating stare, he looked at Stella.

"We're at a stalemate. Oliver Bennet was working undercover for us—he knew something was going on at the crime lab. Arrest rates had skyrocketed over the years and it wasn't due to any evidence they were testing. It was all coming down to eyewitness testimony, the most unreliable form of evidence a prosecutor can use. All of a sudden, crimes with little to no physical evidence were being solved at unprecedented levels, witnesses were coming forward in droves, and people were getting arrested, charged, and prosecuted at record levels. If no witness came forward, shaky evidence was presented to clinch the case."

"At trial?"

"No trial. They almost always take a plea bargain before it goes to trial."

"Innocent people?" Stella asked, outraged.

"Well, that's just it. Innocent? No. Innocent of the particular crime they were charged with? Maybe."

"Well, now I'm right back to square one. Who benefits from that?" Stella felt more confused than when she'd woken up that morning. Gibson just stared at her. "Other criminals?" Stella said uncertainly.

"Exactly."

"Murphy told me that Bennet was unemployed at the time of his death," Stella said, looking at Gibson for his reaction. He sighed and rubbed a hand across his face.

"He was. He lost his job—budget cuts city-wide—and got so angry that he refused to tell us what was going on in the lab. He'd spent nearly a year cataloging who worked on what cases for us and said he had a big report he was ready to share. He lost his job and, frankly, lost his desire to do good."

"He turned rogue?"

Gibson shook his head. "Not rogue—just angry. He wasn't reliable, and he wanted money for his information. We were willing to pay, but it was taking too long for him. We got the call that he'd been shot, and that was that."

Stella grimaced. That was certainly not that. "You think Cheryl is working with Murphy to... what? Plant evidence?"

He stared out the windshield. "Someone in that lab isn't doing their job. Bennet knew who it was, but he didn't tell us—or didn't tell me." He looked up at Murphy's house.

"Why would it be Cheryl? Why not one of the other forensic scientists?"

"It was something Murphy said about how she knows

how to get the job done."

Stella grimaced again, thinking about her comments from the night before. It didn't look good. They sat next to each other silently for a few long moments before she reached for the door.

"Stay in touch, Stella—and be careful."

"Thanks a lot," she snarked, stepping onto the driveway. She started to head up to the house, but Gibson called out. "They're out of town on a cruise. I'm house-sitting."

"Why the heck did we just leave, then? Why didn't we just talk here?"

"I needed some ice cream," he said with a grin. He walked past her and headed into the house. She stood in the driveway and watched him close the door.

Stella sat in her car, head swimming from Gibson's information dump. Finally, she took out her notebook and made some notes. She wrote *Criminals benefit from other criminals going to jail. Gang gets more powerful?*

According to his father, Cas had gotten behind on payments, and his gang would only call it even if he killed Bennet. But how did the gang know Bennet was the informant? She looked up at Murphy's house. Was he in cahoots with a drug gang? Was Gibson working with Murphy? Could she trust that he was investigating the man he was housesitting for? Was Gibson was telling her the truth, or was he just trying to cover his own tracks?

She drove away with only one certainty—trust no one. She needed to find another path up this mountain.

# 32

On the drive back to her apartment, Stella realized that she needed to start from the beginning of both of the recent murders. Who had called in tips about the crimes? When had the calls come in? Which dispatcher answered the calls? Which officers had been first on-scene? These were all things she could find by making public requests for information, and she had been sloppy in her journalism up to this point. That was going to change.

Next, she wanted more time inside the crime lab. She needed to understand how it worked, so she could understand who might be working the system. That's where being a TV journalist gave her an edge.

It might not have been easy to convince Cheryl to give her an interview, but somebody higher up in the city would love the idea of a feel-good piece about the lab—especially if budget cuts had created unhappy employees. After all, everybody loved free press.

It was almost noon by the time Stella got back home, and the apartment was empty with no signs that Janet and Jason had ever been there. The coffee pot was washed and the coffee mugs had been rinsed and placed in the dishwasher. Stella stared in shock at the clean kitchen. Something had changed with Janet, and she couldn't wait to find out what it was.

She made a few calls on her cell phone, so the information she needed would be ready when she started her workday, and then she started the process of getting ready for work.

With the hairdryer on high, she couldn't hear her phone when it rang, but she saw the screen light up on the countertop. She pounced.

"Kevin, thanks so much for getting back to me. I know Fridays can be hectic."

The mayor couldn't have been kinder. He loved talking to the media. "No problem, Stella. What do you need?"

She bit her lip, hoping to phrase everything so as not to raise any alarms. "I had someone stop me this morning at the ice cream parlor," she said, spinning a tale she hoped would work. "They just happened to have seen a forensic scientist at a scene recently and were so impressed with the professionalism. I think they've been expecting the TV show version and were surprised that, in real life, the investigators don't wear stilettos and tank tops," Stella laughed.

"It really got me thinking that I'd love to do a story on how the crime lab actually works. The reality doesn't match up with the TV show, does it? There isn't a team of five scientists working together on one case, right?" She closed her eyes, hating how asinine she sounded. Her comments, however, were well-received.

"That's exactly right. That department does more in a day than most people do in a week, and they do it with a smaller budget every year."

Stella jumped. "That's what I mean, Kevin! They do a great job, and the people of Knoxville should know about it. Those scientists are exactly who you want waiting in the wings when something goes wrong. They're so professional and so good at their jobs."

"It's unusual to have outsiders in the lab, but I think we can make it work. Let me talk to Jack Neahy, the head of the crime lab. Of course, you might want my two cents on how important they are to the city?"

"Yes, that's a great idea," Stella said, grinning.

"All right. I'll get back to you later today. Thanks for the call."

She set down her cell phone and did a silly dance in front of the mirror. It worked! She needn't have worried about the mayor suspecting something was up. This was the mayor, after all—he didn't have enough between the ears to worry about anything other than his own press. This would be good.

Instead of driving straight to work, she drove downtown and parked outside the 911 call center. She went through the security checks to get into the building and then waited for the shift supervisor to come out.

"Stella Reynolds?" came a bored voice across the desk.

"Yes. Thanks for your time today," she simpered, standing.

The man facing her was stocky and bald with glasses perched, forgotten, on his forehead. "I've got the 911 transcripts for you."

Stella took the papers from his outstretched hand and leaned against the desk. "Carl?" she said, reading his name tag. "Do you remember if there was anything unusual about either of those two calls?"

He shrugged and took the papers back, patting his front pocket absent-mindedly. "What calls are they? I just grabbed them off the printer." He finally located his glasses on top of his head and counted through the pages in his hands, adding. "It'll be a dollar twenty-five for the copies, by the way."

She set her voluminous bag on the counter and started searching through it for her wallet. "It's the two recent homicides—the Bennet shooting and the Rockman arson-murder."

"Hmm," he said, scanning through the call logs. "I wasn't working either day. Sorry," he added with an apologetic smile. Stella's fingers finally closed around her wallet, and she handed Carl two dollar bills. "No change, sorry," he said.

"That's fine. Listen, is there any chance I can talk to some of the dispatchers who took the calls?"

He shuffled through the papers again and scratched his head. "It looks like Bernie took calls on both." Carl was walking backward to the door, keen to move on with his day.

"Bernie, you said? Does he have a direct line?"

"She, and no." He had one foot through the door and was still moving away.

"Is she in today?" she asked a little louder to make sure she had his attention.

Stella stared at him long enough that he finally sighed and walked back to the desktop. He picked up a phone, punched in some numbers, and then waited, sighing loudly every few seconds.

"Bernie? There's some news lady here to see you. If you don't have time, that's—" While he listened to Bernie's response, Stella resisted the urge to grab the phone from him. "Okay," he said, shrugging to himself. He looked up at Stella. "I guess she'll be right out." Before she could thank him, he turned and walked through a door into the call center.

Soon, a short, older woman walked into the lobby. Her gray hair looked like it had been cut at a barber shop, and she had a calm air about her that fit with her job description.

"Yes?" she asked, looking inquisitively at her.

Stella introduced herself before asking about the calls. "I guess I was just wondering if anything stuck out to you as unusual."

Bernie wore the dispatcher uniform—a light blue Polo shirt with the city's logo stitched into the fabric by her heart. She leaned onto the counter and chewed a wad of gum with unusual ferocity.

"Well, aside from the fact that they even happened..." She took the call logs from Stella's outstretched hand. "Thanks." As she scanned the pages, she started nodding. "Oh, yeah, that's right. I'd forgotten about that." At her look, she elaborated. "This guy who called in the shooting was very no-nonsense—all business. A lot of times, people want to wait on the phone with me until emergency responders arrive. Not this guy, though. He hung up before I'd even entered the address into the system." She flipped through the papers until she got to the calls about the fire. "Same kind of thing—at least with this first call about the fire—but not as unusual." She looked up at Stella. "Most calls about a house fire are short and sweet. Unless, of course, you're trapped inside," she added offhandedly.

Stella's eyes widened. "How many calls came in about the fire?"

Bernie shuffled through the papers again. "Looks like ten, eleven? I took the first one. It came in, oh, I don't know, fifteen minutes before the other calls." She spread out the papers and confirmed the times. "Yup, it looks like it was fourteen minutes to be exact."

"The caller didn't give a name?"

"No, but that's not too uncommon, either. A vacant house goes up in flames—no one wants to be identified in that kind of neighborhood."

Stella thanked Bernie for her time and left with the papers. She sat in her car in the parking lot and read through each report, but they seemed like dead ends.

While she was driving back to the station for her last work day of the week, her cell phone rang. It was the mayor.

"Stella, I've got some great news. The head of the crime lab says the story's a go. It took a little pressure from me—some greasing of the wheels—but he finally agreed to it. You'll be interviewing Cheryl Calmet. She's been with the department for years and is a really great forensic scientist. That only problem is that he says it has to be tomorrow at noon. Is shooting the story on a Saturday okay for you?"

"Absolutely. We'll be there."

"They're starting a tricky case on Monday and need the lab clear of contaminants. You can thank me tomorrow," the mayor added, and she could practically see his delighted smile through the phone.

After they hung up, she immediately placed another call. "Del, I'm gonna need a photographer."

# 33

Back at the office, Stella sat at her desk in relative silence. The newsroom was deserted, and the few coworkers she did see were busy pounding out scripts. She, alone, had no part in the day's early evening newscast, and Del glared at her across the newsroom from the raised platform of the assignment desk. Stella dropped her head into her hands. She was supposed to be logging her interview from earlier that afternoon. Her human interest piece on a fundraiser for military families would run the following week, but she couldn't focus.

She was trying to make sense of the Bennet homicide—who might be guilty, who could be trusted, and when she might see another gun pointed her way.

She checked her email, hoping for a tip from her anonymous source, but the inbox was empty. Resting her head on her hands on the desktop, she tried to clear her mind.

She muttered a list of names. "Dave Gibson, Brian Murphy, Kevin Lewis, Cheryl Calmet." She took a deep breath and continued, "Harrison Keys, Cas Rockman, Rufus Mills, and random gang members in an Escalade."

There were too many players and not enough space in Stella's head to sort them out. Just as she started going through the names again, she heard her name from the overhead speaker in the newsroom. "Stella Reynolds, you have a visitor in the lobby."

It was just the distraction she needed to keep from driving herself crazy, so she got up from her desk and walked through the newsroom to the lobby. The receptionist sat behind a glass wall. Penny had been at the station for decades, and she looked at Stella over her glasses with disapproval.

"He says you know him, but he doesn't have an appointment. He was quite insistent that I page you."

Stella peeked around the corner. To her surprise, she saw Harrison Keys sitting in the lobby. "It's okay, Penny."

"You know, visitors are supposed to call ahead. They're not supposed to just show up unannounced. It's in chapter forty-two of the station handbook."

She looked from Penny to Harrison and back again. "Well, I didn't know he was coming, and he probably doesn't have a station handbook," she said with a half-smile.

The receptionist chewed on her lip and nodded. She opened the door and motioned for Harrison to follow her. When they'd gotten about halfway down the hallway toward the conference room, she said, "What's going on? Is everything okay?"

Harrison shook his head, but remained quiet as he followed Stella down the hall. He didn't speak until she had closed the conference room door behind them and they were both sitting at the table.

"I don't think Cas is gonna make it. Things are getting bad at the jail." Harrison sat at the edge of his seat, his foot tapping out a furious beat. Change in his pocket jingled, and Stella felt herself getting jittery from all the nervous energy he was trying to contain.

"Has he been threatened?"

Harrison leaped out of his chair. "Of course he's been threatened, and it's getting worse." He paced in front her. The room was small and she could tell that the pacing was unsatisfying. Harrison made a step in one direction, a quick pivot, and two shorter steps to go back.

He finally huffed out a breath and sat back down, keeping his foot tapping. "I couldn't do anything to protect him when he was growing up, because I was in jail. Now he needs protection in jail and I can't do anything from the outside. It's not right. Something's got to change."

She thought the answer was obvious. "Let's call the jail.

It's their job to make sure the inmates behave themselves and everyone stays safe. I'm sure they can make sure he's safe."

Harrison barked out a laugh and looked at her with derision. "Do you believe that crap? There's no one who can enforce rules in jail—especially not the people who are paid to do it. There are too many ways to get around the rules—too many ways to hurt someone, if you want to." He ran both hands over his head before standing up again. "I just came to tell you that, if you have any idea what's going on or any clue as to who really killed those people, you have to act on it now. Cas isn't going to last much longer, and I'm not gonna let anything happen to him."

He grabbed the doorknob and yanked it open with such force that it rebounded off the wall and slammed shut again after he walked out. Stella stared in shock and took in the faces of the producers she could see through a large window between the rooms. With stunned expressions, they watched as Harrison strode past them toward the lobby.

Stella pulled the door open and rushed after him. "Harrison," she called. "Harrison, wait!"

His stride didn't falter, but he stopped just before he got to the door to the lobby.

"Don't do anything rash! I'm close—I think I might be able to get to the bottom of things soon."

He snorted. "Soon isn't good enough. Soon is just a word. It means nothing to someone in Cas' situation." He stormed outside. This time, Stella caught the door before it slammed, and she let it close softly. She pressed her forehead against the cool glass as she watched Harrison disappear through the parking lot.

*Soon.* The word kept showing up in her life, and she was beginning to hate it.

# 34

Leverage—she needed it and she didn't have it. Stella realized she was going to have to expand her usual investigative sources, because the inside was too tangled. She was too uncertain about who was good and who was bad.

She slumped back in her seat and stared at the ceiling, thinking. Finally, inspiration struck, and she picked up the phone and called the only person she could think of who might be able to help.

He answered on the second ring and didn't seem at all surprised to hear from her. "I'd love to do what I can. Meet me for dinner tonight and we can talk it over." After they set up the details, Stella hung up.

She tapped a new set of numbers into her phone, and someone picked up after six rings. "It's Stella. I need cell phone records for two phone numbers."

The voice on the other end of the line laughed incredulously. "Stella who?"

She smiled grimly. "Listen, Agent Jones, I'd be happy to talk to your supervisor about your behavior over these last several weeks... otherwise, we can take care of this right now by you doing me this one small favor." Her demand was met by a heavy sigh, and she pumped her fist into the air victoriously. She gave Jones the phone numbers she wanted him to subpoena. "I need this information as soon as you can get it."

"No problem, Stella. It usually takes about three weeks—maybe four."

"Jones, I need this sooner. Close of business today, or I'll make some calls."

She held her breath, hoping she hadn't gone too far,

when she finally heard Jones blow out another irritated sigh. "I'll see what I can do."

"Email them to me as soon as you get them."

"Done."

She gave him her information and they disconnected. She blew out a breath and sat back in her chair, feeling like she was finally getting there. Halfway up the mountain, at least.

An hour later, she was sitting across the table from Sampson Foster. "I like this restaurant," he said, looking around with appreciation. "Food's good and it's crowded, but not loud. That's hard to find." He nodded sharply to himself and started to butter a roll from the basket.

Stella unfolded her napkin. "How much longer will you be in town?" she asked, wondering if his next stop was North Dakota or Washington, D.C.

"I'll be here for a few more days. I'm in no rush to leave, now that my daughter has finally agreed to not only talk to me, but also to get to know me. It's something I've been waiting for these last fifteen years." She was struck by Sampson's emotional tone and raw honesty. The waiter came over, and he ordered a seven and seven. "What's going on, Stella? If it's a question about some sort of criminal case, it seems like the police should be investigating."

"Exactly," she said, blowing out a frustrated sigh. She spent the next twenty minutes explaining everything about Cas' initial arrest in the Bennet shooting, the gang threatening her, and the thought that someone from police and forensics might be working in some capacity and for some reason with that very same drug gang. When she finally finished, she sat back in her seat, took a few gulps of ice water, and looked at Sampson expectantly.

He sat in silence for several minutes, chewing over the information in his head. He finally asked a single question. "Where's the money?"

Stella felt her eyebrows scrunch together. "Huh?"

"In a case like this, you've got to follow the money.

Who's got more of it than they should? Who doesn't have enough? Who used to have some and now doesn't have any? That's where I'd start."

"Well," she said leaning forward, "obviously, the drug gang has money. They're getting to sell more drugs than they would otherwise."

"Who else?" Sampson asked calmly.

Stella looked up at the ceiling, searching for the answer. "Hmm," she said, stretching her mind. "I'm sure the people involved at police and forensics aren't doing this for fun. I guess they're getting a cut."

"Yes, that's where I would start digging." Sampson drained his drink and motioned to the waiter for a refill.

Stella took a slow sip of water and felt her stomach drop. She'd just had a thought that really didn't prove anything, but that also didn't look good. Stella's friend, Annie, lived in a gorgeous house with top-of-the-line finishes and beautiful cars in the driveway, and right now she was on a cruise. It didn't exactly sound like it could be funded by the salary of the average cop. She had been hoping her research would show that Murphy was innocent, but this thought seemed only to confirm that he must have been in on something bad.

"Don't like what you're finding?" Sampson asked with a look of pity on his face. "Sometimes, when you start digging, you wish you'd never disturbed the ground, at all."

She nodded, lost in thought. She was missing something. If Gibson was telling the truth—if criminals were benefitting from whatever was going on—she needed more information.

She thought back to the officer she'd met at the undercover drug buy outside her apartment. He'd said he was on a drug task force, so he should have a lot of background information and maybe even some history on what gang came to power when. She dug into her purse and found his card.

"Excuse me, Sampson, but I think I've got to go," she said, gathering her bags and standing so suddenly that her napkin fell to the ground.

"Go get 'em, Stella. Let me know if I can do anything else," he said, draining his second cocktail.

"Thanks," she said, heading for the door. She pressed her phone against her ear and listened to it ring. "This is Stella Reynolds from CBS4. I'm not sure if you remember me, but we met outside my apartment a few weeks ago."

"Sure. Red hair, hit the ground like a tank—I remember."

Stella pursed her lips, not liking the description. "Do you have time to talk?"

"Finally," he said, sounding relieved. "I thought you'd never call."

# 35

Stella stirred her water with a tiny black straw and watched the ice cubes jostle around inside the glass. She was across the table from Brad Stott in a booth at a seedy bar in East Knoxville. Because it was early, they were the only ones there, but a full staff of bartenders stood behind the bar, ready for the Friday night crowd to show up.

"You said you'd been waiting for me to call. Why?" Stella asked, looking up at Stott through her eyelashes to check his reaction.

"I talked to Gibson this morning. We figured you'd have some questions."

The news surprised her, but it seemed to confirm that Gibson had been telling the truth earlier. She glanced at her watch and grimaced. Her dinner break was stretching longer than usual and she needed to get back to work soon to get ready for her eleven o'clock live shot. She looked back up at Stott.

"I'm trying to piece together what's going on."

Stott nodded and took a sip of his Coke. "How's it going?"

"What I need from you is a little history on drug trafficking in the City of Knoxville. I've been here for almost two years and I've never heard anyone complain about drug problems beyond what you'd normally expect for a city this size."

Stott nodded again and set his glass down. "What you have to understand is that drugs used to be a bigger problem here. About ten years ago, when Kevin Lewis became mayor for the second time, he started a drug task force to really target the problem in Knoxville."

"Did it work?" she asked.

"Almost immediately, drug crimes were slashed in half. It was unprecedented—people had never seen anything like it. The mayor was actually flying to other cities all over the country to talk about the process and how it worked. It was revolutionary."

Stella sat back, surprised. "How did it work?"

Stott sighed. "How did it really work, or how did the mayor say it worked? They're two different things."

"Let's start with how the mayor said it worked," Stella said, shrugging.

"All right. According to the mayor, we specifically targeted areas where crime rates were high—certain neighborhoods and specific street corners. We had cops walking the beat, getting out of their cars, and interacting with the people who lived in the worst neighborhoods. To hear Lewis talk, the relationship between officers and residents improved dramatically. People started calling in crimes and stepping forward with information, because they wanted to get police involved to improve the neighborhoods."

"But?"

"That's not what was actually happening." Stott paused to take a sip of soda. "Instead, the original head of the drug task force picked one group of drug dealers to back—the Cobras. By working directly with the gang's top honchos, they were able to destroy rival drug dealers. Members of the Cobras were coming forward, accusing other dealers of crimes. They had corroborating witnesses—probably girlfriends and mothers—and two things happened. First, there were hundreds of people in jail within months, and second, gang violence dropped to almost zero. There weren't any rival gangs, anymore. There was no violence between groups, because there weren't other groups."

Stella sat back, stunned. "How could that happen? Didn't anyone notice what this guy was doing?"

"Who would have noticed?"

"Other members in the drug task force, of course!"

"There weren't any other members. The drug task force was one person. Brian Murphy."

Stella sucked in a breath. "What about the beat officers who patrolled the neighborhoods on foot?" she asked, remembering the first part of Stott's history lesson.

"Sure, they were there, but they weren't on the task force. They were just regular patrol officers—newbies. They didn't know anyone or any better, and they did what they were told. They probably didn't even know what Murphy told the mayor about their amazing success."

"How do you know?" she asked suspiciously.

"I was one of those beat officers," Stott said, looking uncomfortable. "I spent five years walking the streets and never saw any improvement in how residents reacted to me. They'd close up shop and head inside when I walked by, like I was the enemy. I saw it with the other officers, too." He shook his head. "You join the force to do good, but all you end up doing is reacting to crimes after the fact and not stopping them."

"When did you realize something was off?"

"Murphy got promoted to head homicide a few years ago, and I was assigned to head up the drug task force. That's when I realized there really wasn't one. Guess what, though? Things didn't change. Drug arrests and prosecutions rates were still high, and the residents were still supposedly working well with the force. When Murphy wasn't heading the program, though, I was able to see that it didn't make sense. There were no happy police-resident partnerships."

"What if the system he put in place was just continuing to work?" Stella asked, looking for holes in his theory.

"What system? All I could see was that some people I'd arrested a dozen times during my first five years on the force suddenly had their records cleared, like they'd never been arrested. They were out of jail, all of them. Some twenty different career drug dealers all saw the light? I doubt it.

"So, I started looking into it. Turned out that every single person who had supposedly stopped dealing drugs was a Cobra. Even the leader of the Cobras—a really bad apple—was in the clear with his arrest record wiped clean."

"Let me take a wild guess about who the leader of this gang is," Stella said, turning to face Stott. "Rufus Mills?"

It was his turn to look surprised. "How did you know that?"

"We've met," she pushed her glass forward and asked the bartender for a refill before turning back to Stott. "Let me get this straight. You've got Detective Murphy deciding to take a drug gang under his wing to help clear rival gang members off the streets, so his favorite gang can have the run of business in town—and what, the mayor turns a blind eye to what's going on?" She looked at him for confirmation.

"That's right."

"How did Murphy pick one gang? Was there some connection?"

"I'll say. He used to work with Rufus Mills years ago."

She gave Stott a funny look. "Are you saying Rufus Mills used to be a cop?"

"No, I'm saying Murphy and Mills worked at the same roofing company when they were teenagers. They might have known each other before then—I don't know."

Facts came crashing into Stella like waves on the beach. She pushed her glass aside as she processed information. "Wait just a minute," she said, feeling a fresh wave of anger overcome her. "A roofing company? Did they work for Tim Tingle?"

Stott looked at her with new respect. "And to think Gibson said you didn't know shit."

# 36

"How is Gibson not a part of this?" Stella asked Stott through narrowed eyes. "He and Murphy have been friends for years. They worked together before they became cops—apparently for the roofing company with Rufus Mills. How do you know he's not involved?"

Stott just looked at her, but he might as well have shrugged. "He helped bring it to my attention, Stella. Without Gibson, I wouldn't know much about what's going on."

Her mouth twisted in disbelief. She'd uncovered connections between too many people, and it seemed unlikely at best that Gibson was innocent. "Where did all the rival gang members go?" Stella asked, staring hard at him. "Even if they're off to jail on drug charges, surely they'll be out again in a couple months. Wouldn't they try to reclaim their turf?"

"You'd be surprised. A lot of this went down during the three strikes laws. If they got busted for selling dope on the corner and it was their third offense, they got locked up for ten or fifteen years. It's a pretty quick way to get rid of a gang, I'll tell you that." Serving fifteen years when you were guilty was one thing, but fifteen when you were innocent? Whoever orchestrated that was pure evil. "Tingle might be orchestrating the whole thing—lots of Cobras work for him. It's a great tax shelter for their drug money, and he pays them a real wage with W2s and the whole nine. He's known for taking care of his employees. He takes care of them and gets a cut of their drug money for his trouble."

"You suspect his girlfriend is involved?"

"It makes sense that she'd be the inside help in the lab.

When eyewitness testimony isn't enough to convince a perp to plea bargain with prosecutors, they trot out some supposed evidence from the crime lab. It works every time. The perp pleads out and goes to jail. Prosecution rates skyrocket without a single case going to trial. The mayor wins, the prosecutor wins, Murphy wins, and the Cobras win."

"Will you go on camera about any of this?" He looked at her with distaste. "Is that a no?"

"That's a hell no."

She walked out to John's car, thinking about how she was sitting on a huge story, but didn't have a single piece of hard evidence tying anyone to any crime. All she had was innuendo and gossip—and a man behind bars for a crime he didn't commit. What she needed was something to link Murphy or Tingle to the drug conspiracy.

She hit the steering wheel in frustration; there had to be an easier way. Taking out her cell phone, intending to call Janet for advice, she stopped short at an email that had come in just minutes ago. It was from her FBI contact and the subject line read *We are even.*

She tapped on the email quickly, eager for the information inside. Jones had sent over call logs for two cell phone numbers. As her eyes crossed at the columns of numbers in front of her, she realized she'd need to print the pages out to analyze them properly. She needed to get back to the office, anyway—it was getting close to news time.

Twenty minutes later, she was sitting at her desk with five pages of single-spaced type in one hand and a highlighter in the other. Detectives Murphy and Gibson made a lot of calls.

The information from the FBI was divided into five columns: the date, the time the call was made, the length of the call, the other phone number involved, and finally, a name associated with that phone number, if there was one.

Jones had sent along a brief message, saying that pre-paid cell phone numbers generally didn't have a name, but cell phone accounts with major carriers did.

The majority of calls to and from both of their cell phones were unlisted, so to speak, which meant that the bulk of their calls involved other cops. The name listed in the identifier column was "City of Knoxville," which wasn't very helpful.

She saw that Murphy and Gibson predictably spoke to each other quite a bit, with their numbers showing up in each other's call logs with the frequency you'd expect of partners.

Another phone number that popped up a lot on Gibson's record belonged to someone named Ophelia Gibson. His mother, maybe, or sister?

She scanned the date column, looking for the days surrounding the Bennet and Rockman shootings, and what she found made her heart stop. She wanted to be absolutely sure though, so she dug the 911 transcripts out of her bag to compare times.

The anonymous call about the Bennet shooting had come in at 10:47 the night before Cas was arrested. She turned her attention to the information from the FBI and saw that Gibson's phone record was clear that night. He only made one call to Ophelia around dinnertime. Murphy, however, had made several calls around that time. First, he'd had an incoming call from an unlisted name at ten o'clock. Fifteen minutes later, there'd been another call from the same number. At 10:47, Murphy had placed a call to 911.

She'd have to listen to the 911 call to be certain, but the length of his call and the length of the anonymous caller's conversation with the 911 dispatcher were exactly the same. If Murphy had called in the shooting, why hadn't he done it in an official capacity? Why had he remained anonymous? It was suspicious, for sure.

She moved down the spreadsheet. The Rockman shooting was more of a challenge. The coroner had told Stella that Luanne Rockman had died around the same time

Bennet was shot. About thirty minutes after Murphy had called 911, the same unlisted number called him. There was one more call between the numbers in the following week.

Stella checked her calendar and saw that the last call between Murphy and the unknown number had come in the same day of the arson—actually, it come in about an hour before she'd gotten pulled from the city council meeting to cover the fire.

Who was this person calling Murphy with alarming precision near the city's two most recent shootings? There was one way to find out. She needed to call the number, herself.

The thought made her nervous, and she glanced hastily around the newsroom. Maybe Stott could find out for her, or maybe the FBI could tell her who owned the phone number. Surely the cell phone company could tell police who the number belonged to? All of that would take time, though, and time was something Cas Rockman was running out of.

She glanced around the newsroom again before picking up her desk phone and punching in the numbers. She wasn't worried that the owner of the phone number would find out it was her calling, because newsroom calls showed up as unlisted, but she still felt oddly nervous.

One ring. Two rings. Stella's heart beat faster. On the third ring, someone answered.

"Tingle. Who's this?"

Stella looked at the receiver in her hand like it was a weapon. She slowly moved it back to the console on the desk and hung it up softly. Had she just spoken to a killer?

Before she could delve too deeply into Cheryl's boyfriend's role in the recent violence in the city, the phone at her desk rang. She jumped like a gunshot had just gone off. Did Tingle somehow figure out who'd been calling? She had to answer—the call would go to voicemail if she didn't.

She picked up the receiver with a slight tremor in her hand. "Hello?" Her voice came out barely above a whisper.

"Stella Reynolds? I can't believe I caught you," a man said, his voice brimming with relief. "I told him there's no way I'd be able to get in touch with you until Monday morning, but it's just amazing that you picked up the phone—and at ten o'clock on a Friday night, no less," the man babbled. He seemed to suddenly remember that she didn't know who was on the line. "This is Kenan Jackson, one of Cas Rockman's lawyers. He wants to talk. Can you get here tomorrow morning?"

# 37

It was 6:45 in the morning, foggy, and oddly muggy for early March. Stella and Ernie stood outside the jail, waiting to get buzzed in.

"They know we're coming, right?" Ernie asked, looking at his watch again.

Stella didn't answer as she checked her phone, but there were no missed calls. She tried Cas' lawyer again to no avail.

Rockman's lawyer had told her the goal was to get her in and out before families started showing up—it was the only way the jail had agreed to the on-camera interview on such short notice. Visitor's day was busy enough for the guards, and they didn't need a news camera clogging up their time.

When Stella had left her apartment that morning, it had been unusually quiet. There was no sign of Janet and Jason, until she got to the parking lot. There, she'd noticed with a grimace that Janet's RV was literally rocking.

Finally, just after seven, she thought she understood the delay. An ambulance pulled out of the jail's garage, leaving the intake area with the siren wailing. The red and white lights looked blurred in the surrounding fog as it drove away.

"There's probably an ambulance here four or five times a day," Ernie said calmly, trying to read Stella's expression.

"Yeah, you're probably right," she answered unconvincingly. She had a bad feeling in the pit of her stomach.

Armed guards ushered them into the facility, a clerk entered their names into the system, and they were both patted down. They walked through metal detectors and Ernie's camera was inspected from lens to battery pack.

Afterward, a captain led them into the bowels of the building, finally showing them into a small interview room where Cas' lawyer was already waiting.

"Cas was just taken to the hospital," Kenan Jackson said without preamble. His face was drawn.

"Just now?" Stella asked. "What happened to him?"

The lawyer took a handkerchief out of his back pocket and wiped his brow, already slick with sweat, despite the cool temperature in the cinderblock room. "I don't think I'm getting the full story, here, but the guards found him when they made the morning rounds and called 911."

Stella put a hand on the table between them to steady herself. "What happened?" she repeated.

"I'm not getting a straight answer from anyone, but I saw him. He was beat to hell, excuse my language," he added hastily, looking at Stella.

"Is there video of the assault—someone to hold accountable?"

The lawyer shook his head. "The jail director says they have nothing, so far. No one's talking, including Cas."

Her anger flared. "You know, that's just great. I'll tell you what, Cas needs to take interest in his own situation. Why won't he talk about what's going on and tell the truth for once?"

The lawyer held out a hand. "No, no, Stella, you don't understand. He can't talk. Cas is in a coma."

She sat softly in a chair. This is exactly what Cas's father had been worried about. He knew that Cas might get hurt on the inside and that no one would able or willing to stop it. She had hoped to break the case wide open before that could happen, but she'd been too late.

She and Ernie collected their gear and walked back out into the murky air with the lawyer. He made a hasty retreat, and Ernie loaded his gear back into the car.

Stella dialed the newsroom. "We've got a story at the jail," she told the weekend assignment editor.

"Yeah, I know. Del told me about your jailhouse interview," Doug said in a bored voice. The kid was still in college and nothing impressed him. He worked the newsroom on the weekend and thought he knew more than everyone else combined.

"No, I'm telling you about some breaking news," she snapped. "Cas Rockman, the man accused in the Bennet homicide, got the snot beat out of him overnight. He's in a coma at the hospital." Satisfied that she'd startled him into silence, she barked out a few instructions and disconnected the call.

"They're going to be live here for the six o'clock tonight," she said to Ernie.

"You?"

"No, the weekend reporter."

She rested her cell phone against her temple, worried. If Cas died, the real shooter might get away with not only his death, but the other two murders, as well. She was also worried that, when Harrison Keys found out his son was in the hospital, he might do something rash that would change the focus of the case from drug gangs and rogue cops to a father searching for revenge.

"The jailhouse interview is obviously dead," she said, wincing at her word choice, "but we've still got the crime lab story later this morning."

Back at the station, she tried to remain positive. Even though they wouldn't get Cas' story, at least she might get some information during her interview with Cheryl. She shook her head, slowly, though—it wasn't enough.

She picked up the phone and called Gibson. "We need to talk. Things have changed, and the story can't wait. It needs to come out now."

"What do you have in mind?"

***

An hour later, Stella was sitting across from Dave Gibson in his house on the west side of town. "Sorry," he said, scrambling to pick up a shirt off the floor. He balled it up and tossed it down the hall. "I wasn't expecting visitors."

She picked her way across the family room and thought

about sitting on the couch, but changed her mind when she spotted a half-eaten bowl of Cheerios on the middle cushion.

"I was just having—" He cut off mid-explanation and glared at her. "It doesn't matter. I pulled the records. Do you want to take a look?"

Stella looked around while Gibson gathered a dozen sheets of paper off the coffee table. He lived in an older part of Knoxville where the houses sat close together on neat, postage stamp-sized yards. It seemed like every other house had a small section of fencing right at the corner of the yard, expertly marking off the property line and nothing else. Gibson's house had white siding and stood just one story tall. On the inside, it was all wood and Formica.

"It's interesting. I wasn't expecting it, that's for sure," he said, handing her the stack of papers. The top page was highlighted in pink and yellow.

"These are Tingle's phone records?"

"Yup. I had to call in a visiting judge for the warrant this morning. Thankfully I know someone at Verizon—otherwise, this would have taken weeks." She looked up and saw him staring at her through narrowed eyes. "I'm not even going to ask how you got Murphy's phone records. It's not easy to access a cop's phone."

Stella bit her lip guiltily and looked at the columns of numbers in front of her. The one that should have listed the name of the account holder of the other phone number was almost all blank.

Gibson noticed her scrutiny and said, "Most of Tingle's calls are coming from and going to pre-paid cell phone numbers—no ID required."

"Hmm. That's going to make this hard, isn't it?" Stella asked, squinting in concentration.

A scanner in the room crackled to life and a dispatcher's nasally voice repeated some code, along with an alert for a drunk man peeing on the sidewalk at an address in

East Knoxville.

"You have a scanner at your house? No wonder there isn't a Mrs. Gibson," she said, looking at the rectangular black box in the corner with distaste. He harrumphed, but didn't answer. She scanned the pages, stopping at a recurring City of Knoxville number on the list. "Detective Murphy?" she said, looking at up at Gibson.

"Yup," Gibson answered grimly. "Look at the section I highlighted in yellow—that's the day of the Bennet shooting. See anything suspicious?"

Stella flipped to the page with the yellow highlighter lines and saw the corresponding calls to Murphy that she'd seen on his call log just the day before. Before Tingle and Murphy had spoken that day, Tingle had called someone else.

"Do you know who this number belongs to?" she asked, pointing to the lines on the spreadsheet. "There's one about an hour before Murphy called 911 that day to report the shooting anonymously and another call from the same number close to twenty minutes later."

"I just dialed it. You should, too."

She found her cellphone at the bottom of her bag. Holding the papers in one hand, she slowly dialed the number in question.

After several rings, a voicemail service picked up and a computerized voice said, "The voicemail box for..." and a man's voice interjected, "Oliver Bennet," before the computer finished with, "is full. Please call back later."

"Oliver Bennet! This is as good as gold!" she crowed, looking at Gibson victoriously.

"It's not enough," he said shortly.

"It's enough to link Tingle and Murphy to Bennet just minutes before he was shot!" she exclaimed.

"Well, what exactly are you suggesting I do with the information?" Gibson finally asked with a glare.

"You need to confront Murphy and Tingle today with the evidence of the phone calls. Their phone records are enough. Can't you get their locations during the calls from the phone company? Can't they triangulate GPS coordinates using the nearest cell phone towers or something geometric-sounding like that?" she asked. "It will tell us for certain if they were near Bennet when he was shot, and that, my friend, is called probable cause!"

"Yes, we can do that, Stella," he said with an exasperated sigh. "I will do that, but that takes time and another warrant. It's certainly not going to happen today."

"Something needs to happen today!" she said, sitting on his couch with a thump, forgetting about the breakfast dishes nearby. The bowl of Cheerios tilted dangerously to one side, and Gibson jumped from the chair and plucked it up before the milk could do any damage to the cushions. "Cas is injured! He might die!"

"There's no rush, then, is there?"

They glared at each other for a moment before Gibson spoke again. "What are you picturing? I tell them what we've got, and you're behind me, recording the whole thing? You think these two are going to confess on camera?"

"Not exactly," Stella said, looking down at her hands. That's actually exactly what she'd been picturing, but his attitude was pissing her off. "More like a hidden camera or two," she added defensively. "My station can set it all up. Pick a location and they'll wire the room. We'll get their reaction to your information on camera!"

He shook his head as he set the bowl on a table sat back down. "It's not going to work. Tingle and Murphy would never fall for that."

"They wouldn't be confessing, though—they'd just be talking to you. Maybe you tell them you want a cut of whatever they're getting! We'll just be recording it, and they won't know until it's too late!"

Gibson was chewing over her idea, and for a moment, she thought she had him. Before he could agree to her plan, though, a tone rang out from the scanner and both Stella and Gibson were startled to attention. This was a tone that meant business.

The dispatcher's nasally voice quickly followed, "Dispatch to all area responders, we have a 10-91 in city center. Repeat, 10-91 at 125 Main Street." A ten-ninety-one meant a body had been found. Stella and Gibson both jumped up from their seats. The dispatcher's voice crackled back to life, "Victim is Cheryl Calmet. I need an ambulance and all available first responders to 125 Main Street, the Knoxville City Crime Lab."

# 38

Gibson popped a siren on the roof of his car and peeled out of the driveway before Stella was even all the way out of his house.

She pulled his door closed and stopped on the porch to call the newsroom. Doug answered again, "I'm on it, Stella. Dawson's on her way with Ernie."

Melanie Dawson was the weekend reporter. She was new to the station, but she did a solid job. Stella knew how big this story was, though. "Let's plan for team coverage. I'm headed that way, too."

"Patricia said you were just working on Specials; that I couldn't use you for spot news," Doug said, confused by the schedule.

"I'm not supposed to be, but that's my beat—it's my turf—and... I, uh, I knew the victim," she said, realizing as she said the words that her neighbor was dead.

Cheryl was dead. What did this mean? Had there been some terrible accident at the lab, or was the truth darker and more awful? Had she been killed because of what she knew—what she'd been a part of?

She jumped into her car, peeling out almost as fast as Gibson had minutes earlier. She had to get to the crime lab. She had to know what had happened.

When she arrived downtown, it looked like the entire city was roped off. Yellow police caution tape blocked the entrance to every parking lot near the crime lab, police department, jail, and morgue. Stella circled the block several times before getting waved through toward the crime lab by a patrol officer.

She parked along the street, turned on her emergency flashers, and waved Ernie and Melanie over when she saw them drive up. Soon, there was a group of local reporters and photographers gathered on the street. A story like this one—still unfolding—meant the media was roped off and not allowed to get too close. There were photographers and reporters milling around the sidewalk, all waiting for information.

One ambulance was parked in front of the crime lab and its back doors were wide open. The lights were flashing out their warning from atop of the vehicle. Police were everywhere, blocking entrances, redirecting traffic, and generally keeping anyone curious who didn't belong away.

"Do you know what's going on?" Melanie asked as soon as Stella walked up.

"I only know what came across the scanners," she answered. "I'm sure you heard it, too. The dispatcher said that a forensic scientist is dead." She didn't add that it was the second forensic scientist to die in recent weeks.

"The victim worked here?" Melanie asked, surprised. "I only heard her name. We didn't know it was an employee." She grabbed her phone to call the information in as Stella sat in the back of the live truck. She knew it would be a long morning of waiting.

Minutes turned to hours and still they waited. This was the weekend, and no one was in a rush—including, for once, the media. The news hole was smaller on the weekends; most stations only had evening newscasts, leaving airwaves free for sporting events and movies to run all day. That meant that, today, there was no rush to meet a deadline for the noon newscast, because there wasn't one.

Finally, around twelve thirty in the afternoon, there was a flurry of activity at the crime lab doors. Three photographers hefted cameras off the sidewalk and onto their shoulders and all the reporters nearby got their notebooks ready, microphones out, just in case.

The first out was a uniformed cop, holding the door open for the gurney that followed. Someone turned off the ambulance lights—there was no reason to hurry anywhere with this victim.

Two EMTs rolled the gurney down the sidewalk and onto the street. They jostled Cheryl's body, zipped in a black bag, into the back of the ambulance. The sound of the doors slamming seemed to announce more than the beginning of a trip to the morgue—it was like a gong announcing the end of a life's journey.

The photographers captured the ambulance's slow drive away, knowing its trip would be short, since the entrance to the morgue was just on the other side of the crime lab. Stella wondered why they hadn't just pushed the gurney around the block, but she figured they had to follow protocol.

Thirty minutes later, Detective Murphy was ready to talk. Photographers crowded around and Melanie held her microphone out to him. Stella stood back, out of the way as the flashbulb of a print photographer's camera clicked and Detective Murphy began his statement.

"It is with great sadness that I relay the news that Cheryl Calmet, a longtime forensic scientist with the crime lab in Knoxville, has died. The circumstances of her death are still being investigated, but at this time, we don't believe there was any foul play." Stella crept closer, eyes narrowed. This reeked of foul play. Murphy continued, "We ask that you give the victim's family and friends privacy while they grieve this terrible loss of life." He nodded as if to thank the media for their time and started taking microphones off of his lapel.

Questions exploded rapid-fire from the gathered reporters.

"How did the victim die?"

"Has anyone been arrested?"

Stella cleared her throat and caught Murphy's eye. "Was there an accident in there? What do you mean there was no foul play?"

He grimaced, but he must have realized that he needed to answer more questions before he could leave. "Right now, we're investigating the possibility that no one else was involved in this death," he said vaguely.

"Are you saying this was a suicide?" someone else asked.

"I'm saying this case is still under investigation. When I'm ready to release more information, I'll be sure to let you know," Murphy snapped.

Stella bit her lip, aware that he wasn't usually so irritable with the media. She had an idea why he was this time.

"What impact will her death have on any open cases at the lab?" Murphy glared at her, and she blanched at the anger radiating from him, but held her gaze steady on his, anyway. The other reporters grew quiet, waiting for his answer as, well.

"It's possible that some cases might be affected. We'll leave it up to the director of the crime lab to determine which, if any, cases need to be re-examined. That's all for now, folks."

Stella walked slowly back to the truck. Cas knew someone was getting away with murder and this morning he'd been rushed to the hospital, close to death. Now, someone with access to information about the crime scenes was dead, and suicide was too convenient—too tidy.

It couldn't be a coincidence. It seemed that anyone who had inside knowledge about what was going on with the Cobras was getting knocked off at an alarmingly rapid pace, and Stella had to wonder if she might be next.

# 39

"Gibson, we've got everything set up from my end," Stella muttered, her eyes darting around the newsroom as she spoke quietly into her cell phone.

It was Thursday afternoon and they'd been working on the plan since Cheryl's death Saturday morning. He was ready to confront Murphy and Tingle about the gang connection, and they'd picked a warehouse on the outskirts of town. Stella had to loop her boss into the situation and Patricia had agreed that Ernie would wire the place for Gibson, as long as their station got first access to the story. Stella would get exclusive interviews about the arrests and exclusive video from the hidden cameras.

In exchange, she and her station agreed to stay far away from the warehouse while the sting was going down. Gibson didn't want to worry about civilians getting caught in the crossfire, and Stella's boss didn't want the extra headache of a wrongful death claim if anything went wrong.

"We lost our HR person with the last round of budget cuts," she'd said with grim determination during their meeting with Gibson over the weekend. "I'd have to handle the paperwork, and I hate HR stuff."

Gibson picked the time. He and Murphy often met to run before work, so he would suggest a new route. An unscheduled bathroom break in the warehouse would be the excuse to get Murphy into the wired room, and then it was up to Gibson to get him to talk.

A photographer would be stationed about a mile away from the scene of the takedown, and Gibson would call with an all-clear, so they could get video of the arrests. Now, it was just hours away from starting.

"It should happen around ten o'clock tomorrow morning." Gibson sounded stoic, but she could hear an underlying excitement—a sense of relief that things would come to a head soon. Although he'd been working on the case for two years, the last several days had seemed twice as long. He was ready to start putting nails in the coffin.

"Ernie is at the warehouse now. Are you sure you have time to meet him out there?"

"Yes. In fact, I need the change of scenery," he answered. "Things are getting weird downtown—Murphy's been holed up in his office and I can't get access to any information about Cheryl's death. Something's up and I just wish I knew what."

"Hopefully we'll get to him first," Stella said and he murmured in agreement. "I'm headed to the crime lab today for a memorial piece on Cheryl. I'll see what I can find out. Anyway, I'll tell Ernie you're on the way and he'll show you where the hidden cameras are, as well as the motion detectors and audio components. As soon as you enter the room, everything that happens will be recorded."

"Good, good. And, Stella? Thanks. I know we haven't always seen eye to eye, but this is going to make a difference. This is going to be the difference."

She carefully placed her cell phone on her desk and leaned back in her chair. The newsroom had no windows, but she could hear the rain pounding on the metal roof with ferocious force. Thunder sounded in the distance and the lights overhead flickered.

"Fire up the generators!" Patricia called. The newsroom couldn't afford to lose power during a storm, so they had huge, independent generators outside the building, just in case.

"I'm on it!" Del called back, standing up at the assignment desk.

While Stella waited for her computer to come back online after the power glitch, she looked down at her desk. She had the picture from Allen Elementary School out and was studying it intently. There were three smiling boys with their arms around each other—Brian Murphy, Kevin Lewis, and someone else. For some reason, she kept circling back to the third friend. She knew the picture was forty years old. The third person, now nearly fifty, might be living in another country or hiking the Appalachian Trail. Heck, he might even be dead. For some reason, however, she couldn't shake the feeling that learning his identity was important.

Her cell phone rang, and she picked it up, glad for the distraction.

"Are you keeping it, or what?" John asked.

"What?" Stella asked, momentarily confused.

"My car! You've had it for two and a half weeks! I'm not going to lie, it was kind of tricky explaining to Katie why you had it in the first place, and now every time we get in your car to go somewhere, I can see her temperature rise," there was a pause before he added, "and not in a good way, okay?"

"John, I'm so sorry. I meant to get it back to you the very next day, but—"

"I know," he interrupted. "Life gets busy. Do you want to make the switch today?"

"Yes, of course!" she said, feeling inexplicably irritated, even though she knew he'd been far too kind, considering the situation. "We can meet downtown."

"I'm stuck at a story right now, but if you have an extra set of keys for your car, that'll work."

"I don't."

"Oh. Well…"

"Listen, I'll just drop your car off at your apartment right now and have Janet drive me over tomorrow morning to get mine. When you get home tonight, just leave my keys in the glove compartment."

"Stella, it's just that—"

"Thanks so much, John. It really was a life-saver."

A silence stretched between them.

"So, you outran the feds, huh?" he asked, trying to inject some humor into the call.

"So far," she said, before hanging up with a terse, "Goodbye, John."

So, Katie didn't like driving around in her car, eh? She felt her face twist into a satisfied smile. *Good.*

She shoved her phone into her bag, along with the picture she'd been examining, and stood up. "Laffy?" she called.

His head popped up over the lockers, his dark hair looking even blacker than usual as it was wet and slicked back. "Let's roll, Reynolds."

He slid a rain cover over his camera and shrugged into one, himself. Stella took an umbrella from under her desk and buttoned up her purple trench coat. Laffy would follow her to John's apartment, Stella would hop in the news car, and they'd be on their way.

"Ready?" he said over the pounding rain. "Go!"

He pushed the door open and the two raced to their cars. By the time she threw herself behind the wheel, she was soaked.

During the drive across town, she tried to tamp down her irritation with John and his girlfriend. After all, she had definitely moved on. She and Lucky talked every other day or so and had standing dinner plans when he was in town. She thought their set up was going to be perfect.

After tucking John's keys into his glove compartment, she hopped into the news car waiting behind her in the lot.

Stella picked up a wet lock of hair that had fallen over her face and tucked it behind her ear. "This is supposed to keep up all day?" she asked with a frown, glaring at the rain bouncing off the pavement.

"Yup," Laffy looked at her with a grin. He turned out of the lot and pointed the news car downtown. "What's your over-under on when we'll be pulled from your story to cover the storm?"

"Hmm. This is a kind of a big story today, and I'm the

only one with access to the director of the crime lab. He's going to talk to us on camera about Cheryl Calmet's death, so I think they'll only pull us if there's a tornado warning."

Laffy turned the windshield wipers to their fastest setting and squinted, trying to make out the edge of the road through the storm. "I'll take your tornado warning and raise you a tornado watch. Ten to one, you'll be standing by a downed tree, talking about the rain by five o'clock tonight." Stella smiled, but remained silent. Laffy sensed her mood and cleared his throat. "I'm sorry to joke. I heard the victim was your neighbor, right? Were you friends?"

"Not good friends, but more than neighbors," Stella answered slowly. She'd been grappling with the situation since the week before, and she couldn't decide if the fact that Cheryl was dead made it more or less likely that she had been involved in whatever was going on between Detective Murphy and the Cobras.

Oliver Bennet had known that someone he worked with was involved, but he'd never told police who it was. Cheryl was a likely candidate and had even made some damning remarks about her job to Stella weeks ago. Add to that the fact that her boyfriend was more than likely involved in the city's two recent homicides, and the picture seemed to get a little clearer.

Had Cheryl been overcome by shame at her role in the false convictions? Had she been unable to live with herself for trading forensics results for money? Surely there had been money involved. Or—and this was the big one that had kept Stella up for nearly a week—had Cheryl's death really been a suicide, at all? She blew out a sigh and Laffy glanced at her before quickly turned back to the road.

"Chin up, Reynolds. You'll be dry by tomorrow— definitely Friday, at the latest." He tapped the brakes and shifted lanes to avoid colliding with a truck that had stopped in the middle of the road for no apparent reason. "Drivers here are bad," he scowled, concentrating on the road.

A flash of lightning streaked down to the ground in the distance and Stella silently counted out the seconds until they heard the thunder. She wondered if the eye of the storm was really ten miles away, as she'd learned as a kid.

Finally, they got off the interstate and the crime lab came into view. Laffy parked the car on the street and handed Stella the microphone. "I'll give you a head start. Hold the door for me when I get there?" he asked.

"Sure," she replied, opening her umbrella through the smallest crack in the door she could manage. The rain howled in, anyway, and she felt her damp skin get slick again.

After racing to the main entrance of the lab, she pressed down the buzzer. In a few seconds, the door lock clunked over and she pulled the door open, rushing into the vestibule. She had just enough time to shake off her raincoat and push her sticky hair off her face before Laffy came charging in from the street. He sprayed her with water as he shuffled past.

"Sorry," he said, taking a towel out of his bag. She reached for it with a smile, and when he immediately used it to dry off his camera, she laughed. "What?" he said, giving the lens one final swipe.

"Nothing, Laffy. Let's go."

Through the now-familiar security screening they went, and then into the elevators up to the third floor, where Cheryl's old boss, Jack Neahy, was waiting on them. The doors opened, and they heard a man talking in the hallway just beyond their field of vision.

"I have to do this damn interview—the mayor insisted. Afterward, we can start cataloguing her open files and cross reference them with Bennet's to see if we need to contact any of the defense attorneys. Oh, and, of course, Yvonne is contesting our divorce settlement again."

Laffy started forward, but Stella snaked out a hand to stop him. "Wait," she mouthed, listening.

The man continued. "If I have to pay that woman any

more money that I don't have—oh, you're here." Neahy stopped talking as he came to the open elevator doors. His face was pale and strained and tiny beads of sweat gathered at his hairline. The head of the crime lab was at least three hundred pounds with narrow shoulders and wide hips. His lab coat was open, revealing dark slacks and a blue button-down dress shirt, the fabric of which was evenly strained at each small, white button.

"Sorry, you can't image the stress of the last week," he said, ushering Stella and Laffy down the hallway. "First, the shock of it all, and then the mounting evidence of... well, that's why you're here, isn't it?" he said, looking at Stella with distaste.

"Excuse me?" she asked, glancing at Laffy. He looked blankly back, and both turned toward the head of the crime lab.

"The media exposure's been intense. I've never had so many people questioning our job. With Cheryl's death, we have to re-examine every case of hers—everything she touched in the lab. Defense attorneys will be clamoring for new hearings and new agreements with their clients. It's going to be a nightmare."

"Yes, I'm sure that was a shock," she said, trying to make sense of his words. It sounded like he was planning to give her more than a memorial piece that day.

"Cheryl didn't have proper documentation on most of her cases. I don't know how you found out, but the mayor said it was best that I talk to you. 'Control the message' is what he said—as if I can control this!

"Closing the crime lab! It'll be the biggest story to hit Tennessee in years. We've got to send all our cases to an outside agency to test and re-test... it's going to be a nightmare with chain of custody issues all the way through. Hundreds of criminal cases will get thrown out and the average wait time for results will skyrocket to at least six months for even the most mundane drug crime." He waddled down the hall, finally pushing open the door to the lab. "It's a nightmare."

"So you said," Stella murmured, holding the door for Laffy, who was carrying the camera, a tripod, and a messenger bag with all his other equipment. Neahy walked behind a counter and looked at them expectantly. While Laffy set up his camera, she clipped the microphone onto the man's lapel.

Her mind was racing. For some reason, the mayor was setting her up with a major exclusive. She didn't know enough details to ask good questions, though, so she was going to have to tiptoe around until she found her footing.

"This could result in dozens of people going free?"

"More like hundreds. We have evidence that Cheryl was entering false results into the system—either not doing the forensics tests, at all, or changing the results to suit her own convictions about the case."

"Why?" she asked, even though she thought she knew.

"We don't know. We have checks and balances in place to prevent this kind of thing—peer review plans and the like—but it mostly comes down to the honor system. The basic tenet of our job is to be honorable and fair and to treat the evidence with respect and approach each case impassively, without judgement. We let the evidence speak for itself. We've been short staffed for months, though—"

"Since Oliver Bennet left?" she interjected.

Neahy paled, but quickly recovered. "Yes, that's right."

He fell silent, and Stella stared at him, trying to wrap her mind around what was happening. "So, you're closing the crime lab?" she finally asked in disbelief.

"Yes, effective immediately. We'll send all of our open cases to an outside lab—probably in Nashville."

"You're saying that any case that Cheryl worked on is suspect?"

"That's exactly right."

"Since she was hired?" Stella asked, her voice breaking in disbelief on the last word. Cheryl said she'd worked at the lab for six years; that was a lot of cases that needed to be revisited. Neahy nodded solemnly. "That will take—"

"Years," he finished with a pained look on his face.

Stella couldn't believe it. She'd been holding out hope that her neighbor wasn't the insider at the lab and that she was a good person. It looked like she'd been wrong, though.

"When will the lab reopen?" she finally asked, trying to focus on the major story at hand.

"It'll take us weeks to catalog everything Cheryl touched and another month to get everything boxed up and sent to Nashville. We'll reopen for local cases sometime this fall."

"How do you know all of this?" Stella asked. What had happened to make Cheryl's boss treat her as a suspect, all of a sudden?

He blew out a heavy puff of air and reached into his pocket. "It's just a photocopy. The original is evidence," he choked out a humorless laugh, "on its way to Nashville, now." He took a lingering look at the paper in his hand before holding it to Stella.

She scanned the sheet. "Is this a suicide note?" When Neahy nodded, she shook herself and started over at the beginning, this time reading slowly, so she wouldn't miss a thing.

The writing took up a whole page of white printer paper, written in loopy cursive with each Y and G taking up the space of two other letters.

*To my colleagues, I'm so sorry for the trouble I have caused. All of this lying and cheating has gotten to be too much for me. I'm afraid I've been gaming the system for some time, and it seems now that there's no way out. Please know that it all started honorably—my desire to put away the bad guys was my sole intent. Sometimes the evidence wasn't enough, though, and I wanted to make sure someone paid for the crime. I knew I'd gone too far and was ready to stop, but Detective Dave Gibson wouldn't let me back out. He wanted me to keep putting away innocent people and I just couldn't do it, anymore. I am tired—so very tired. Cheryl Calmet.*

When she finally dropped the paper to her side, her mouth was hanging open.

"I know. It's a shock to all of us. Cheryl was one of the best. At least, we thought she was. We'll have to pull all of her old files and reexamine all the cases—and that's if the evidence is still round. In drug cases, especially, things are disposed of after just a year or two." He shook his head, as if still not believing she had made so much extra work for his team.

Stella shook her head, too. She couldn't believe it. Cheryl was dead and a finger of blame was pointed squarely at Detective Gibson. There was only one problem. She knew the handwriting on the page didn't belong to Cheryl. Her handwriting was neat and precise, almost like keystrokes from a typewriter. In fact, she had a sample of it in her purse from the Post-it note Cheryl had left on Stella's door with her phone number weeks ago.

This wasn't a suicide note—it was evidence of a murder. A shiver ran down Stella's spine. Someone in this very lab had planted evidence in this case and hundreds of others. They had possibly killed two co-workers to keep news of their criminal activity silent, too. Her racing mind was interrupted when Neahy spoke again.

"Well, what else do you need, Stella? I'm sure you can understand how busy we'll be around here until we can sort all this out." He looked expectantly at her photographer, who looked uncertainly back at Stella. This story was so big and unexpected that she could tell he didn't know what other video they might need to fill out the package.

"Gibson?" Stella asked weakly, not able to do more than say his name.

"I heard they're on their way to arrest him right now. There's another exclusive for you," Neahy said with a sigh. "Detective Murphy's been working on this secretly since we found the note last weekend, trying to cross all the Ts and dot all the Is."

"I'll bet," Stella said quietly as she turned toward the

door. Things were moving too fast, and no matter what she figured out, she couldn't seem to stay ahead of this story. She was still clutching the photocopied paper of Cheryl's supposed confession when a familiar-looking child walked into the lab space.

He had a pale, round face with a squashed nose and nonexistent chin. Stella started, recognizing him immediately from the picture she'd spent hours poring over from Allen Elementary School. This was the third boy—the final friend of Murphy and the mayor. He wasn't dead or hiking the Appalachian Trail, but somehow, he was inexplicably still ten years old.

She knew she was staring, floored by the child's very existence, when Neahy spoke from behind her. "Ryan, what are you doing here?" The boy stared back at Stella like she was crazy, and she blinked, trying to unlock her eyes from his face. "Stella Reynolds, I'd like you to meet my son, Ryan. He's in fifth grade and supposed to be in school right now," he added with a bit of concern mixed with disapproval.

"Where do you go to school, Ryan?" Stella asked, weakly. He didn't answer, and she turned to look at the head of the crime lab.

Just before Neahy spoke, a grin lit up his face. "He goes to Allen Elementary, just like his old man."

# 40

Things were finally making sense, but not in the way Stella imagined. Jack Neahy was the insider at the crime lab. He'd been friends with Murphy and the mayor since elementary school, and he must have been getting kickbacks for his participation. Had he killed Cheryl and Oliver Bennet to hide his crimes? Even if he hadn't pulled the trigger, his final act had been to plant a suicide note from Cheryl and create a spectacle so big and distracting that he and his friends could slide under the radar. Maybe they all felt the heat of Gibson's investigation and were trying to get out before they got caught.

She said goodbye to Neahy and his son in a daze and rode the elevator down to the lobby, her mind both blank and racing.

She and Laffy stood in the vestibule, watching the rain bounce off the sidewalk on the other side of the glass door.

"Stella, we need to call this in. This is huge. Team coverage, at least, and probably live at five. We should get the mayor on the phone and the police chief live tonight..." Laffy had his phone pressed to one ear, waiting for someone in the newsroom to pick up.

"The chief is out, remember?" she said absently.

"I've always hated that Gibson guy," Laffy continued, as if Stella hadn't spoken. "I'm not surprised to find he's involved, ya know?" he said. "Hey!" he shouted as Stella grabbed the phone from his ear and disconnected the call.

"Gibson! We've got to warn him!" she said, pushing Laffy out the door into the pouring rain. He shoved his camera under his sweatshirt and glared at her.

When they were sitting in the car minutes later, he

looked at her reproachfully. "My rain gear wasn't even on, Stella. That's really bad for the camera!"

"I'm sorry! I'm sorry! It's just—we're out of time! I need you to take me to the business district now!"

"I can't!" At her look, he continued, "I'm running a live shot at Neyland for sports tonight. I have just enough time to drop you back at the station before I head over."

Stella groaned. "It's pouring rain—surely the spring football game will be canceled!"

"That's where I'm headed, until they tell me otherwise," Laffy answered mutinously. As he started up the car, she had an idea.

"Can you drop me off at my apartment? It's on the way. I'll borrow my roommate's car."

"No problem," he said, cranking the windshield wipers up to full-speed again.

During the ten-minute drive to her apartment, the weather improved slightly and the driving rain became more of a mist. Dark clouds to the west threatened, though, and Stella knew this was just a break in the storm.

"Thanks, Laffy," she said as she hopped out of the news car.

She scanned the parking lot for Janet's car. "Uhh..." Her roommate wasn't supposed to work until later that night, but her car was gone. "I just can't catch a break!" Stella exclaimed, realizing her mistake. Laffy was gone, Janet's car wasn't there, and now Stella was stuck on the wrong side of town without a ride.

She tried Gibson's cell phone, but there was no answer. She took a calming breath and tried to think. He'd said his sting operation would happen tomorrow morning. It was still early at only three-thirty in the afternoon. She had plenty of time to find Gibson at the business park and tell him he was walking squarely into a trap. Based on Cheryl's supposed suicide note, they were setting the groundwork to pin the whole thing on him, and she couldn't let that happen.

She tapped another number into her phone.

"Newsroom, Patricia." Her boss picked up the call, and for a moment, Stella was speechless, not sure how to convey everything that she had just learned in the last thirty minutes.

"Hello?"

"Patricia, it's Stella. Where's Ernie?"

"Just back from your warehouse. He was missing a few connectors and was going to head back out, but I sent Jim to finish the job."

Stella was momentarily distracted by this information. "Jim? Why not just have Ernie finish things? You know, just so we're sure that... uh...you know, it's all—"

"I had to pull Ernie," Patricia interrupted. "Nev called off sick and I need Ernie back at the station to edit the shows." Silence filled the airwaves between the two women. "All he has to do is connect two or three wires. I think he can handle it," Patricia finally said, her voice brisk.

Stella wasn't sure, but she didn't argue. There was too much else to discuss. She filled Patricia in on all they'd learned from Jack Neahy.

"They're closing the crime lab?" she asked.

"Yes, but don't you see? That's just to distract us from the main story!"

"Well, they sure did. I need you live at five on this. See if you can get the mayor. I'll put Melanie on the defense angle, and we'll need a response from the public defender's office on what this means for anyone convicted on evidence results from the crime lab over the last six years. Good God, network will want a piece of this!"

"Patricia, I can't! I need to warn Gibson. This is a distraction—a way to get the focus off the real story, which is that someone at the police department, a local business owner, and maybe even the mayor are working with a drug gang!"

"I understand, but that's tomorrow's story. No matter who's guilty—Cheryl or someone else—today's story is that the crime lab is closing. This will impact the entire criminal justice system in the city and I need you on it. Stations all over the country will probably want a piece of this—I'll offer national hits at 5:10, 5:40, and 6:10. Are you ready for the national feeds, Stella?" Patricia's voice was excited. This was her dream, long-extinguished, and she was happy to deliver Stella to the big leagues, instead.

She gulped. A national story broadcast live across the country was a major opportunity. It would be phenomenal video for her résumé tape. "Patricia," she said, not altogether believing what she was about to say. "Give the story to someone else. I have to get to Gibson, first—I have to warn him."

"You can warn him after the news," Patricia said, trying another tack.

"I need to get to him now, so he can stay ahead of things!" She took a deep breath. "So far, anyone who has questioned what's happening is dead. Oliver Bennet is dead, Cas Rockman is one step away, and his mom was killed just because he knew too much. Cheryl Calmet must have gotten too curious, and now they've got Gibson in their sights. I have to warn him—he has to know."

There was a pause while her boss considered Stella's words. Finally, she said, "Okay, but don't forget you're on that list, too. Come right back to the station afterward. I need you on this for the eleven. Wait, hold on—"

There was muffled speaking on the other end of the call and, after a moment, Patricia came back on the line. "Ernie wants to know if you can bring back that old car phone? I guess he brought it over to show Gibson and left it in the warehouse by mistake."

While she spoke, Stella's eyes scanned the parking lot and street beyond. An idea was forming, and she hurried off the phone. "Sure, no problem, Patricia. I'll be back as soon as I can."

She disconnected the call and shouted a cry of victory—not because of what Patricia had said, although she was glad she'd be able to take her story back for the late night news—but because of a certain house on wheels she'd just caught sight of. She finally knew how she was going to get to the business district.

She walked briskly to Janet's RV and found the key on her ring. As she climbed behind the wheel, her heart rate accelerated and her body remembered the last time she'd been inside.

Stella shook out her suddenly trembling hands. "No one else here today," she reminded herself out loud, but she still thoroughly scanned the inside of the vehicle. When she was satisfied that there were no men with guns nearby, she cranked over the engine.

It took her three tries to dislodge the giant motorhome from its slot on the street, but she finally managed to free the RV. As she barreled down the road, she left a message for Janet, explaining why she was borrowing the vehicle.

It was 3:42 in the afternoon—barely enough time to get her crime lab story together, if she'd been headed right to the station. Instead, she was driving in the opposite direction, toward Gibson and the business district. She tried him on his phone again, but the call went right to voicemail. It was difficult to know whether he chose not to answer, or if he even had cell service to begin with.

The business district was located in the lowest part of the city, and cell service there was spotty at best. It had actually been a story several years ago. Here was a business park with no cell service, and the tenants were livid. The owners had pledged to pay for additional towers to serve the area, but the promises had been largely not kept.

The misty weather had given way to heavier rains again, and Stella searched the area around the steering wheel, finally finding a knob that controlled the windshield wipers and headlights.

She pulled into the deserted parking lot and the stark building looked lonely. Only a few cars were in the lot, and she picked out Gibson's Jeep, as well as an old, maroon, rusted-out Taurus that looked like it had been abandoned by the Dumpster years ago. Nearby office spaces were full with cars moving in and out of the parking lots and employees racing in and out of the building at light speed to try and beat the rain, but Gibson had chosen this building for a reason. He said it was owned by the city—bought up at auction two years earlier—but nobody could decide what to do with it, so it had sat empty since then.

He said he'd have a team of undercover officers ready to go by the time Murphy showed up the following day, ostensibly to discuss the identity of the crime lab insider. Gibson planned to surprise him with his intel, hope for a confession to be caught on camera, and then, at his signal, have his officers move in for the arrest.

Once Murphy was behind bars, Tingle would be arrested. Gibson wouldn't say, yet, whether the mayor would be questioned. Stella thought he was waiting for more information before he involved the city's top elected official in a scandal of this magnitude.

She stood outside the white metal edifice and shook off a feeling of unease. She guessed Murphy didn't know where to find Gibson that afternoon, but their plan needed tweaking if he was about to take the fall for everything that had happened over the last few weeks—or years.

Rain bounced off the sidewalk and hit her legs, and the longer she stood there, the wetter she got. Something was keeping her from taking the final two steps, though. She finally squared her shoulders and pulled the door open.

The inside was just as blank as the exterior. Worn carpet covered the floor with some brighter rectangles of color bordered by deep grooves showing her where the previous tenants had placed their office furniture. Stella walked through the first room and down a hallway lit only by windows along one side. Dim light from the stormy skies lent a gloomy air that seemed to stifle her breathing.

Ernie had told her that the wired room was in the back, so she moved past several open doors revealing empty offices before finally pushing through the door at the end of the hallway. She caught sight of Gibson and felt relieved, only realizing until she lay eyes on him that she'd been half-anticipating something going wrong.

He then turned to face her and she gasped, finally seeing the entire scene in front of her.

Gibson was sitting on a chair, bleeding from a nasty gash on his head. One eye was swollen shut and his hands were cuffed behind him. He wasn't alone. Brian Murphy and Tim Tingle were standing across from him. Murphy's gun was out, trained on Gibson, and as Stella took a step back in surprise, Tingle's arm raised and had a gun pointed at her.

"Oh, crap," she said, her stomach dropping to her toes.

She froze and watched Tingle walk toward her with a grim smile on his face. "Come on in, Stella. What a nice surprise."

# 41

Her feet might have grown roots—it was that difficult to move. She wasn't even sure which way she wanted to run, but before she could decide, Tingle waved his gun at her threateningly and motioned to an empty chair next to Gibson. Fear made her body unresponsive, though, and she still stood frozen in place.

"Oh, for God's sake," he snarled, stalking toward her and grabbing her roughly around the arm.

She gasped from pain before she managed to clamp her mouth shut defiantly, and she stumbled along after Cheryl's boyfriend, barely managing to keep her feet under her before he slammed her into a chair next to Gibson. The only furniture in the whole place was spaced out across the room. Besides the chairs she and Gibson now occupied, a card table pushed up against the far wall, and another folding chair near the door.

She could just make out where a bookcase had been attached to the wall. The yellow hadn't been painted behind the bookcase and now the eggshell blue rectangle was all that was left to show where the piece of furniture had been.

"Well?" Tingle asked. His face was red and his eyebrows were drawn together angrily. He must have been talking to her, but she'd gotten distracted by paint colors. Paint colors! She admonished herself to pay attention.

"What?"

"Who knows that you're here?" Tingle was seething, and little spit bubbles formed at the corners of his mouth. Rage radiated off of him in waves.

"I d-d-don't know," she stammered. He stepped closer and moved his gun swiftly across his body. Stella closed her eyes, bracing for the hit, but it never came.

She opened her eyes slowly and saw that Murphy had stopped the assault. He was the yin to Tingle's yang. He was calm, cool, and unfazed by whatever turn of events had led him to the warehouse the day before Gibson had planned.

"Not her face," Murphy said, smiling sadly at her, as he dropped his arm. Tingle recovered and launched a blow that smashed into her ribs and knocked the wind right out of her. She felt her mouth open and close soundlessly as she tried to take in air, but her lungs felt squashed flat. She finally heaved in a breath and sagged back against her chair, cringing from the sharp pain in her side.

"Got an answer, now?" Tingle asked with a sneer.

"I don't know. A few," Stella gasped. When he cocked his arm back again, she quickly added, "My boss, a photographer, and probably other people at the station!" Her coat was hanging open, and she noticed the top of the travel hairspray can that Matthew Mason had given her weeks ago peeking out from the inside pocket. Thank God Tingle hadn't hit her on that side.

"Shit," Tingle said, dropping his arm and looking at Murphy. "I told you this was a mistake."

"He's coming, right?" Murphy asked.

"Yes. Should be here now," Tingle answered, looking at the door. "Must be running late."

"Then just wait. He can take care of everything—we'll be fine."

She glanced around the room, searching for the hidden cameras Ernie had set up earlier in the day. One was supposed to look like an air vent and another was camouflaged into a ceiling tile. All she saw were some large, ragged holes above her head.

"What are you looking for?" Tingle snarled. "These?" At an odd crunching sound, she looked over to see him stomping on a pile of electronics. "Thought you were going to go undercover on us? Idiot." With a sense of growing horror, Stella realized the hidden cameras weren't hidden, at all. Her mouth dropped open.

"How... what..." she was at a loss for words, but realized just how dangerous her situation was. She noticed Ernie's antique car phone on the floor and realized sadly that she might not be able to get it back to him.

"Gibson," Murphy said, his voice low, "why don't you explain to your new partner what happened?"

He grimaced and shook his head, but Tingle kicked him sharply. "They got here early," he groaned in pain.

Murphy turned to see what she was looking at. "What's that?" he asked, walking over. The sound of the zipper filled the silence, and he stared into the bag silently for a moment. "What is this?" he repeated, turning to Stella.

"It's just an old c-c-car phone," she stammered.

"I don't like it—could be recording us," he muttered to Tingle. Before she could react, she and Gibson were being plucked off their chairs and pushed out the door.

A sudden crash made her jump, and she turned back to see that Murphy had crushed the plastic and metal phone into a dozen pieces. A panicked laugh almost escaped her. If they had just destroyed an item least-likely to cause them any trouble, what would they do to her? To Gibson?

She didn't know what their plan was, but maybe they didn't, either, because minutes later, they all stopped to stare at Janet's RV in the middle of the parking lot.

"What is that?" Tingle asked, glaring at the motorhome with distaste.

"That's the perfect place to wait," Murphy said, pushing Gibson toward the RV. "Is Janet in there?" he asked when he got close to the door.

"No," Stella said dully. She hated that he knew so much about her—even her roommate's name. There was no way to lie or be evasive when he already knew the answers. "I borrowed it to get here."

She looked bitterly at Gibson. How had he let this happen? That's when it hit her. She could, at least, play dumb. They had no idea what she knew. It was worth a try.

"What's going on here, Murphy? Why is Cheryl's boy-friend here?" She ignored Gibson, but felt him stiffen at her questions.

"I think you know," he said, his eyes darting toward the cabin door again. He pushed it open and cleared the inside of the RV. "We can talk in here. It's much more private," he added grimly.

She felt the pain in her side and the fear in her stomach and somehow knew that, if she walked into that RV, she would never walk back out. She was about to become a statistic of the crooked crime lab and police force—a statistic no one would ever know about.

In a last mad attempt at freedom, she reached into her coat pocket and pulled out the travel-size can of hairspray. In one move, she popped the cap off and pressed down on the nozzle. White Rain shot straight into Tingle's face—a direct hit—and his eyes scrunched up in pain as he batted the can out of her hands with a scream of rage. Before she could pivot and run, though, Murphy shoved her into the RV from behind.

"My eyes! My eyes!" Tingle shouted, staggering into the main part of the cabin.

He blindly reached for the sink in the kitchenette and turned the faucet on. Of course, nothing happened; the RV wasn't connected to a water source.

He turned his angry, streaming eyes on her. "You think you can mace me, you stupid—"

Murphy stepped between them. "Moron, it was hair-spray—you'll be fine."

She glared at the bottle through the open door, lying useless on the ground, just out of reach. *Stupid gentle mist. The stream from a pump might have bought me more time to escape.* Now she was exactly where she didn't want to be, and she might as well blame it on Matthew Mason.

While Tingle let the rain clean off his face outside, Stella looked around Janet's RV. Striped sheets were balled up in the corner, tucked under the bench, plastic wine glasses lay sideways in the sink, and the open trash can had two empty bottles of wine inside. In any other circumstance, she would have been impressed with Janet's game. She certainly knew how to keep a man's interest. Now, however, it was the furthest thing from her mind.

Murphy didn't look at her, and that made her even angrier. "Brian," she said, using his first name for the second time in her life. "Brian, why? Why are you involved in this?"

He didn't answer, and by then, Tingle was back inside, patting his face dry with a handkerchief. He laughed—a loud, joyless sound that reverberated around the small space. "Why? Stella, we've been involved in this since before you were born."

"What are you talking about?" she asked desperately.

"When I took over the roofing company, it was pathetic. Sales barely covered the cost of operating, and there were three employees, including me and Brian. We were tired—so damn tired—of this life, of this system, and of the injustices of being born poor. So, we decided to change things—rig the system, so we would benefit, for once."

"How?" Stella asked. She might as well understand everything—it might have been the last thing she ever did. She chanced a look at Gibson who stared straight ahead with dead eyes.

"By making our own system. It started small; I knew a guy who was selling drugs to make money, but he kept running into trouble with the cops. So, I gave him a job, and working for me gave him legitimacy. He wasn't the guy on the corner selling dope in the middle of the day who cops could easily pick off. He had a real job with regular hours, and that gave him cover when the cops came calling. We realized that it could give a lot of people cover, so I employed a fleet of his friends. We were able to scale the business dramatically—"

At that, Murphy snorted. Tingle stopped and turned toward him with a curious look on his face. "You've been to too many Rotary Club meetings, Tingle. 'Scale the business dramatically.' Listen to yourself," Murphy said derisively.

Tingle forced a smile onto his face and turned back to Stella. "Let's just say business was booming. The dozens of people we hired essentially worked for free—their real money came from dealing drugs on job sites. Instead of taking a cut of their profits, I got free labor. It let me outbid just about any company back then, and that forced my competition out of business. When I was the only game in town, I slowly raised my rates until I was making a huge profit on each job. In the meantime, my employees were making huge profits dealing drugs on the job."

"But?" Stella prompted when he fell silent.

He had taken on a reflective tone. His gun was by his side, and he rubbed his face with his other hand until his fingers stuck to the skin by his temple. Hairspray. He glared at Stella.

"The competition on the streets was too stiff. My guys stopped bringing in the money, and I realized we needed to annihilate not just my roofing competition, but their drug dealing competition, too."

"So, you had Murphy join the force?"

"We needed an inside guy. He was the perfect candidate."

She turned to the detective with a look of distaste. "So, you've always been the bad guy, huh?" she shook her head. Poor Annie.

Murphy didn't answer, and before she could say anything else, Tingle broke in. He was gloating and couldn't help but finish his story. "We started putting away other dealers—I've never seen a plan work so well."

"Just one big, happy family, huh?"

"That's just it. It was! For once, we all had a family—a first for many of us. You don't know what it's like, not being able to rely on anyone. Everyone needs a family."

"Just when did you decide to start offing the mothers of certain members of the family?" she asked through gritted teeth. The shock of the situation was wearing off, and her side hurt like a bitch.

Murphy blanched, but Tingle smiled. "You know about Rockman's mother?"

Stella nodded, and his grin spread. The sight was cold and filled her stomach with dread.

"He's here," Murphy interrupted, lifting the blinds on the small, rectangular windows and looking at someone outside. Stella felt a cool rush of wind as the door was pushed open, and rain drops swept into the RV before the door banged shut. She didn't turn to see who'd arrived, though, and instead plowed forward. She was finally learn-ing the truth—finally getting some answers.

"Cas wouldn't kill Oliver Bennet for you, so you killed Oliver Bennet and Cas' mother? Where's the logic in that?"

"I did what had to be done. That's business, Stella."

His answer turned Stella's stomach, and she finally looked away. Her eyes locked with those of the man now standing at the threshold of the RV. "Rufus Mills," she said, and heard her voice quiver. "Fancy meeting you here."

# 42

Stella listened hard for sirens, thinking that, surely, by now, someone would be coming to her rescue. All she could hear, however, was the thundering rain storm pounding against the metal roof of the RV.

Rufus Mills looked warily around the crowded space, his tiger eyes circling back to her face. "What did you say?" he asked. His voice was low and gravelly, like the slow, yet powerful rumble of thunder from a storm still ten miles away.

Tingle put his gun in the waistband of his pants. "Glad you're here. Things have gone to hell. We came here to silence Gibson, but then she showed up. We need to get rid of her, too. There's no telling how much she knows."

"I know how much she knows," Murphy said with a frown, "because you just told her everything."

"Not everything," she interjected. "Who killed Cheryl?" Turning to Tingle, she asked, "Did you kill your own girlfriend? What happened?"

He glared at Stella and growled, "Don't talk about her. Don't you dare talk about her."

She looked at him in surprise. The angry, red color on his face had faded, and in its absence, Tingle looked pale. The dark circles under his eyes stood out in sharp contrast to his sallow skin, almost like he'd been unable to sleep for days. Was he grieving Cheryl? Was this regret—sorrow— over her death, or guilt that he killed her? She wanted to find out.

Before she could ask, though, he cleared his throat. "It doesn't matter what she knows, because she's not going to be talking to anyone anytime soon."

"What did you say?" Rufus asked again, and Stella realized he was talking to her.

Her mouth immediately went as dry as the desert. "Huh?" was all she could manage under his unwavering eyes.

"About Rockman's mom. What did you say?"

The room fell silent, and Stella felt the weight of his words. He was angry, but she didn't think it was directed at her. She cleared her throat. "I asked your boss why he killed Cas' mom. If you guys are a big family, why would he do that?"

Rufus' stare hardened and she felt his anger shift to Tingle. "Is that true?" He turned to Murphy. "You said her death wasn't related. You told me it was a random shooting."

Stella snorted. "They called each other just before she was shot and then set the fire together a week later to cover their tracks."

Tingle crossed his arms over his chest. "Rockman didn't step up. We needed him to step up, and he didn't. So, I fixed things and sent a message to the next person who might have thought about not doing their part."

"You knew?" Rufus turned to Murphy. "You knew he did that?"

"After the fact," Murphy said, measuring his words. "He called me and I cleaned it up. The body was hidden for a week before we set the fire."

Rufus leveled a disappointed glare at Tingle and turned toward the door.

"Where are you going?" Tingle shouted. "We need you to—to fix this—"

Rufus stopped, but he didn't turn back when he spoke. "The first rule of the Cobras is you don't mess with family, Tingle. Don't you know that?"

Stella fought an insane urge to laugh—she felt like she was watching a strange version of *Fight Club*.

Rufus took another step toward the door when Tingle lashed out. "You idiot! You're going to ruin everything.

We're hanging by a thread, and you're going to walk away? We need you to help now, or this whole thing blows up. Rockman didn't step up and look where that got him. He's in jail, with his mother gone. If you don't help, we're all gonna go down, man, okay? All of us."

Rufus was a big guy—he had broad shoulders and thick, muscular arms and legs—so Stella was surprised by his speed. He pivoted and swung, and somehow, seconds later, Tingle was at the other end of the RV, lying half on the bed in the back room. Stella blinked. She hadn't actually seen Rufus' fist make contact and only saw Tingle lying there, dazed. Before he could recover, though, Rufus stalked over and snatched the gun from his waistband.

"You don't threaten me," he snarled, "and you don't mess with family." He leaned down and one meaty arm jabbed out, away from his body. The sound of his fist connecting with Tingle's head and the resulting crack of knuckle to skull was sickening.

While the man lay on the floor, knocked out cold, Rufus flipped open the barrel of the gun and emptied the bullets from the chamber. They fell with soft thuds against the worn carpet. He wiped the gun off with the tail of his shirt and then banged the bathroom door open and tossed the weapon into the toilet.

"Let's go," he said, looking at Murphy.

Murphy shook his head, though. "I can't."

Rufus nodded slowly, and all three watched him walk out the door as silence descended on the group. Stella didn't know if she should get up and run to safety, or if safety had found her inside the RV.

Gibson opened his mouth to speak and then shut it wordlessly. Murphy backed into the captain's chair of the RV and sat heavily.

Stella finally stood. "What happens now?" she asked the room at large.

Murphy grimaced. "Nothing. Looks like Tingle had a terrible accident—maybe he needs a lawyer. You've got nothing on me."

"So much for family, huh?"

He shrugged, but she thought she understood. Someone had to take the fall, and Murphy was going to pin it all on Tingle and probably Rufus Mills.

Stella bit her lip. There was much she wanted to say, but she thought she had a chance of making it out of this trailer alive, and she wasn't going to get into an argument with Murphy just then.

She looked over at Gibson who was still frozen in his chair, and then crossed the RV and opened the door. Her bag was lying just feet away, where she'd dropped it in shock earlier. She grabbed it, leaned against the open RV door, and took out her cell phone. Miraculously, it was dry. She pressed three numbers and waited.

"911. What is your emergency?" came a woman's crisp voice on the other end.

"I need police and a medic in the business district," she said, looking back at Tingle still lying prone on the floor. She scanned the face of the building, looking for the address, relayed it to the dispatcher, and hung up without waiting for the questions that would follow.

Within minutes, they heard the wail of a siren in the distance. She looked at her watch. It was 4:58 PM. Even with everything she'd just been through, her internal clock was ticking down to the five o'clock news deadline.

Murphy stalked past her, out of the RV, and waved to the arriving officer.

"He's going to pin it all on you," Stella said, shaking her head. "They've got a fake suicide note from Cheryl all lined up."

"What?" Gibson asked, stunned. Murphy had unlocked his handcuffs, but he hadn't moved.

She shook her head, put the key into the ignition, and cranked over the engine, so she could power up the electronics. She flipped the TV on and then turned to Gibson.

"I'm sure it'll be all over the news," she said, putting the TV on the right channel. He still didn't say anything, and she snapped. "So, that's it? He gets away with it, because we don't have any video? Can't you still file a report about what you know—what we heard?"

Gibson slowly shook his head. "I can't believe it." They looked out the front windshield to see Murphy laughing with the responding officer. They flagged down the EMTs from the ambulance and turned toward the RV. "I've got next to nothing. He might become chief before I can do anything."

The sound of the news starting distracted Stella, and she turned toward the tiny screen.

**CHET**

**Good evening, Knoxville. Major breaking news tonight, as the city crime lab closes for business.**

**ANDREA**

**It might be the biggest scandal to rock the city ever. Piper Collins is live with the exclusive.**

Stella sighed. Piper got her big story. Piper would get the network hits at 5:11 and 6:11. Piper would have amazing material for her résumé tape. All Stella had was a possible broken rib—and some explaining to do to Janet.

She moved out of the RV, so EMTs could tend to Tingle, and she stared dully at Murphy as he chatted with his colleagues like nothing had happened. She knew they still had the cell phone records, which definitely proved a connection between Murphy, Tingle, and the shootings, but she had a feeling those could be explained away without any other corroborating evidence.

If Gibson didn't make a full report, the story would die right then. There would be no justice for Cas Rockman, no justice for his mother, no justice for Oliver Bennet, and no justice for Cheryl Calmet. Even worse, there would be no sunshine pointed on the dozens or even hundreds of people wrongly convicted over the years by lying witnesses, faulty evidence, and rogue police work.

When her cell phone rang, she almost didn't answer it. She was so disheartened that she couldn't imagine doing anything as normal as talking on the phone. She pressed a button, anyway, though, and held the phone to her ear.

"Stella, I got your message about borrowing the RV." Janet sounded breathless. It must have already been busy at the bar.

"Yeah. Sorry I just kind of took it..." Stella trailed off, unable to feign too much interest in the conversation.

"Did you, uh... you didn't turn on the TV system, did you?" She paused for a moment and then continued, "I only ask, because I just wanted to warn you... uh, I mean... I guess I'm just saying you shouldn't watch the TV."

Stella watched Gibson climb out of the RV and call her over. Murphy followed with a look of grim determination on his face—he wasn't going to give him a chance to narc on him. Stella had trouble reading his expression; it wasn't the same one he'd had just moments ago. He looked... victorious. While she was still trying to figure out what had changed, Janet spoke again.

"I only say that because I don't want—I'm just worried you might... ha, ha..." It was the uncomfortable laugh that finally drew Stella's attention away from Gibson.

"Janet, what are you talking about?" she asked.

"Listen, I'm just saying that Jason and I have been experimenting with making our own, uh... videos, if you know what I mean... and the system he set up is motion-activated. There are about five cameras hidden all around that RV. He sells home security systems, didn't I tell you?

"Anyway, we didn't want to miss any of the action, no matter where our love took us, you know? When you turn the entertainment system on, it will play back the last recorded session. It takes about five minutes to warm up, but it's automatic play-back." Her voice took on a haughty tone. "So, what I'm telling you, Stella, is that, unless you want to watch me and Jason as we reenacted the Kim Kardashian-Ray J sex tape last night, then don't turn on the TV, okay?"

Stella stared, open-mouthed, at the RV just feet away.

"Stella? Don't get all judgmental on me. I really like this

guy, and..." she dropped her phone to her side and stumbled forward. After pulling the door to the RV open, she stepped aside as Murphy was heading out—in handcuffs.

The captain was talking in a low, official voice. With a start, Stella realized she was reading Murphy his Miranda Rights.

She allowed them to pass and stepped into the RV, and her eyes were immediately drawn to the tiny TV screen. She caught the tail end of Rufus Mills' powerful demonstration that left Tingle unconscious, and she sank onto the bench seat by the door, her knees suddenly too weak to hold her up.

"Does this mean..." she trailed off, too hopeful to say the words out loud.

"Stella, it was all recorded from the moment we walked into this damn RV. Everything Tingle and Murphy said was recorded! I was just sitting here, planning out my early retirement from the force, when it started playing back. We got them!" Gibson smiled, and it made him look ten years younger.

When the screen went to black, she didn't waste any time. She lifted her cell phone back up, disconnected from Janet, who was still rattling away about best sexual positions for home recordings, and called the station.

"I need a live truck and a conference call with everyone in management in about five minutes. I've got an exclusive on a major breaking news story. If we hurry, we can get it on for six." She heard a throat clear again and looked at Gibson after she disconnected her call. "What?"

"Wasn't me," he said with a shrug.

She turned to the door and saw Jim standing there with his camera slung over his shoulder. "Hey there, Stella. Just a tip—you guys are never going to keep this quiet with all the police and medics here. You've probably already blown your cover—and this RV sticks out like a sore thumb." He shook his head. "I'll head into the warehouse and finish the set-up Ernie started this afternoon. I want to make sure everything's in working order, if this thing actually goes down tomorrow morning, you know?"

She stared at the inept photographer, speechless for a moment. Before she could gather her thoughts, though, his eyes widened.

"Whoa. You're watching porn out here? Didn't figure you for that, Stella."

As she looked at him with confused distaste, she heard the moaning. She turned around to look back at the small TV in time to see Janet and Jason in all their glory. She froze and took in the bouncing flesh, the sounds of slapping skin, and the looks of ecstasy.

Gibson was staring at her with a smile on his face. "Can't turn away, can you?" he asked, fighting a laugh.

"No, it's not that... I just realized that this video was filmed right on this bench!" She jumped off the seat and dove for the power switch.

The last thing she heard before the screen went black was Janet's voice. "Oh, God, oh, yes! This is going to be epic!"

It certainly was.

# 43

"Standby, Stella. Show open in two minutes." Melissa stood behind the camera, and Ernie was just visible behind her, holding a reflector panel so the light from the setting sun outside shined softly onto Stella's face. She nodded and connected her IFB cord.

After what felt like seconds later, Melissa gave the final cue to standby. Stella took a deep breath, trying to find a sense of calm, knowing that her day wasn't anywhere close to being over. She glanced at her notebook one last time and heard the anchors read the intro to her story.

**Chet**
**Good evening, Knoxville. Tonight at six, we begin with breaking news—an exclusive story you'll see only on CBS4.**

**Andrea**
**A local business owner is under arrest, along with the head of the crime lab and a finalist for the Knoxville police chief position.**

**Chet**
**Stella Reynolds is live with all the details in this still-developing situation. Stella?**

**Stella**
**Chet, Andrea, the ramifications of today's arrests are still unknown, but this day will go down as one of the darkest in Knoxville history. Hundreds of criminal cases could be overturned, convictions thrown out, and the unsolved crime rate in the city will skyrocket, all because untrustworthy people aspired to greatness at the expense of honesty, justice, and truth.**

**Tonight, much of the truth finally came out. Our hidden cameras caught confessions, violence, and shocking**

disinterest in upholding the law. You will see it all unfold in full-color later, during our eleven o'clock newscast. For now, I can tell you that Knoxville Police Detective Brian Murphy is under arrest, charged with homicide, dereliction of duty, abuse of power, and arson. Local business owner, Tim Tingle of Tingle Roofing, is under guard at the hospital and charged with homicide, drug dealing, complacency in drug crimes, and money laundering. Finally, Jack Neahy, the head of the crime lab, has been relieved of duty. Officials tell me he could face charges related to doctoring evidence and lying under oath.

There will be so much more tonight at eleven, but for now, Chet, Andrea, back to you.

Chet

Stella, how many people will face charges in this case?

She saw Melissa roll her eyes, and she bit her lip to keep her smile at bay.

Stella

Many people will face charges, Chet, including, as I said, Detective Brian Murphy, Tim Tingle, and Jack Neahy. More on that—and hidden video confessions of their crimes—is coming up later, only on CBS4. For now, reporting live, I'm Stella Reynolds. Back to you.

They got the all-clear from the producer back at the station, and Stella unhooked herself from all the wires and cords. They had a bevy of employees at the scene, and Melissa, Ernie, and even Bob were lurking in the background, getting perp walks and interviews. She felt someone standing close, though, and when she turned, she saw that Gibson was finally done giving his statement to police.

"Hey," she said, shifting from one foot to the other.

He nodded toward some camp chairs someone had set up at the edge of the parking lot, and they walked over in silence. Once they were both seated, Stella nodded at the bandages covering his head.

"Are you okay?" she asked.

He touched his head lightly and winced. "Yup. It hurts like a you-know-what, but the EMT says I don't have a concussion."

"What happened?" she asked. "How did Murphy and Tingle find you today?"

"Remember that I called that visiting judge to get Tingle's phone records?" Stella nodded, and he continued, "I guess they're golfing buddies. He called Murphy after signing the warrant. When I suggested we meet out here tomorrow morning, he picked up Tingle and they did a drive-by to check out the place. They saw my car parked out front and ambushed me right after your first photographer, Ernie, left." He shook his head and his cheeks colored. "I should have had backup watching the place from the minute I got here. I just didn't know who to trust—who might have been working with Murphy."

"Rufus?" Stella asked, taking out her notebook with pen poised and ready.

"Gone. His place was cleaned out by the time police got there. Not a trace."

"Cleaned out? What, in the last hour? The furniture, clothes—all gone?"

"Even the walls and countertops were wiped clean. Forensics from Nashville couldn't find a single print. The guy might as well not even exist."

Stella put her notebook down. Nashville was two and a half hours away. "How'd they get here so fast?"

"They were already here to inventory the crime lab."

Stella nodded. "Rufus worked for Tingle Roofing for decades. Didn't he have a summer home, car, anything to his name?"

"Not that we can find. He lived a very simple life and must have saved every penny. We'll find the money—we'll try to find him."

"Is anyone else involved?"

"No. Well, we don't know." Gibson sighed and gingerly

touched his head again. "It's been going on for so long that it will take a while to peel away the layers and find out if anyone else was in-the-know. Murphy says the mayor wasn't involved—he just happily benefitted from the improved crime stats."

Stella tapped her pen against her lips. "Do you believe him?"

Gibson leaned back in his seat. "Honestly, he probably didn't ask too many questions. He's negligent, but not a criminal."

She nodded. "So, who killed Cheryl? That suicide note was fake." She watched Gibson closely for his reaction.

"I don't know. Tingle, or maybe Neahy. It's going to be hell testing evidence that's already been compromised. We'll do our best, but we might never know."

She rolled her shoulders, trying to release some of the tension from the last few hours. "Ernie says it's all there, from the moment the door to the RV opened until Murphy was cuffed."

Gibson didn't answer as he stared at the only remaining ambulance, waiting to take him to the hospital. Finally, he looked at Stella with a frown. "Cas is awake—woke up from his coma this afternoon. He was able to write out a statement for police, and we've got two guys on the inside identified. They say Detective Brian Murphy told them that, if they got to Cas, they'd get out of jail early for good behavior."

Her jaw dropped. "What? Murphy?"

"He's rotten, Stella. I know you'd like to put the blame on Rufus and Tingle, but Brian was in it with them from day one. He's not a nice person."

Crunching gravel announced the arrival of someone, and they looked up in time to see Andrea, one of the anchors at Stella's station, pull up.

"Bringing out the top dogs for this story, huh?" he asked. He sat up a little straighter in the camp chair and Stella saw him suck in his gut. She bit back a smile—the grouchy cop was clearly star-struck by Andrea's presence.

"This story's too big for one reporter," Stella said, watching Gibson stare.

The anchor was about ten years older than Stella, and she had long, brown hair that was styled back in a twist. She was bone thin, had perfectly-applied makeup and tasteful jewelry, and was wearing a black, sleeveless shift dress and three-inch heels. Andrea balanced awkwardly on the gravel as she walked over, and Gibson jumped up to steady her.

"Oh, thank you, officer," she said with a genuine smile on her lips. She turned to Stella, "Patricia says we're doing a big overnight shift together. I'm taking over the crime lab angle for Piper." Andrea leaned close and dropped her voice, so only Stella could hear, "She bombed her network hits. It was awful!" She stood up straight again. "Patricia wants us live here for the eleven, and then new versions and soundbites for the morning news. You'll be live for network starting at seven tomorrow morning!"

She turned to watch an ambulance drive away and gasped when she saw a long line of cars coming down the two-lane drive. All the TV stations, newspapers, and a good number of gawkers were descending on the little-used business park building like never before. Her exclusive story would be on every outlet by that evening. Of course, no one else would have the hidden camera video or Murphy's perp walk, and the thought made her smile.

Stella left Andrea and Gibson and walked back to her photographers at the live truck. They discussed the plan for the eleven o'clock newscast in detail, laying out who would do what and when. She wrote and voiced her package for the late news, handed her script to Melissa, and left the truck to get some air.

That's when she came face to face with John. He was smiling, but something was off. "Great job today, Stella. You scooped everyone—again."

"They sent you to cover the story?" she asked.

"Yup. Playing catch up to you—again."

After an awkward silence, she said, "I'm sorry about keeping your car for so long. It's just that this story was all-consuming—"

"I know. I get it," he said, crossing his arms. "I do. You have nothing to explain."

"Then why do I feel like, I don't know, like something's wrong?"

John stepped back and looked over her head at the building. "Katie is switching programs—doesn't like her cohorts at UT. She'll head to Florida next month."

"Oh, wow. Will you go with her?"

"No. I think it's a good time for... for us to be apart."

"Oh." Stella stared at John, not sure of what to say. She bit her lip. Although they hadn't dated for years, he seemed to be trying to tell her something without telling her something.

"I feel like you should know that Lucky and I are kind of..."

He nodded. "I figured. It's okay." She nodded and watched John walk away.

"Not many men can stand being with someone who's better at their job than them—especially a job that's under the microscope, like ours," Andrea said, coming up from behind her.

Stella flicked a tear away. Where had that come from? "I don't know what you're talking about."

"Sure," Andrea said with a sad smile on her face. "Sure."

Stella blinked twice and took a deep breath. She didn't know the woman well; they were co-workers, but they spoke to each other across the airwaves more than in person. Her job was to find news out of the building, and Andrea's was to anchor it from inside. She knew the woman was single—divorced, maybe—and had been in Knoxville for six years.

"Are you speaking from experience?" she finally asked.

"I don't know what you're talking about," Andrea answered, using Stella's words. She looked sadly into the distance before turning to her with a small smile. "Is that the mayor?" she asked, shielding her eyes against the setting sun as she looked past the media area in the parking lot.

Stella smiled. "Sure is. He can't stand to miss an interview, can he?"

Andrea grimaced. "I'm going to hide in the truck—do you mind? He's asked me out a half dozen times, and I just don't have the energy today."

The mayor was striding toward her, and instead of answering, she headed his way. "Kevin, news travels fast, eh?"

"Stella, I knew you'd need official sound on this situation."

"Will it be weird to talk about your childhood friend tonight?" she asked, watching him closely. After all, no one really knew how deep his connection to Murphy ran.

"More like acquaintance, Stella, and the truth will out, as they say." He grabbed his buzzing phone out of his pocket, and after a quick glance, he held up a finger. "Can you give me one minute while I send this email—urgent business—and then I'll be ready."

She shrugged, but Kevin's eyes were already glued to the tiny screen in front of him. While she waited, she waved her photographer over and took out her own phone to check for messages.

"All right, then. I'm ready when you are," Kevin said, tapping the screen one last time before putting his phone back into his pocket.

Stella made to do the same when the ping of an incoming message distracted her. She looked down at her phone, intending only to see who it was from, when a tiny gasp escaped her lips. Anonymous had sent one last email.

She tapped the screen and her eyes scanned the message. *Great job. Way to persevere. By the way, nice jacket.*

She got a funny feeling and slowly lifted her eyes from the screen to find Kevin staring at her intently.

"The purple really brings out the green in your eyes."

"You're my anonymous source?" she whispered, shocked. Kevin nodded, his mouth set in a determined line. "Why not just launch an internal investigation? Why all the smoke and mirrors?"

"There wasn't time."

"Why not?"

"It's just... I needed to make sure Luanne Rockman got justice."

"Why?" Stella asked. It's not that she didn't feel the same way, but she wondered why the mayor cared about that particular victim when so many people had to have been wronged over the years.

Kevin wrinkled his nose, as if annoyed to reveal his connection. She thought he owed it to her, though, so she stared unwaveringly at him until he blinked. "She was my seventh grade teacher. My parents pulled me out of public school after sixth grade, and I was miserable in the new private school, but Mrs. Rockman made a difference. She was a great woman."

"Again, I have to ask—why not just launch an internal investigation? You certainly had the power to do that!"

"Stella, come on. What do I have to gain by investigating my own city's great results on crime?"

"That's exactly what you did, though—through me."

"Right, through you! I won't be blamed for hundreds of criminal cases being thrown out of court and the inevitable lawsuits and general distrust of the system that will plague Knoxville for years."

"You won't?" Stella shook her head, trying to follow his train of thought.

"No. You will." At her look, he hastily added, "And, of course, Detective Murphy, Tim Tingle, and Jack Neahy. You, however, are the one people will connect to this terrible story and not me. Politically, I couldn't take that kind of heat."

She frowned, not liking the picture he was painting. "That's not going to happen."

Kevin smiled lightly. "We'll see. In the meantime, however, I'm glad we could clean up the city offices. It's really a win-win."

"Yeah, but... you used me," Stella said angrily. "You put me in danger for something you should have done, frankly, years ago."

Kevin turned serious. "Some of us have to live here, Stella. You'll be heading to greener pastures soon enough, so it doesn't matter if people don't like you in Knoxville. It matters for me."

Melissa tapped her on the shoulder. "Are you ready?" she said, motioning to the mayor with her chin. She hefted the camera onto her shoulder and handed the microphone to her. "I'm rolling."

"Let's do this," the mayor said.

Stella stared at him numbly. She'd underestimated him in a big way, and she wondered if he was right.

# 44

One month later, Stella was still reeling from the fallout of the story. Eighteen people had been released from jail within weeks of her big overnight shift after an emergency panel of judges looked over their cases and determined that the evidence used to convict them had been undeniably tainted. Another three hundred cases were still under review. City council hired a forensics expert out of Washington, D.C., to oversee new rules and operating procedures for the Knoxville crime lab, which would remain closed until fall.

In the meantime, Detective Brian Murphy was relieved of his duties while he awaited trial from the county jail. Tim Tingle was found to be a nuisance prisoner, and in an unusual move, he'd been transferred to the state penitentiary until his trial, which was slated to start the same week as Murphy's. Jack Neahy had a heart attack when officers went to the crime lab to arrest him the day the story broke, and he had been in the hospital under guard ever since. His case was proceeding, even though his lawyer argued that he shouldn't face charges because of his medical condition.

Almost every day, Stella and her colleagues covered stories that had to do with their scheme of corroborating with the Cobras. Bank records showed hundreds of thousands of dollars in cash deposits in all three men's accounts. Tingle's tax filings were being pulled from the last twenty years and scrutinized. Dozens of half-finished roofing projects needed a new company to come in and finish the job.

Rufus Mills was still missing.

Of course, Annie had disowned Stella as a friend, and

she could feel her staring angrily at her each time they met across the courtroom. They hadn't exchanged a word since Murphy's arrest.

In addition, she covered many of the prisoner's release days, which were some of the only stories that made her feel happy with her job. It was good to know she'd made a difference.

On this particular day, she was in court, somewhat surprised to be covering the release hearing for Cas Rockman. After he missed out on the initial rush of prisoners being set free, Stella figured he would simply be transferred across the state to stand trial in Nashville after the Bennet charges were officially dropped.

No one had reported on Cas and his supposed link to a Nashville cold case, and try as she might, Stella couldn't get any official confirmation. Nashville police refused to return her calls, and though Gibson was sticking with his story that Cas really had been identified in their murder investigation, Stella's boss was insistent that she get confirmation about the story from two sources before moving forward.

Cas' father sat in the front row of the courtroom, ready to welcome his son home again. It was what he'd been working for since the very first day she'd met him outside the jail two months ago.

A door opened behind the bench and a middle-aged woman walked out, black robes swirling. The court bailiff spoke, "All rise. The honorable Rebecca Borchers presides."

Judge Borchers sat down. "Please be seated. We are here today for the release hearing for Cas Rockman. I have read statements from both sides and am prepared to make a ruling. Are there any additional comments from the defense?"

Rockman's striking, young public defender stood up from the defense table. "Thank you, Your Honor. I only want to reiterate that my client has spent far too long in jail for a crime he did not commit. He lost his opportunity to say goodbye to his mother at her funeral, and he is looking forward to having time to reconnect with his father." She stared thoughtfully at Cas for a moment, and Stella thought she might have more to say. Instead, she sat next to her client.

"Thank you, Ms. Owens." Judge Borchers nodded and turned to the prosecutor in the case. "What say you, Mr. Davenport?"

An older, harried-looking man stood up wearily from the desk across from Cas. Stella had watched Stu Davenport in a dozen cases over the last few weeks, and he had a script he seemed to follow in every case. First, a plea for time, then an assurance that his office was working overtime to re-interview witnesses, and finally a request that the judge not assume anyone was innocent when they had already been found guilty beyond a reasonable doubt. In every case, so far, the judge had immediately and without delay ruled in favor of letting the defendant out of jail.

Today, however, there was a break in protocol.

"Your honor, as outlined in my brief, this case has extenuating circumstances, and I ask you to reconsider our appeal. The City of Nashville needs more time to get their murder case against Mr. Rockman together—"

"Your honor," Ms. Owens said, standing up so quickly that her chair would have toppled over if a man in the front row hadn't caught it. She continued without a break, "As we vehemently stated in our brief, the evidence gathered against my client violates his fourth and fifth amendment rights. *Mapp v. Ohio* clearly states that the court must exclude evidence seized in violation of the Fourth Amendment, and I would submit that taking a DNA sample from my client when he was illegally arrested for a crime he did not commit by a rogue officer of the law—"

The judge banged her gavel. "Order in the court. Order!"

Stella's fingers instinctively moved to her cell phone.

There it was—confirmation on the Nashville cold case. She was desperate to call it in, but she'd have to wait. If Cas might go free on a technicality, the story was even bigger than they'd imagined.

Stella looked at Rockman's father and their eyes locked. His were unapologetic, and all of a sudden, she felt ill. Had he known all along? Before she could recover from the blow, the judge's voice broke through her grim thoughts.

"Mr. Davenport, sit down! It is my turn to speak." The judge straightened the papers in front of her and took her time, now that she had the courtroom's full attention. "In my eighteen years on the bench, I have never seen a system so corrupt—so bankrupt of moral fiber and scruples—as the one we are dealing with today. Mr. Rockman should never have been in jail, his DNA swab should never have been taken, and evidence of his past crimes should never have been known to us."

Rockman's shoulders slumped in relief. His lawyer, however, leaned in and whispered something that made him sit back up.

"With that said," the judge continued, "now we do know that Mr. Rockman's DNA was present at the scene of an unsolved murder." She glared at him. "Your lawyer is correct, though. *Mapp v. Ohio* requires that we throw out that DNA evidence tying you to the crime. It does not, however, require that we forget what we know." She looked down her nose at the defendant who stared back unflinchingly, until his lawyer tapped his arm and he looked away.

"It is this court's decision, therefore, that the charges of homicide against you in the death of Oliver Bennet should be dismissed and you should be released from jail immediately. However, Mr. Rockman, you should know that police will be watching you. If you do anything wrong, and I mean anything—jaywalking, loitering, throwing a cigarette butt on the ground, instead of into an approved container—you will be arrested, booked into jail, and swabbed, and then it's game over for you. Do I make myself clear?"

Cas muttered, "Yes, ma'am."

While the lawyers and judge signed the final papers for his release, Stella recalled Cheryl's words that had seemed so horrifying to her weeks before. She'd said that, even if the system occasionally got an innocent person, "chances are that they've probably done something wrong along the way."

Cas was exactly the kind of person and case Cheryl had been describing. Her words had seemed so terrible back then, but as Stella looked coolly at Cas, celebrating his victory with his lawyer, she now understood that the issue wasn't always black and white.

*** 

Hours later, her face was buried in the couch cushion in her apartment. She couldn't even think about it, it made her sick to her stomach.

"Stop it. Stop it right there," Janet said, and she heard her plop down in the chair opposite her. "It's not your fault—it's Murphy's, Tingle's, and Neahy's."

"I know that... in my head," Stella said, her voice muted through the pillow. It was after midnight and she should have been in bed. Instead, she looked up at her roommate. "It's just—did you see her face? The way she yelled at me?"

Janet started to nod, but Stella waved her off and picked up the remote from the coffee table. "No, you need to really look at her face." She pressed some buttons and the TV came to life. After pressing a few more, the DVR was cued up to that evening's newscast. Stella hit play and watched the end of her live shot unfold again in real time. Despite her misgivings about Cas' innocence, her news director had insisted that she interview him live for the news that evening.

**Stella**
**Cas, what will you do, now that you're a free man?**

#### Cas

There's lots of sadness, still. My mom is dead and I have to live with that. I'm just going to spend time with my father and take it one day at a time.

The camera followed Cas as he embraced his father. As the two men walked away, Stella had started to wrap up her live shot.

#### Stella

Once again, Cas Rockman is a free man tonight, cleared of the homicide charge against him after the judge determined that he was wrongfully arrested on tainted evidence from the crime lab. He is prisoner number nineteen to be released after recent events.

Rockman says he'll go home for a steak dinner—

Just then, from the right side of the screen, a wailing woman gestured toward Stella, her face ablaze with fury.

#### Woman

My daughter's murder won't be solved because of you!

She spit the words out, like they'd cost her years of her life. The camera gobbled it up, like a scene from a movie.

#### Stella

I'm sorry, Chet, Andrea, we'll send it back to you—

#### Woman

Cas Rockman killed my daughter! For five years, we've had no answers, and finally last week, we got some! Now his lawyer says police can't use the evidence. It's because of you that my family won't get justice!

Stella had faltered, unable to talk, and finally Andrea took the live shot back to the anchor desk and carried on with the rest of the day's news.

She hit pause and looked up at Janet.

"By the end, you had her calmed down, though, right? She knew who to blame and it wasn't you!" she said, as if that fixed everything.

Stella nodded slowly. Eventually, she had been able to get the woman calmed down and she'd even done a proper interview that she'd turned into a story for the eleven o'clock news. Cas had refused to comment, though, and his father had only glared angrily at the grieving mother.

"I just can't believe this is happening," Stella said, flopping back into the pillow. "How many other criminals are going to walk because of my story?"

"Not because of your story! It's the job of the police and prosecutors to prove people guilty. They're the ones to blame, Stella. The system failed these victims—you didn't." Janet clarified. After a pause, she cleared her throat delicately. "I actually wanted to talk to you about something."

"What?" she asked the pillow.

"I—I'm going to move in with Jason."

Stella sat up and looked at Janet in wonder. "What?"

"Well, things are going really well, and he asked me to, and I thought it was time, you know?" She felt a smile stretch across her face. "Don't do that. It's not a big deal. It just makes sense. It's really a financial decision more than anything..."

"You like him," Stella said, her problems forgotten for the moment. "You really like him, don't you?"

Janet chucked a pillow and hit her squarely in the face. "Don't be a bitch about this, Stella." She crowed out a laugh. "There's something else."

Still smiling, she sat back on the couch and looked at her roommate expectantly. "What?"

"I think you should take that job. There's nothing holding you here, anymore. John's moved on, Lucky's traveling more than ever, and you don't really like it here, anymore." She motioned to the TV, still frozen on Stella's look of confusion.

The grimace was back, and now it was her turn to chuck the pillow. She missed her roommate by an arm's length, though. "I don't know."

"What don't you know?" Janet asked, refusing to let her ignore the situation.

"It's just—it's a big job, and I don't know if I'm ready."

"Hell yeah, it's a big job. The weekend anchor in Columbus, Ohio! You'll be making more money as an anchor and getting the experience you'll need to launch you to network, someday. Isn't this what you want?" Janet asked.

"Objection, leading the witness," she answered without looking up.

"Stella."

The silence stretched for so long that she finally looked at her roommate. "Yes, it's an amazing opportunity. I just... I need some time to really think it over."

"When do they need their answer?"

"This week—I have until the end of this week." Stella rolled over so her back was to Janet, and she stayed that way until she heard her leave.

When she was alone again, she flopped onto her back and stared at the ceiling. The story from her big overnight shift had gone national. She'd fronted it for her station and all the CBS affiliates for days, even getting a slot on the CBS morning news show. When the dust had settled from the initial stories, she'd gotten a call from the NBC affiliate in Columbus, Ohio. They had a weekend anchor position they wanted to fill. Now she just had to decide if she was ready to take it.

Lucky was in a different city every week for the Sprint Cup Series, and she guessed they didn't need Knoxville, anymore. They could meet up on their days off anywhere.

The hiring manager in Ohio had told her she'd be working with excellent, award-winning photographers every day, and she'd be paired with a long-time anchor at the station. He'd hinted that their main female anchor would be retiring soon and that they'd look internally to fill the slot. It sounded luxurious and exciting, but frankly, it also sounded exhausting. Maybe that's what she needed, though.

Ole Boy leaned his head against Stella's shoulder and she sat up, her daydreams punctured by reality. The dog! She couldn't take the job, obviously. Who would watch

Ole Boy? Before she could come down from her high, though, her roommate called out from the kitchen.

"I'm taking the dog. He likes me more, anyway."

Stella smiled. There was nothing holding her back. She was heading for her next adventure just as soon as she could pack up her bags.

###

# ABOUT THE AUTHOR

Libby Kirsch is an Emmy award-winning television news journalist. She draws on her rich history of making embarrassing mistakes on live TV, and is happy to finally indulge her creative writing side, instead of always having to stick to the facts.

Libby grew up in Columbus, Ohio and now lives with her husband and children in Ann Arbor, Michigan. Yes, Thanksgiving weekend* is tense.

For more information, check out her website at www.LibbyKirschBooks.com

*Also known as College Football Rivalry Weekend.

## THE STELLA REYNOLDS MYSTERY SERIES

THE BIG LEAD

THE BIG INTERVIEW

THE BIG OVERNIGHT

THE BIG WEEKEND
(coming February 2017)

For updates on new releases or to connect with the author, go to www.LibbyKirschBooks.com

Made in the USA
San Bernardino, CA
15 May 2017